# HERCULE POIROT

went looking for a killer. This is what he found:

- A bloody hatchet
- A piece of poisoned wedding cake
- The corpse of an eccentric widow whose face had been smashed beyond recognition
- A housekeeper who listened at keyholes
- Two nieces greedy for money and men
- And a bunch of quarrelsome relatives who needed cash and weren't fussy about how to get it

When he added them all up, Hercule Poirot had everything except one clue.

And he could get that only from the killer!

**Books by Agatha Christie**

Published by POCKET BOOKS

# Agatha Christie

# Funerals Are Fatal

(Original British title: *After the Funeral*)

PUBLISHED BY POCKET BOOKS NEW YORK

The characters, places, incidents, and situations in this book are imaginary and have no relation to any person, place, or actual happening.

POCKET BOOKS, a Simon & Schuster division of
GULF & WESTERN CORPORATION
1230 Avenue of the Americas, New York, N.Y. 10020

Copyright 1953 by Agatha Christie Mallowan

Published by arrangement with Dodd, Mead & Company

ISBN: 0-671-83173-9

First Pocket Books printing June, 1954

20   19   18   17   16

POCKET and colophon are trademarks of Simon & Schuster.

Printed in the U.S.A.

# FOR JAMES

In memory of happy days at Abney

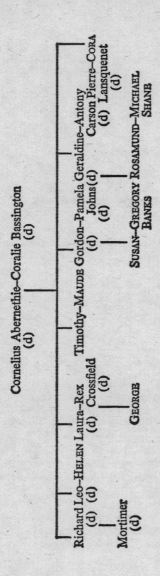

THE ABERNETHIE FAMILY.

Those designated in CAPITAL AND SMALL CAP letters were present at the funeral of RICHARD ABERNETHIE.

SUSAN BANKS: Richard's other niece, and the only one who'd inherited his brains.

GREGORY BANKS: Susan's volatile husband. The family's acceptance of him had to be wanted in a chemist's shop . . . . . . . . . . . . . . . . . . . . . . . . . . . . . . 7

CORA LANSQUENET: Richard's sister who had an unhappy habit of blurting out unpleasant truths. . . . 5

MISS GILCHRIST: Cora's devoted housekeeper. . . . . . . . . . . . . . . . . . . . . . . . . . . . . . . . . . . . . . . . . . . . . . .

# Cast of Characters

# Funerals Are Fatal

Old Lanscombe moved totteringly from room to room, pulling up the blinds. Now and then he peered with screwed up rheumy eyes through the windows.

Soon they would be coming back from the funeral. He shuffled along a little faster. There were so many windows.

Enderby Hall was a vast Victorian house built in the Gothic style. In every room the curtains were of rich faded brocade or velvet. Some of the walls were still hung with faded silk. In the green drawing room, the old butler glanced up at the portrait above the mantelpiece of old Cornelius Abernethie for whom Enderby Hall had been built. Cornelius Abernethie's brown beard stuck forward aggressively, his hand rested on a terrestrial globe, whether by desire of the sitter, or as a symbolic conceit on the part of the artist, no one could tell.

A very forceful looking gentleman, so old Lanscombe had always thought, and was glad that he himself had never known him personally. Mr Richard had been *his* gentleman. A good master, Mr Richard. And taken very sudden, he'd been, though of course the doctor had been attending him for some little time. Ah, but the master had never recovered from the shock of young Mr Mortimer's death. The old man shook his head as he hurried through a connecting door into the White Boudoir. Terrible, that had been, a real catastrophe. Such a fine upstanding young gentleman, so strong and healthy. You'd never have thought such a thing likely to happen to him. Pitiful, it had been, quite pitiful. And Mr Gordon killed in the war. One thing on top of another. That was the way things went nowadays. Too much for the master, it had been. And yet he'd seemed almost himself a week ago.

The third blind in the White Boudoir refused to go up as it should. It went up a little way and stuck. The springs were weak—that's what it was—very old, these blinds were, like everything else in the house. And you couldn't get these old things mended nowadays. Too old fashioned, that's what they'd say, shaking their heads in that silly superior way—as if the old things weren't a great deal better than the new ones! *He* could tell them that! Gimcrack, half the new stuff was—came to pieces in your hand. The material wasn't good, or the craftsmanship either. Oh yes, *he* could tell them.

Couldn't do anything about this blind unless he got the steps. He didn't like climbing up the steps much, these days, made him come over giddy. Anyway, he'd leave the blind for now. It didn't matter since the White Boudoir didn't face the front of the house where it would be seen as the cars came back from the funeral—and it wasn't as though the room was ever used nowadays. It was a lady's room, this, and there hadn't been a lady at Enderby for a long while now. A pity Mr Mortimer hadn't married. Always going off to Norway for fishing and to Scotland for shooting and to Switzerland for those winter sports, instead of marrying some nice young lady and settling down at home with children running about the house. It was a long time since there had been any children in the house.

And Lanscombe's mind went ranging back to a time that stood out clearly and distinctly—much more distinctly than the last twenty years or so, which were all blurred and confused and he couldn't really remember who had come and gone or indeed what they looked like. But he could remember the old days well enough.

More like a father to those young brothers and sisters of his, Mr Richard had been. Twenty-four when his father had died, and he'd pitched in right away to the business, going off every day as punctual as clockwork, and keeping the house running and everything as lavish as it could be. A very happy household with all those young ladies and gentlemen growing up. Fights and quarrels now and again, of course, and those governesses had had a bad time of it! Poor spirited creatures, governesses, Lanscombe had always despised them. Very spirited the young ladies had been. Miss Geraldine in particular. Miss Cora, too, although she was so much younger. And now Mr Leo was dead, and Miss Laura gone too. And Mr Timothy such a sad invalid. And Miss Geraldine dying somewhere abroad. And Mr Gordon killed in the war. Although he was the eldest, Mr Richard himself turned out the strongest of the lot. Outlived them all, he had—at least not quite because Mr Timothy was still alive and little Miss Cora who'd married that unpleasant artist chap. Twenty-five years since he'd seen her and she'd been a pretty young girl when she went off with that chap, and now he'd hardly have known her, grown so stout—and so arty crafty in her dress! A Frenchman her husband had been, or nearly a Frenchman—and no good ever came of marrying one of *them!* But Miss Cora had always been a bit—well, *simple like* you'd call it if she'd lived in a village. Always one of them in a family.

She'd remembered *him* all right. "Why, it's Lanscombe!" she'd said and seemed ever so pleased to see him. Ah, they'd all been fond of him in the old days and when there was a dinner party they'd crept down to the pantry and he'd given them jelly and Charlotte Russe when it came out of the dining room. They'd all known old Lanscombe, and now there was hardly anyone who remembered. Just the younger lot whom he could never keep clear in his mind and who just thought of him as a butler who'd been there a long time. A lot of strangers, he had thought, when they all arrived for the funeral—and a seedy lot of strangers at that!

Not Mrs Leo—she was different. She and Mr Leo had come here off and on ever since Mr Leo married. She was a nice lady, Mrs Leo—a *real* lady. Wore proper clothes and did her hair well and looked what she was. And the master had always been fond of her. A pity that she and Mr Leo had never had any children . . .

Lanscombe roused himself; what was he doing standing here and dreaming about old days with so much to be done? The blinds were all attended to on the ground floor now, and he'd told Janet to go upstairs and do the bedrooms. He and Janet and the cook had gone to the funeral service in the church but instead of going on to the Crematorium they'd driven back to the house to get the blinds up and the lunch ready. Cold lunch, of course, it had to be. Ham and chicken and tongue and salad. With cold lemon soufflé and apple tart to follow. Hot soup first —and he'd better go along and see that Marjorie had got it on ready to serve, for they'd be back in a minute or two now for certain.

Lanscombe broke into a shuffling trot across the room. His gaze, abstracted and uncurious, just swept up to the picture over this mantelpiece—the companion portrait to the one in the green drawing room. It was a nice painting of white satin and pearls. The human being round whom they were draped and clasped was not nearly so impressive. Meek features, a rosebud mouth, hair parted in the middle. A woman both modest and unassuming. The only thing really worthy of note about Mrs Cornelius Abernethie had been her name—Coralie.

For over sixty years after their original appearance, Coral Cornplasters and the allied "Coral" foot preparations still held their own. Whether there had ever been anything outstanding about Coral Cornplasters nobody could say—but they had appealed to the public fancy. On a foundation of Coral Cornplasters there had arisen this neo-Gothic palace, its acres of gardens, and the money that had paid out an income to seven sons and daughters and had allowed Richard Abernethie to die three days ago a very rich man.

ii

Looking into the kitchen with a word of admonition, Lanscombe was snapped at by Marjorie, the cook. Marjorie was young, only twenty-seven, and was a constant irritation to Lanscombe as being so far removed from what his conception of a proper cook should be. She had no dignity and no proper appreciation of his, Lanscombe's, position. She frequently called the house "a proper old mausoleum" and complained of the immense area of the kitchen, scullery and larder saying that it was a "day's walk to get round them all." She had been at Enderby two years and only stayed because, in the first place the money was good, and in the second because Mr Abernethie had really appreciated her cooking. She cooked very well. Janet, who stood by the kitchen table, refreshing herself with a cup of tea, was an elderly housemaid who, although enjoying frequent acid disputes with Lanscombe, was nevertheless usually in alliance with him against the younger generation as represented by Marjorie. The fourth person in the kitchen was Mrs Jacks who "came in" to lend assistance where it was wanted and who had much enjoyed the funeral.

"Beautiful it was," she said with a decorous sniff as she replenished her cup. "Nineteen cars and the church quite full and the Canon read the service beautiful, I thought. A nice fine day for it, too. Ah, poor dear Mr Abernethie, there's not many like him left in the world. Respected by all, he was."

There was the note of a horn and the sound of a car coming up the drive, and Mrs Jacks put down her cup and exclaimed: "Here they are."

Marjorie turned up the gas under her large saucepan of creamy chicken soup. The large kitchen range of the days of Victorian grandeur stood cold and unused, like an altar to the past.

The cars drove up one after the other and the people issuing from them in their black clothes moved rather uncertainly across the hall and into the big green drawing room. In the big steel grate a fire was burning, tribute to the first chill of the Autumn days and calculated to counteract the further chill of standing about at a funeral.

Lanscombe entered the room, offering glasses of sherry on a silver tray.

Mr Entwhistle, senior partner of the old and respected firm of Bollard, Entwhistle, Entwhistle and Bollard, stood with his back to the fireplace warming himself. He accepted a glass of sherry, and surveyed the company with his shrewd lawyer's gaze. Not all of them were personally known to him, and he was under the necessity of sorting them out, so to speak. Introductions before the departure for the funeral had been hushed and perfunctory.

Appraising old Lanscombe first, Mr Entwhistle thought to himself, "Getting very shaky, poor old chap—going on for ninety I shouldn't wonder. Well, he'll have that nice

little annuity. Nothing for *him* to worry about. Faithful
soul. No such thing as old fashioned service nowadays.
Household helps and baby sitters, God help us all! A sad
world. Just as well, perhaps, poor Richard didn't last his
full time. He hadn't much to live for."

To Mr Entwhistle who was seventy-two, Richard
Abernethie's death at sixty-eight was definitely that of a
man dead before his time. Mr Entwhistle had retired from
active business two years ago, but as executor of Richard
Abernethie's will and in respect for one of his oldest
clients who was also a personal friend, he had made the
journey to the North.

Reflecting in his own mind on the provisions of the
will, he mentally appraised the family.

Mrs Leo, Helen, he knew well, of course. A very charming woman for whom he had both liking and respect.
His eyes dwelt approvingly on her now as she stood near
one of the windows. Black suited her. She had kept her
figure well. He liked the clear cut features, the springing
line of grey hair back from her temples and the eyes that
had once been likened to cornflowers and which were still
quite vividly blue.

How old was Helen now? About fifty-one or two, he
supposed. Strange that she had never married again after
Leo's death. An attractive woman. Ah, but they had been
very devoted, those two.

His eyes went on to Mrs Timothy. He had never
known her very well. Black didn't suit her—country
tweeds were her wear. A big sensible capable-looking
woman. She'd always been a good devoted wife to Timothy. Looking after his health, fussing over him—fussing over him a bit too much, probably. Was there really
anything the matter with Timothy? Just a hypochondriac,
Mr Entwhistle suspected. Richard Abernethie had suspected so, too. "Weak chest, of course, when he was a
boy," he had said. "But blest if I think there's much
wrong with him now." Oh well, everybody had to have
some hobby. Timothy's hobby was the all absorbing one
of his own health. Was Mrs Tim taken in? Probably not
—but women never admitted that sort of thing. Timothy
must be quite comfortably off. He'd never been a spend-
thrift. However, the extra would not come amiss—not in

these days of taxation. He'd probably had to retrench his scale of living a good deal since the war.

Mr Entwhistle transferred his attention to George Crossfield, Laura's son. Dubious sort of fellow Laura had married. Nobody had ever known much about him. A stockbroker he had called himself. Young George was in a solicitor's office—not a very reputable firm. Good looking young fellow—but something a little shifty about him. He couldn't have too much to live on. Laura had been a complete fool over her investments. She'd left next to nothing when she died five years ago. A handsome romantic girl, she'd been, but no money sense.

Mr Entwhistle's eyes went on from George Crossfield. Which of the two girls was which? Ah yes, that was Rosamund, Geraldine's daughter, looking at the wax flowers on the malachite table. Pretty girl, beautiful, in fact—rather a silly face. On the stage. Repertory companies or some nonsense like that. Had married an actor, too. Good looking fellow. "*And* knows he is," thought Mr Entwhistle who was prejudiced against the stage as a profession. "Wonder what sort of a background *he* has and where he comes from."

He looked disapprovingly at Michael Shane with his fair hair and his haggard charm.

Now Susan, Gordon's daughter, would do much better on the stage than Rosamund. More personality. A little too much personality for everyday life, perhaps. She was quite near him and Mr Entwhistle studied her covertly. Dark hair, hazel—almost golden—eyes, a sulky attractive mouth. Beside her was the husband she had just married —a chemist's assistant, he understood. Really, a chemist's assistant! In Mr Entwhistle's creed girls did not marry young men who served behind a counter. But now of course, they married *anybody!* The young man who had a pale nondescript face and sandy hair seemed very ill at ease. Mr Entwhistle wondered why, but decided charitably that it was the strain of meeting so many of his wife's relations.

Last in his survey Mr Entwhistle came to Cora Lansquenet. There was a certain justice in that, for Cora had decidedly been an afterthought in the family. Richard's youngest sister, she had been born when her mother was just on fifty, and that meek woman had not survived her tenth pregnancy (three children had died in infancy). Poor little Cora! All her life, Cora had been rather an embarrassment—growing up tall and gawky, and given to blurting out remarks that had always better have remained unsaid. All her elder brothers and sisters had been very kind to Cora, atoning for her deficiencies and covering her social mistakes. It had never really occurred to anyone that Cora would marry. She had not been a very attractive girl, and her rather obvious advances to visiting young men had usually caused the latter to retreat in some alarm. And then, Mr Entwhistle mused, there had come the Lansquenet business—Pierre Lansquenet, half French, whom she had come across in an Art school where she had been having very correct lessons in painting flowers in water colours. But somehow she had got into the Life class and there she had met Pierre Lansquenet and had come home and announced her intention of marrying him. Richard Abernethie had put his foot down—he hadn't liked what he saw of Pierre Lansquenet and suspected that the young man was really in search of a rich wife. But whilst he was making a few researches into Lansquenet's antecedents, Cora had bolted with the fellow and married him out of hand. They had spent most of their married life in Brittany and Cornwall and other painters' conventional haunts. Lansquenet had been a very bad painter and not, by all accounts, a very nice man, but Cora had remained devoted to him and had never forgiven her family for their attitude to him. Richard had generously made his young sister an allowance and on that they had, so Mr Entwhistle believed, lived. He doubted if Lansquenet had ever earned any money at all. He must have been dead now twelve years or more, thought Mr Entwhistle. And now here was his widow, rather cushion-like in shape and dressed in wispy artistic black with festoons of jet beads, back in the home of her girlhood, moving about and touching things and exclaiming with pleasure when she recalled some childish memory. She made very little pretence of grief at her brother's death. But then, Mr Entwhistle reflected, Cora had never pretended.

Re-entering the room Lanscombe murmured in muted tones suitable to the occasion:

"Luncheon is served."

## 2

AFTER THE delicious chicken soup, and plenty of cold viands accompanied by an excellent *chablis,* the funeral atmosphere lightened. Nobody had really felt any deep grief for Richard Abernethie's death since none of them had had any close ties with him. Their behaviour had been suitably decorous and subdued (with the exception of the uninhibited Cora who was clearly enjoying herself) but it was now felt that the decencies had been observed and that normal conversation could be resumed. Mr Entwhistle encouraged this attitude. He was experienced in funerals and knew exactly how to set correct funeral timing.

After the meal was over, Lanscombe indicated the library for coffee. This was his feeling for niceties. The time had come when business—in other words, The Will —would be discussed. The library had the proper atmosphere for that with its bookshelves and its heavy red velvet curtains. He served coffee to them there and then withdrew closing the door.

After a few desultory remarks, everyone began to look tentatively at Mr Entwhistle. He responded promptly after glancing at his watch.

"I have to catch the 3.30 train," he began.

Others, it seemed, also had to catch that train.

"As you know," said Mr Entwhistle, "I am the executor of Richard Abernethie's will—"

He was interrupted.

"*I* didn't know," said Cora Lansquenet brightly. "Are you? Did he leave me anything?"

Not for the first time, Mr Entwhistle felt that Cora was too apt to speak out of turn.

Bending a repressive glance at her he continued:

"Up to a year ago, Richard Abernethie's will was very simple. Subject to certain legacies he left everything to his son Mortimer."

"Poor Mortimer," said Cora. "I do think all this infantile paralysis is *dreadful.*"

"Mortimer's death, coming so suddenly and tragically, was a great blow to Richard. It took him some months to rally from it. I pointed out to him that it might be advisable for him to make new testamentary dispositions."

Maude Abernethie asked in her deep voice:

"What would have happened if he *hadn't* made a new will? Would it—would it all have gone to Timothy—as the next of kin, I mean?"

Mr Entwhistle opened his mouth to give a disquisition on the subject of next of kin, thought better of it, and said crisply:

"On my advice, Richard decided to make a new will. First of all, however, he decided to get better acquainted with the younger generation."

"He had us up on appro," said Susan with a sudden rich laugh. "First George and then Greg and I, and then Rosamund and Michael."

Gregory Banks said sharply, his thin face flushing:

"I don't think you ought to put it like that, Susan. On appro, indeed!"

"But that was what it was, wasn't it, Mr Entwhistle?"

"Did he leave *me* anything?" repeated Cora.

Mr Entwhistle coughed and spoke rather coldly:

"I propose to send you all copies of the will. I can read it to you in full now if you like but its legal phraseology may seem to you rather obscure. Briefly it amounts to this: After certain small bequests and a substantial legacy to Lanscombe to purchase an annuity, the bulk of the estate—a very considerable one—is to be divided into six equal portions: Four of these, after all duties are paid, are to go to Richard's brother Timothy, his nephew George Crossfield, his niece Susan Banks, and his niece Rosamund Shane. The other two portions are to be held upon trust and the income from them paid to Mrs Helen Abernethie, the widow of his brother Leo; and to his sister Mrs Cora Lansquenet, during their lifetime. The capital after their death to be divided between the other four beneficiaries or their issue."

"That's *very* nice!" said Cora Lansquenet with real appreciation. "An income! How much?"

"I—er—can't say exactly at present. Death duties, of course will be heavy and—"

"Can't you give me any idea?"

Mr Entwhistle realised that Cora must be appeased.

"Possibly somewhere in the neighbourhood of three to four thousand a year."

"Goody!" said Cora. "I shall go to Capri."

Helen Abernethie said softly:

"How very kind and generous of Richard. I do appreciate his affection towards me."

"He was very fond of you," said Mr Entwhistle. "Leo was his favourite brother and your visits to him were always much appreciated after Leo died."

Helen said regretfully:

"I wish I had realised how ill he was—I came up to see him not long before he died, but although I knew he *had* been ill, I did not think it was serious."

"It was always serious," said Mr Entwhistle. "But he did not want it talked about and I do not believe that anybody expected the end to come as soon as it did. The doctor was quite surprised, I know."

" 'Suddenly, at his residence,' that's what it said in the paper," said Cora nodding her head. "I wondered, then."

"It was a shock to all of us," said Maude Abernethie. "It upset poor Timothy dreadfully. So sudden, he kept saying. So *sudden.*"

"Still it's been hushed up very nicely, hasn't it?" said Cora.

Everybody stared at her and she seemed a little flustered.

"I think you're all quite right," she said hurriedly. "*Quite* right. I mean—it can't do any good—making it public. Very unpleasant for everybody. It should be kept strictly in the family."

The faces turned towards her looked even more blank.

Mr Entwhistle leaned forward:

"Really, Cora, I'm afraid I don't quite understand what you mean."

Cora Lansquenet looked round at the family in wide-eyed surprise. She tilted her head on one side with a bird-like movement.

"But he *was* murdered, wasn't he?" she said.

### 3

TRAVELLING TO London in the corner of a first class carriage Mr Entwhistle gave himself up to somewhat uneasy thought over that extraordinary remark made by Cora Lansquenet. Of course Cora was a rather unbalanced and excessively stupid woman, and she had been noted, even as a girl, for the embarrassing manner in which she had blurted out unwelcome truths. At least, he didn't mean *truths*—that was *quite* the wrong word to use. Awkward statements—that was a much better term.

In his mind he went back over the immediate sequence to that unfortunate remark. The combined stare of many startled and disapproving eyes had roused Cora to a sense of the enormity of what she had said.

Maude had exclaimed, *"Really,* Cora!" George had said, "My dear Aunt Cora." Somebody else had said, "What *do* you mean?"

And at once Cora Lansquenet, abashed, and convicted of enormity, had burst into fluttering phrases.

"Oh I'm sorry—I didn't mean—oh, of course, it was very stupid of me, but I did think from what he said— Oh, of course I know it's quite all right, but his death was so *sudden*— Please forget that I said anything at all—I didn't mean to be so stupid—I know I'm always saying the wrong thing. . . ."

And then the momentary upset had died down and there had been a practical discussion about the disposition of the late Richard Abernethie's personal effects. The house and its contents, Mr Entwhistle supplemented, would be put up for sale.

Cora's unfortunate *gaffe* had been forgotten. After all, Cora had always been, if not subnormal, at any rate embarrassingly *naive*. She had never had any idea of what should or should not be said. At nineteen it had not mattered so much. The mannerisms of an *enfant terrible* can persist to then, but an *enfant terrible* of nearly fifty is decidedly disconcerting. To blurt out unwelcome truths—

Mr Entwhistle's train of thought came to an abrupt check. It was the second time that that disturbing word had occurred. *Truths.* And why was it so disturbing? Because, of course, that had always been at the bottom of the embarrassment that Cora's outspoken comments had caused. It was because her *naive* statements had been either true or had contained some grain of truth that they had been so embarrassing!

Although in the plump woman of forty-nine, Mr Entwhistle had been able to see little resemblance to the gawky girl of earlier days, certain of Cora's mannerisms had persisted—the slight birdlike twist of the head as she brought out a particularly outrageous remark—a kind of air of pleased expectancy. In just such a way had Cora once commented on the figure of the kitchenmaid. "Mollie can hardly get near the kitchen table, her stomach sticks out so. It's only been like that the last month or two. I wonder *why* she's getting so fat?"

Cora had been quickly hushed. The Abernethie household was Victorian in tone. The kitchenmaid had disappeared from the premises the next day, and after due inquiry the second gardener had been ordered to make an honest woman of her and had been presented with a cottage in which to do so.

Far off memories—but they had their point. . . .

Mr Entwhistle examined his uneasiness more closely. What was there in Cora's ridiculous remarks that had remained to tease his subconscious in this manner? Presently he isolated two phrases. "I did think from what he said—" and "his death was so sudden . . ."

Mr Entwhistle examined that last remark first. Yes, Richard's death could, in a fashion, be considered sudden. Mr Entwhistle had discussed Richard's health both with Richard himself and with his doctor. The latter had indicated plainly that a long life could not be expected. If Mr Abernethie took reasonable care of himself he might live two or even three years. Perhaps longer—but that was unlikely. In any case the doctor had anticipated no collapse in the near future.

Well, the doctors had been wrong—but doctors, as they were the first to admit themselves, could never be sure about the individual reaction of a patient to disease. Cases given up, unexpectedly recovered. Patients on the way to recovery, relapsed and died. So much depended on the vitality of the patient. On his own inner urge to live.

And Richard Abernethie, though a strong and vigorous man, had had no great incentive to live.

For six months previously his only surviving son, Mortimer, had contracted infantile paralysis and had died within a week. His death had been a shock greatly augmented by the fact that he had been such a particularly strong and vital young man. A keen sportsman, he was also a good athlete and was one of those people of whom it was said that he had never had a day's illness in his life. He was on the point of becoming engaged to a very charming girl and his father's hopes for the future were centered in this dearly loved and thoroughly satisfactory son of his.

Instead had come tragedy. And besides the sense of personal loss, the future had held little to hold Richard Abernethie's interest. One son had died in infancy, the second without issue. He had no grandchildren. There was, in fact, no one of the Abernethie name to come after him, and he was the holder of a vast fortune with wide business interests which he himself still controlled to a certain extent. Who was to succeed to that fortune and to the control of those interests?

That this had worried the old man deeply, Entwhistle knew. His only surviving brother was very much of an invalid. There remained the younger generation. It had been in Richard's mind, the lawyer thought, though his friend had not actually said so, to choose one definite successor, though minor legacies would probably have been made. Anyway, as Entwhistle knew, within the last six months Richard Abernethie had invited to stay with him, in succession his nephew George, his niece Susan and her husband, his niece Rosamund and her husband, and his sister-in-law, Mrs Leo Abernethie. It was amongst the first three so the lawyer thought, that Abernethie had looked for his successor. Helen Abernethie, he thought, had been asked out of personal affection and even possibly as someone to consult, for Richard had always held a high opinion of her good sense and practical judgment. Mr Entwhistle also remembered that sometime during that six months period Richard had paid a short visit to his brother Timothy.

The net result had been the will which the lawyer now carried in his brief case. An equable distribution of property. The only conclusion that could be drawn, therefore, was that he had been disappointed both in his nephew, and in his nieces—or perhaps in his nieces' husbands.

As far as Mr Entwhistle knew, he had not invited his sister, Cora Lansquenet to visit him—and that brought the lawyer back to that first disturbing phrase that Cora had let slip so incoherently—"but I did think from what he *said*—"

What had Richard Abernethie said? And when had he said it? If Cora had not been to Enderby, then Richard Abernethie must have visited her at the artistic village in Berkshire where she had a cottage. Or was it something that Richard had said in a letter?

Mr Entwhistle frowned. Cora, of course, was a very stupid woman. She could easily have misinterpreted a phrase, and twisted its meaning. But he did wonder what the phrase could have been. . . .

There was enough uneasiness in him to make him consider the possibility of approaching Mrs Lansquenet on the subject. Not too soon. Better not make it seem of importance. But he *would* like to know just what it was that Richard Abernethie had said to her which had led her to pipe up so briskly with that outrageous question:

*"But he was murdered, wasn't he?"*

## ii

In a third class carriage, further along the train, Gregory Banks said to his wife:

"That aunt of yours must be completely bats!"

"Aunt Cora?" Susan was vague. "Oh, yes, I believe she was always a bit simple or something."

George Crossfield, sitting opposite, said sharply:

"She really ought to be stopped from going about saying things like that. It might put ideas into people's heads."

Rosamund Shane, intent on outlining the cupid's bow of her mouth with lipstick murmured vaguely:

"I don't suppose anyone would pay any attention to what a frump like that says. The most peculiar clothes and lashings and lashings of jet—"

"Well, I think it ought to be stopped," said George.

"All right, darling," laughed Rosamund, putting away her lipstick and contemplating her image with satisfaction in the mirror. "You stop it."

Her husband said unexpectedly:

"I think George is right. It's so easy to set people talking."

"Well, would it matter?" Rosamund contemplated the question. The cupid's bow lifted at the corners in a smile. "It might really be rather fun."

"Fun?" Four voices spoke.

"Having a murder in the family," said Rosamund. "Thrilling, you know!"

It occurred to that nervous and unhappy young man Gregory Banks that Susan's cousin, setting aside her attractive exterior might have some faint points of resemblance to her Aunt Cora. Her next words rather confirmed his impression.

"If he was murdered," said Rosamund, "who do you think did it?"

Her gaze travelled thoughtfully round the carriage.

"His death has been awfully convenient for all of us," she said thoughtfully. "Michael and I are absolutely on our beam ends. Mick's had a really good part offered to him in the Sandborne show if he can afford to wait for it. Now we'll be in clover. We'll be able to back our own show if we want to. As a matter of fact there's a play with a simply wonderful part—"

Nobody listened to Rosamund's ecstatic disquisition. Their attention had shifted to their own immediate future.

"Touch and go," thought George to himself. "Now I can put that money back and nobody will ever know. . . . But it's been a near shave."

Gregory closed his eyes as he lay back against the seat. Escape from bondage.

Susan said in her clear rather hard voice, "I'm very sorry, of course, for poor old Uncle Richard. But then he *was* very old, and Mortimer had died, and he'd nothing to live for and it would have been awful for him to go on as an invalid year after year. *Much* better for him to pop off suddenly like this with no fuss."

Her hard confident young eyes softened as they watched her husband's absorbed face. She adored Greg. She sensed vaguely that Greg cared for her less than she cared for him—but that only strengthened her passion. Greg was hers, she'd do anything for him. Anything at all. . . .

### iii

Maude Abernethie, changing her dress for dinner at Enderby (for she was staying the night), wondered if she ought to have offered to stay longer to help Helen out with the sorting and clearing of the house— There would be all Richard's personal things. . . . There might be letters. . . . All important papers, she supposed, had already been taken possession of by Mr Entwhistle. And it really was necessary for her to get back to Timothy as soon as possible. He fretted so when she was not there to look after him. She hoped he would be pleased about the will and not annoyed. He had expected, she knew, that most of Richard's fortune would come to *him*. After all, he was the only surviving Abernethie. Richard could surely have trusted *him* to look after the younger generation. Yes, she was afraid Timothy *would* be annoyed. . . . And that was so bad for his digestion. And really, when he was annoyed, Timothy could become quite unreasonable. There were times when he seemed to lose his sense of proportion. . . . She wondered if she ought to speak to Dr Barton about it. . . . Those sleeping pills—Timothy had been taking far too many of them lately—he got so angry when she wanted to keep the bottle for him. But they could be dangerous—Dr Barton had said so—you could get drowsy and forget you'd taken them—and then take more. And then anything might happen! There certainly

weren't as many left in the bottle as there ought to be. . . .
Timothy was really very naughty about medicines. He
wouldn't listen to her. . . . He was very difficult sometimes.

She sighed—then brightened— Things were going to
be much easier now. The garden, for instance—

iv

Helen Abernethie sat by the fire in the green drawing
room waiting for Maude to come down to dinner.

She looked round her, remembering old days here with
Leo and the others. It had been a happy house. But a
house like this needed *people*. It needed children and servants and big meals and plenty of roaring fires in winter.
It had been a sad house when it had been lived in by one
old man who had lost his son. . . .

Who would buy it, she wondered? Would it be turned
into a Hotel, or an Institute, or perhaps one of those
Hostels for young people? That was what happened to
these vast houses nowadays. No one would buy them to
live in. It would be pulled down, perhaps, and the whole
estate built over. It made her sad to think of that, but she
pushed the sadness aside resolutely. It did one no good to
dwell on the past. This house, and happy days here, and
Richard, and Leo, all that was good, but it was over. She
had her own activities and friends and interests. Yes, her
interests. . . . And now, with the income Richard had left
her, she would be able to keep on the villa in Cyprus and
do all the things she had planned to do.

How worried she had been lately over money—taxation—all those investments going wrong. . . . Now, thanks
to Richard's money, all that was over. . . .

Poor Richard. To die in his sleep like that had been really a great mercy. . . . *Suddenly on the 22nd*—she supposed that that was what had put the idea into Cora's
head. Really Cora was outrageous! She always had been.
Helen remembered meeting her once abroad, soon after
her marriage to Pierre Lansquenet. She had been particularly foolish and fatuous that day, twisting her head sideways and making dogmatic statements about painting,
and particularly about her husband's painting, which must

have been most uncomfortable for him. No man could like his wife appearing such a fool. And Cora was a fool! Oh, well, poor thing, she couldn't help it, and that husband of hers hadn't treated her too well.

Helen's gaze rested absently on a bouquet of wax flowers that stood on a round malachite table. Cora had been sitting beside it when they had all been sitting round waiting to start for the church. She had been full of reminiscences and delighted recognitions of various things and was clearly so pleased at being back in her old home that she had completely lost sight of the reason for which they were assembled.

"But perhaps," thought Helen, "she was just less of a hypocrite than the rest of us. . . ."

Cora had never been one for observing the conventions. Look at the way she had plumped out that question: "But he *was* murdered, wasn't he?"

The faces all round, startled, shocked, staring at her! Such a variety of expressions there must have been on those faces. . . .

And suddenly, seeing the picture clearly in her mind, Helen frowned. . . . There was something wrong with that picture . . .

Something . . . ?

Somebody . . . ?

Was it an expression on someone's face? Was that it? Something that—how could she put it?—ought not to have been there . . . ?

She didn't know . . . she couldn't place it . . . but there had been something—somewhere—*wrong*.

v

Meanwhile, in the buffet at Swindon, a lady in wispy mourning and festoons of jet was eating bath buns and drinking tea and looking forward to the future. She had no premonitions of disaster. She was happy.

These cross country journeys were certainly tiring. It would have been easier to get back to Lytchett St. Mary via London—and not so very much more expensive. Ah, but expense didn't matter now. Still, she would have had to travel with the family—probably having to talk all the way. Too much of an effort.

No, better to go home cross country. These bath buns were really excellent. Extraordinary how hungry a funeral made you feel. The soup at Enderby had been delicious—and so was the cold soufflé.

How smug people were—and what hypocrites! All those faces—when she'd said that about murder! The way they'd all looked at her!

Well, it had been the right thing to say. She nodded her head in satisfied approval of herself. Yes, it had been the right thing to do.

She glanced up at the clock. Five minutes before her train went. She drank up her tea. Not very good tea. She made a grimace.

For a moment or two she sat dreaming. Dreaming of the future unfolding before her. . . . She smiled like a happy child.

She was really going to enjoy herself at last. . . . She went out to the small branch line train busily making plans. . . .

## 4

MR ENTWHISTLE passed a very restless night. He felt so tired and so unwell in the morning that he did not get up.

His sister who kept house for him, brought up his breakfast on a tray and explained to him severely how wrong he had been to go gadding off to the North of England at his age and in his frail state of health.

Mr Entwhistle contented himself with saying that Richard Abernethie had been a very old friend.

"Funerals!" said his sister with deep disapproval. "Funerals are absolutely fatal for a man of your age! You'll be taken off as suddenly as your precious Mr Abernethie was if you don't take more care of yourself."

The word "suddenly" made Mr Entwhistle wince. It also silenced him. He did not argue.

He was well aware of what had made him flinch at the word *suddenly.*

Cora Lansquenet! What she had suggested was definitely quite impossible, but all the same he would like to find out exactly why she had suggested it. Yes, he would go down to Lytchett St. Mary and see her. He could pretend that it was business connected with probate, that he needed her signature. No need to let her guess that he had paid any attention to her silly remark. But he would go down and see her—and he would do it soon.

He finished his breakfast and lay back on his pillows and read the *Times.* He found the *Times* very soothing.

It was about a quarter to six that evening when his telephone rang.

He picked it up. The voice at the other end of the wire was that of Mr James Parrott, the present second partner of Bollard, Entwhistle, Entwhistle and Bollard.

"Look here, Entwhistle," said Mr Parrott, "I've just been rung up by the police from a place called Lytchett St. Mary."

"Lytchett St. Mary?"

"Yes. It seems—" Mr Parrott paused a moment. He seemed embarrassed. "It's about a Mrs Cora Lansquenet. Wasn't she one of the heirs of the Abernethie estate?"

"Yes, of course. I saw her at the funeral yesterday."

"Oh? She was at the funeral, was she?"

"Yes. What about her?"

"Well," Mr Parrott sounded apologetic. "She's—it's really *most* extraordinary—she's been—well—*murdered.*"

Mr Parrott said the last word with the uttermost deprecation. It was not the sort of word, he suggested, that ought to mean anything to the firm of Bollard, Entwhistle, Entwhistle and Bollard.

*"Murdered?"*

"Yes—yes—I'm afraid so. Well, I mean, there's no doubt about it."

"How did the police get on to us?"

"Her companion, or housekeeper, or whatever she is—a Miss Gilchrist. The police asked for the name of her nearest relative or of her solicitors. And this Miss Gilchrist seemed rather doubtful about relatives and their addresses, but she knew about us. So they got through at once."

"What makes them think she was murdered?" demanded Mr Entwhistle.

Mr Parrott sounded apologetic again.

"Oh well, it seems there can't be any doubt about *that*—I mean it was a hatchet or something of that kind—a very violent sort of crime."

"Robbery?"

"That's the idea. A window was smashed and there are some trinkets missing and drawers pulled out and all that, but the police seem to think there might be something —well—phony about it."

"What time did it happen?"

"Sometime between two and four this afternoon."

"Where was the housekeeper?"

"Changing library books in Reading. She got back about five o'clock and found Mrs Lansquenet dead. The police want to know if we've any idea of who could have been likely to attack her. I said," Mr Parrott's voice sounded outraged, "that I thought it was a most unlikely thing to happen."

"Yes, of course."

"It *must* be some half-witted local oaf—who thought there might be something to steal and then lost his head and attacked her. That must be it—eh, don't you think so, Entwhistle?"

"Yes, yes . . ." Mr Entwhistle spoke absentmindedly.

Parrott was right, he told himself. That was what must have happened. . . .

But uncomfortably he heard Cora's voice saying brightly:

"But he *was* murdered, wasn't he?"

Such a fool, Cora. Always had been. Rushing in where angels fear to tread. . . . Blurting out unpleasant truths. . . . *Truths!*

That blasted word again . . .

ii

Mr Entwhistle and Inspector Morton looked at each other appraisingly.

In his neat precise manner Mr Entwhistle had placed at the Inspector's disposal all the relevant facts about Cora Lansquenet. Her upbringing, her marriage, her widowhood, her financial position, her relatives.

"Mr Timothy Abernethie is her only surviving brother and her next of kin, but he is a recluse and an invalid, and is quite unable to leave home. He has empowered me to act for him and to make all such arrangements as may be necessary."

The Inspector nodded. It was a relief for him to have this shrewd elderly solicitor to deal with. Moreover he hoped that the lawyer might be able to give him some assistance in solving what was beginning to look like a rather puzzling problem.

He said:

"I understand from Miss Gilchrist that Mrs Lansquenet had been North, to the funeral of an elder brother, on the day before her death?"

"That is so, Inspector. I myself was there."

"There was nothing unusual in her manner—nothing strange—or apprehensive?"

Mr Entwhistle raised his eyebrows in well simulated surprise.

"Is it customary for there to be something strange in the manner of a person who is shortly to be murdered?" he asked.

The Inspector smiled rather ruefully.

"I'm not thinking of her being 'fey' or having a premonition. No, I'm just hunting around for something—well, something out of the ordinary."

"I don't think I quite understand you, Inspector," said Mr Entwhistle.

"It's not a very easy case to understand, Mr Entwhistle. Say someone watched the Gilchrist woman come out of the house at about two o'clock and go along to the village and the bus stop. This someone then deliberately takes the hatchet that was lying by the woodshed, smashes the kitchen window with it, gets into the house, goes upstairs, attacks Mrs Lansquenet with the hatchet—and attacks her savagely. Six or eight blows were struck." Mr Entwhistle flinched—"Oh, yes, quite a brutal crime. Then the

intruder pulls out a few drawers, scoops up a few trinkets
—worth perhaps a tenner in all, and clears off."

"She was in bed?"

"Yes. It seems she returned late from the North the
night before, exhausted and very excited. She'd come into
some legacy as I understand?"

"Yes."

"She slept very badly and woke with a terrible
headache. She had several cups of tea and took some
dope for her head and then told Miss Gilchrist not to disturb her till lunch-time. She felt no better and decided to
take two sleeping pills. She then sent Miss Gilchrist into
Reading by the bus to change some library books. She'd
have been drowsy, if not already asleep, when this man
broke in. He could have taken what he wanted by means
of threats, or he could easily have gagged her. A hatchet,
deliberately taken up with him from the outside, seems
excessive."

"He may just have meant to threaten her with it," Mr
Entwhistle suggested. "If she showed fight then—"

"According to the medical evidence there is no sign
that she did. Everything seems to show that she was lying
on her side sleeping peacefully when she was attacked."

Mr Entwhistle shifted uneasily in his chair.

"One does hear of these brutal and rather senseless
murders," he pointed out.

"Oh yes, yes, that's probably what it will turn out to
be. There's an alert out, of course, for any suspicious
character. Nobody local is concerned, we're pretty sure of
that. The locals are all accounted for satisfactorily. Most
people are at work at that time of day. Of course her cottage is up a lane outside the village proper. Anyone could
get there easily without being seen. There's a maze of
lanes all round the village. It was a fine morning and
there has been no rain for some days so there aren't any
distinctive car tracks to go by—in case anyone came by
car."

"You think someone came by car?" Mr Entwhistle
asked sharply.

The Inspector shrugged his shoulders. "I don't know.
All I'm saying is there are curious features about the case.
These, for instance—" He shoved across his desk a hand-

ful of things—a trefoil-shaped brooch with small pearls, a brooch set with amethysts, a small string of seed pearls, and a garnet bracelet.

"Those are the things that were taken from her jewel box. They were found just outside the house shoved into a bush."

"Yes—yes, that *is* rather curious. Perhaps if her assailant was frightened at what he had done—"

"Quite. But he would probably then have left them upstairs in her room . . . Of course a panic may have come over him between the bedroom and the front gate."

Mr Entwhistle said quietly:

"Or they may, as you are suggesting, have only been taken as a blind."

"Yes, several possibilities . . . Of course this Gilchrist woman may have done it. Two women living alone together—you never know what quarrels or resentments or passions may have been aroused. Oh yes, we're taking that possibility into consideration as well. But it doesn't seem very likely. From all accounts they seemed to be on quite amicable terms." He paused before going on. "According to you nobody stands to gain by Mrs Lansquenet's death?"

The lawyer shifted uneasily.

"I didn't quite say that."

Inspector Morton looked up sharply.

"I thought you said that Mrs Lansquenet's source of income was an allowance made to her by her brother and that as far as you knew she had no property or means of her own."

"That is so. Her husband died a bankrupt, and from what I knew of her as a girl and since, I should be surprised if she had ever saved or accumulated any money."

"The cottage itself is rented, not her own, and the few sticks of furniture aren't anything to write home about, even in these days. Some spurious 'cottage oak' and some arty painted stuff. Whoever she's left them to won't gain much—if she's made a will, that is to say."

Mr Entwhistle shook his head.

"I know nothing about her will. I had not seen her for many years, you must understand."

"Then what exactly did you mean just now? You had something in mind, I think?"

"Yes. Yes, I did. I wished to be strictly accurate."

"Were you referring to the legacy you mentioned? The one that her brother left her? Had she the power to dispose of that by will?"

"No, not in the sense you mean. She had no power to dispose of the capital. Now that she is dead, it will be divided amongst the five other beneficiaries of Richard Abernethie's will. That is what I meant. All five of them will benefit automatically by her death."

The Inspector looked disappointed.

"Oh, I thought we were on to something. Well, there certainly seems no motive there for anyone to come and swipe her with a hatchet. Looks as though it's some chap with a screw loose—one of these adolescent criminals, perhaps—a lot of them about. And then he lost his nerve and bushed the trinkets and ran . . . Yes, it must be that. Unless it's the highly respectable Miss Gilchrist and I must say that seems unlikely."

"When did she find the body?"

"Not until just about five o'clock. She came back from Reading by the 4.50 bus. She arrived back at the cottage, let herself in by the front door, and went into the kitchen and put the kettle on for tea. There was no sound from Mrs Lansquenet's room, but Miss Gilchrist assumed that she was still sleeping. Then Miss Gilchrist noticed the kitchen window, the glass was all over the floor. Even then, she thought at first it might have been done by a boy with a ball or a catapult. She went upstairs and peeped very gently into Mrs Lansquenet's room to see if she was asleep or if she was ready for some tea. Then of course, she let loose, shrieked, and rushed down the lane to the nearest neighbor. Her story seems perfectly consistent and there was no trace of blood in her room or in the bathroom, or on her clothes. No, I don't think Miss Gilchrist had anything to do with it. The doctor got there at half past five. He puts the time of death not later than four o'clock—and probably much nearer to two o'clock, so it looks as though whoever it was, was hanging round waiting for Miss Gilchrist to leave the cottage."

The lawyer's face twitched slightly. Inspector Morton

went on: "You'll be going to see Miss Gilchrist, I suppose?"

"I thought of doing so."

"I should be glad if you would. She's told us, I think, everything that she can, but you never know. Sometimes in conversation, some point or other may crop up. She's a trifle old-maidish—but quite a sensible practical woman —and she's really been most helpful and efficient."

He paused and then said:

"The body's at the mortuary. If you would like to see it—"

Mr Entwhistle assented though with no enthusiasm.

Some few minutes later he stood looking down at the mortal remains of Cora Lansquenet. She had been savagely attacked and the henna dyed fringe was clotted and stiffened with blood. Mr Entwhistle's lips tightened and he looked away queasily.

Poor little Cora. How eager she had been the day before yesterday to know whether her brother had left her anything. What rosy anticipations she must have had of the future. What a lot of silly things she could have done —and enjoyed doing—with the money.

Poor Cora. . . . How short a time those anticipations had lasted.

No one had gained by her death—not even the brutal assailant who had thrust away those trinkets as he fled. Five people had a few thousands more of capital—but the capital they had already received was probably more than sufficient for them. No, there could be no motive there.

Funny that murder should have been running in Cora's mind the very day before she herself was murdered.

*"It was murder, wasn't it?"*

Such a ridiculous thing to say. Ridiculous! Quite ridiculous! Much too ridiculous to mention to Inspector Morton.

Of course, after he had seen Miss Gilchrist . . .

Supposing that Miss Gilchrist, although it was unlikely, could throw any light on what Richard had said to Cora.

*"I thought from what he said—"* What *had* Richard said?

"I must see Miss Gilchrist at once," said Mr Entwhistle to himself.

### iii

Miss Gilchrist was a spare faded-looking woman with short iron grey hair. She had one of those indeterminate faces that women around fifty so often acquire.

She greeted Mr Entwhistle warmly.

"I'm *so* glad you have come, Mr Entwhistle. I really know *so little* about Mrs Lansquenet's family, and of course I've never never had anything to do with a *murder* before. It's too dreadful!"

Mr Entwhistle felt quite sure that Miss Gilchrist had never before had anything to do with murder. Indeed, her reaction to it was very much that of his partner.

"One *reads* about them, of course," said Miss Gilchrist, relegating crimes to their proper sphere. "And even *that* I'm not very fond of doing. So *sordid,* most of them."

Following her into the sitting room Mr Entwhistle was looking sharply about him. There was a strong smell of oil paint. The cottage was overcrowded, less by furniture which was much as Inspector Morton had described it, than by pictures. The walls were covered with pictures, mostly very dark and dirty oil paintings. But there were water colour sketches as well, and one or two still lifes. Smaller pictures were stacked on the window seat.

"Mrs Lansquenet used to buy them at sales," Miss Gilchrist explained. "It was a great interest to her, poor dear. She went to all the sales round about. Pictures go so cheap, nowadays, a mere song. She never paid more than a pound for any of them, sometimes only a few shillings and there was a wonderful chance, she always said, of picking up something worthwhile. She used to say that this was an Italian Primitive that might be worth a lot of money."

Mr Entwhistle looked at the Italian Primitive pointed out to him dubiously. Cora, he reflected, had never really known anything about pictures. He'd eat his hat if any of these daubs were worth a five pound note!

"Of course," said Miss Gilchrist, noticing his expression, and quick to sense his reaction. "I don't know much myself, though my father was a painter—not a very successful one, I'm afraid. But I used to do water colours

myself as a girl and I heard a lot of talk about painting
and that made it nice for Mrs Lansquenet to have someone she could talk to about painting and who'd understand. Poor dear soul, she cared so much about artistic
things."

"You were fond of her?"

A foolish question, he told himself. Could she possibly
answer "no"? Cora, he thought, must have been a tiresome woman to live with.

"Oh *yes,*" said Miss Gilchrist. "We got on *very* well together. In some ways, you know, Mrs Lansquenet was
just like a child. She said anything that came into her
head. I don't know that her *judgment* was always very
good—"

One does not say of the dead—"She was a thoroughly
silly woman"— Mr Entwhistle said, "She was not in any
sense an intellectual woman."

"No—no—perhaps not. But she was very shrewd, Mr
Entwhistle. Really very shrewd. It quite surprised me
sometimes—how she managed to hit the nail on the head."

Mr Entwhistle looked at Miss Gilchrist with more interest. He thought that she was no fool herself.

"You were with Mrs Lansquenet for some years, I
think?"

"Three and a half."

"You—er—acted as companion and also did the—er
—well—looked after the house?"

It was evident that he had touched on a delicate subject. Miss Gilchrist flushed a little.

"Oh yes, indeed. I did most of the cooking—I *quite*
enjoy cooking—and did some dusting and light housework. None of the *rough*, of course." Miss Gilchrist's tone
expressed a firm principle. Mr Entwhistle who had no
idea what "the rough" was, made a soothing murmur.

"Mrs Panter from the village came in for that. Twice a
week regularly. You see, Mr Entwhistle, I could not have
contemplated being in any way a *servant*. When my little
teashop failed—such a disaster—it was the war, you
know. A delightful place. I called it the Willow Tree and
all the china was blue willow pattern—sweetly pretty—
and the cakes *really* good—I've always had a hand with
cakes and scones. Yes I was doing really well and then

the war came and supplies were cut down and the whole thing went bankrupt—a war casualty, that is what I always say, and I try to think of it like that. I lost the little money my father left me that I had invested in it, and of course I had to look round for something to do. I'd never been trained for anything. So I went to one lady but it didn't answer at all—she was so rude and overbearing and then I did some office work—but I didn't like that at all, and then I came to Mrs Lansquenet and we suited each other from the start—her husband being an artist and everything." Miss Gilchrist came to a breathless stop and added mournfully: "But how I loved my dear dear little teashop. Such *nice* people used to come to it!"

Looking at Miss Gilchrist, Mr Entwhistle felt a sudden stab of recognition—a composite picture of hundreds of ladylike figures approaching him in numerous Bay Trees, Ginger Cats, Blue Parrots, Willow Trees and Cosy Corners, all chastely encased in blue or pink or orange overalls and taking orders for pots of china tea and cakes. Miss Gilchrist had a Spiritual Home—a ladylike teashop of Ye Olde Worlde variety with a suitable genteel clientele. There must, he thought, be large numbers of Miss Gilchrists all over the country, all looking much alike with mild patient faces and obstinate upper lips and slightly wispy grey hair.

Miss Gilchrist went on:

"But really I must not talk about myself. The police have been very kind and considerate. Very kind indeed. An Inspector Morton came over from headquarters and he was *most* understanding. He even arranged for me to go and spend the night at Mrs Lake's down the lane but I said 'No.' I felt it my duty to stay here with all Mrs Lansquenet's nice things in the house. They took the—the—" Miss Gilchrist gulped a little—"the body away, of course, and locked up the room, and the Inspector told me there would be a constable on duty in the kitchen all night— because of the broken window—it has been reglazed this morning, I am glad to say—where was I?—Oh yes, so I said I should be *quite* all right in my own room, though I must confess I *did* pull the chest of drawers across the door and put a big jug of water on the window-sill. One never knows—and if by any chance it *was* a maniac—one does hear of such things . . ."

Here Miss Gilchrist ran down. Mr Entwhistle said quickly:

"I am in possession of all the main facts. Inspector Morton gave them to me. But if it would not distress you too much to give me your own account—?"

"Of course, Mr Entwhistle. I know *just* what you feel. The police are so impersonal, are they not? Rightly so, of course."

"Mrs Lansquenet got back from the funeral the night before last," Mr Entwhistle prompted.

"Yes, her train didn't get in until quite late. I had ordered a taxi to meet it as she told me to. She was very tired, poor dear—as was only natural—but on the whole she was in quite good spirits."

"Yes, yes. Did she talk about the funeral at all?"

"Just a little. I made her a cup of Ovaltine—she didn't want anything else—and she told me that the church had been quite full and lots and lots of flowers—oh! and she said that she was sorry not to have seen her other brother —Timothy—was it?"

"Yes, Timothy."

"She said it was over twenty years since she had seen him and that she hoped he would have been there, but she quite realised he would have thought it better not to come under the circumstances, but that his wife was there and that she'd never been able to stand Maude—oh dear, I *do* beg your pardon, Mr Entwhistle—it just slipped out—I never meant—"

"Not at all. Not at all," said Mr Entwhistle encouragingly. "I am no relation, you know. And I believe that Cora and her sister-in-law never hit it off very well."

"Well, she almost said as much. 'I always knew Maude would grow into one of those bossy interfering women,' is what she said. And then she was very tired and said she'd go to bed at once—I'd got her hot water bottle in all ready—and she went up."

"She said nothing else that you can remember specially?"

"She had no *premonition*, Mr Entwhistle, if that is what you mean. I'm sure of that. She was really, you know, in remarkably good spirits—apart from tiredness and the—the sad occasion. She asked me how I'd like to go to Capri. To Capri! Of course I said it would be too wonderful—it's a thing I'd never dreamed I'd ever do—and she said, 'We'll go!' Just like that. I gathered—of course it wasn't actually *mentioned*—that her brother had left her an annuity or something of the kind."

Mr Entwhistle nodded.

"Poor dear. Well, I'm glad she had the pleasure of planning—at all events." Miss Gilchrist sighed and murmured wistfully, "I don't suppose I shall ever go to Capri now. . . ."

"And the next morning?" Mr Entwhistle prompted, oblivious of Miss Gilchrist's disappointments.

"The next morning Mrs Lansquenet wasn't at all well. Really, she looked dreadful. She'd hardly slept at all, she told me. Nightmares. 'It's because you were overtired yesterday,' I told her, and she said maybe it was. She had her breakfast in bed, and she didn't get up all the morning, but at lunchtime she told me that she still hadn't been able to sleep. 'I feel so restless,' she said. 'I keep thinking of things and wondering.' And then she said she'd take some sleeping tablets and try and get a good sleep in the afternoon. And she wanted me to go over by bus to Reading and change her two library books, because she'd finished them both on the train journey and she hadn't got anything to read. Usually two books lasted her nearly a week. So I went off just after two and that—and that—was the last time—" Miss Gilchrist began to sniff. "She must have been asleep, you know. She wouldn't have heard anything and the Inspector assures me that she didn't suffer. . . . He thinks the first blow killed her. Oh dear, it makes me quite sick even to *think* of it!"

"Please, please. I've no wish to take you any further over what happened. All I wanted was to hear what you could tell me about Mrs Lansquenet before the tragedy."

"Very natural, I'm sure. Do tell her relations that apart from having such a bad night she was really very happy and looking forward to the future."

Mr Entwhistle paused before asking his next question. He wanted to be careful not to lead the witness.

"She did not mention any of her relations in particular?"

"No, no, I don't think so." Miss Gilchrist considered. "Except what she said about being sorry not to see her brother Timothy."

"She did not speak at all about her brother's decease? The—er—cause of it? Anything like that?"

"No."

There was no sign of alertness in Miss Gilchrist's face. Mr Entwhistle felt certain there would have been if Cora had plumped out her verdict of murder.

"He'd been ill for some time, I think," said Miss Gilchrist vaguely, "though I must say I was surprised to hear it. He looked so very vigorous."

Mr Entwhistle said quickly:

"You saw him—when?"

"When he came down here to see Mrs Lansquenet. Let me see—that was about three weeks ago."

"Did he stay here?"

"Oh—no—just came for luncheon. It was quite a surprise. Mrs Lansquenet hadn't expected him. I gather there had been some family disagreement. She hadn't seen him for years, she told me."

"Yes, that is so."

"It quite upset her—seeing him again—and probably realizing how ill he was—"

"She knew that he was ill?"

"Oh yes, I remember quite well. Because I wondered—only in my own mind, you understand—if perhaps Mr Abernethie might be suffering from softening of the brain. An aunt of mine—"

Mr Entwhistle deftly sidetracked the aunt.

"Something Mrs Lansquenet said caused you to think of softening of the brain?"

"Yes. Mrs Lansquenet said something like 'Poor Richard. Mortimer's death must have aged him a lot. He sounds quite senile. All these fancies about persecution and that someone is poisoning him. Old people get like that.' And of course, as I knew, that is only too *true*. This aunt that I was telling you about—convinced the servants were trying to poison her in her food and at last would eat only boiled eggs—because, she said, you couldn't get inside a boiled egg to poison it. We humoured her, but if it had been nowadays I don't know *what* we should have done. With eggs so scarce and mostly foreign at that, so that boiling is always risky."

Mr Entwhistle listened to the saga of Miss Gilchrist's aunt with deaf ears. He was very much disturbed.

He said at last, when Miss Gilchrist had twittered into silence:

"I suppose Mrs Lansquenet didn't take all this too seriously?"

"Oh no, Mr Entwhistle, she *quite* understood."

Mr Entwhistle found that remark disturbing too, though not quite in the sense in which Miss Gilchrist had used it.

*Had* Cora Lansquenet understood? Not then, perhaps, but later. Had she understood only too well?

Mr Entwhistle knew that there had been no senility about Richard Abernethie. Richard had been in full possession of his faculties. He was not the man to have persecution mania in any form. He was, as he always had been, a hard-headed business man—and his illness made no difference in that respect.

It seemed extraordinary that he should have spoken to his sister in the terms that he had. But perhaps Cora, with her odd childlike shrewdness had read between the lines, and had crossed the t's and dotted the i's of what Richard Abernethie had actually said.

In most ways, thought Mr Entwhistle, Cora had been a complete fool. She had no judgment, no balance, and a crude childish point of view, but she had also the child's uncanny knack of sometimes hitting the nail on the head in a way that seemed quite startling.

Mr Entwhistle left it at that. Miss Gilchrist, he thought, knew no more than she had told him. He asked whether she knew if Cora Lansquenet had left a will. Miss Gilchrist replied promptly that Mrs Lansquenet's will was at the Bank.

With that and after making certain further arrangements he took his leave. He insisted on Miss Gilchrist's accepting a small sum in cash to defray present expenses and told her he would communicate with her again, and in the meantime he would be grateful if she would stay on at the cottage while she was looking about for a new post.

That would be, Miss Gilchrist said, a great convenience and really she was not at all nervous.

He was unable to escape without being shown round the cottage by Miss Gilchrist, and introduced to various pictures by the late Pierre Lansquenet which were crowded into the small dining room and which made Mr Entwhistle flinch—they were mostly nudes executed with a singular lack of draughtsmanship but with much fidelity to detail. He was also made to admire various small oil sketches of picturesque fishing ports done by Cora herself.

"Polperro," said Miss Gilchrist proudly. "We were there last year and Mrs Lansquenet was delighted with its picturesqueness."

Mr Entwhistle, viewing Polperro from the southwest, from the northwest, and presumably from the several other points of the compass, agreed that Mrs Lansquenet had certainly been enthusiastic.

"Mrs Lansquenet promised to leave me her sketches," said Miss Gilchrist wistfully. "I admired them so much. One can really see the waves breaking in this one, can't one? Even if she forgot, I might perhaps have just *one* as a souvenir, do you think?"

"I'm sure that could be arranged," said Mr Entwhistle graciously.

He made a few further arrangements and then left to interview the Bank Manager and to have a further consultation with Inspector Morton.

# 5

"Worn out, that's what you are," said Miss Entwhistle in the indignant and bullying tones adopted by devoted sisters towards brothers for whom they keep house. "You shouldn't do it, at your age. What's it all got to do with you, I'd like to know? You've retired, haven't you?"

Mr Entwhistle said mildly that Richard Abernethie had been one of his oldest friends.

"I daresay. But Richard Abernethie's dead, isn't he? So

I see no reason for you to go mixing yourself up in things that are no concern of yours and catching your death of cold in these nasty draughty railway trains. And murder, too! *I* can't see why they sent for you at all."

"They communicated with me because there was a letter in the cottage signed by me, telling Cora the arrangements for the funeral."

"Funerals! One funeral after another, and that reminds me. Another of these precious Abernethies has been ringing you up—Timothy, I think he said. From somewhere in Yorkshire—and *that's* about a funeral, too! Said he'd ring again later."

A personal call for Mr Entwhistle came through that evening. Taking it, he heard Maude Abernethie's voice at the other end.

"Thank goodness I've got hold of you at last! Timothy has been in the most terrible state. This news about Cora has upset him dreadfully."

"Quite understandable," said Mr Entwhistle.

"What did you say?"

"I said it was quite understandable."

"I suppose so." Maude sounded more than doubtful. "Do you mean to say it was really murder?"

(*"It was murder, wasn't it?"* Cora had said. But this time there was no hesitation about the answer.)

"Yes, it was murder," said Mr Entwhistle.

"And with a hatchet, so the papers say?"

"Yes."

"It seems *quite* incredible to me," said Maude, "that Timothy's sister—his own sister—can have been murdered with a *hatchet!*"

It seemed no less incredible to Mr Entwhistle. Timothy's life was so remote from violence that even his relations, one felt, ought to be equally exempt.

"I'm afraid one has to face the fact," said Mr Entwhistle mildly.

"I am really *very* worried about Timothy. It's so bad for him all this! I've got him to bed now but he insists on my persuading you to come up and see him. He wants to know a hundred things—whether there will be an inquest, and who ought to attend, and how soon after that the funeral can take place, and where, and what funds there are, and if Cora expressed any wishes about being cremated or what, and if she left a will—"

Mr Entwhistle interrupted before the catalogue got too long.

"There is a will, yes. She left Timothy her executor."

"Oh dear, I'm afraid Timothy can't undertake anything—"

"The firm will attend to all the necessary business. The will's very simple. She left her own sketches and an amethyst brooch to her companion, Miss Gilchrist and everything else to Susan."

"To Susan? Now I wonder why Susan? I don't believe she ever saw Susan—not since she was a baby anyway."

"I imagine that it was because Susan was reported to have made a marriage not wholly pleasing to the family."

Maude snorted.

"Even Gregory is a great deal better than Pierre Lansquenet ever was! Of course marrying a man who serves in a shop would have been unheard of in my day—but a chemist's shop is much better than a haberdasher's—and at least Gregory seems quite respectable." She paused and added: "Does this mean that Susan gets the income Richard left to Cora?"

"Oh no. The capital of that will be divided according to the instructions of Richard's will. No, poor Cora had only a few hundred pounds and the furniture of her cottage to leave. When outstanding debts are paid and the furniture sold I doubt if the whole thing will amount to more than at most five hundred pounds." He went on: "There will have to be an inquest, of course. That is fixed for next Thursday. If Timothy is agreeable, we'll send down young Lloyd to watch the proceedings on behalf of the family." He added apologetically: "I'm afraid it may attract some notoriety owing to the—er—circumstances."

"How very unpleasant! Have they caught the wretch who did it?"

"Not yet."

"One of these dreadful half baked young men who go about the country roving and murdering, I suppose. The police are so incompetent."

"No, no," said Mr Entwhistle. "The police are by no means incompetent. Don't imagine that, for a moment."

"Well, it all seems to me quite extraordinary. And *so* bad for Timothy. I suppose you couldn't possibly come down here, Mr Entwhistle? I should be *most* grateful if you could. I think Timothy's mind might be set at rest if you were here to reassure him."

Mr Entwhistle was silent for a moment. The invitation was not unwelcome.

"There is something in what you say," he admitted. "And I shall need Timothy's signature as executor to certain documents. Yes, I think it might be quite a good thing."

"That is splendid. I am so relieved. Tomorrow? And you'll stay the night? The best train is the 11.20 from St. Pancras."

"It will have to be an afternoon train, I'm afraid. I have—" said Mr Entwhistle, "other business in the morning . . ."

## ii

George Crossfield greeted Mr Entwhistle heartily but with, perhaps, just a shade of surprise.

Mr Entwhistle said, in an explanatory way, although it really explained nothing:

"I've just come up from Lytchett St. Mary."

"Then it really was Aunt Cora? I read about it in the papers and I just couldn't believe it. I thought it must be someone of the same name."

"Lansquenet is not a common name."

"No, of course it isn't. I suppose there is a natural aversion to believing that anyone of one's own family can be murdered. Sounds to me rather like that case last month on Dartmoor."

"Does it?"

"Yes. Same circumstances. Cottage in a lonely position. Two elderly women living together. Amount of cash taken really quite pitifully inadequate one would think."

"The value of money is always relative," said Mr Entwhistle. "It is the need that counts."

"Yes—yes, I suppose you're right."

"If you need ten pounds desperately—then fifteen is more than adequate. And inversely also. If your need is for a hundred pounds, forty-five would be worse than useless. And if it's thousands you need, then hundreds are not enough."

George said with a sudden flicker of the eyes: "I'd say *any* money came in useful these days. Everyone's hard up."

"But not *desperate*," Mr Entwhistle pointed out. "It's the desperation that counts."

"Are you thinking of something in particular?"

"Oh no, not at all." He paused then went on. "It will be a little time before the estate is settled, would it be convenient for you to have an advance?"

"As a matter of fact, I *was* going to raise the subject. However, I saw the Bank this morning and referred them to you and they were quite obliging about an overdraft."

Again there came that flicker in George's eyes, and Mr Entwhistle, from the depths of his experience, recognised it. George, he felt certain, had been, if not desperate, then in very sore straits for money. He knew at that moment, what he had felt sub-consciously all along, that in money matters he would not trust George. He wondered if old Richard Abernethie, who also had had great experience in judging men, had felt that. Mr Entwhistle was almost sure that after Mortimer's death, Richard Abernethie had formed the intention of making George his heir. George was not an Abernethie, but he was the only male of the younger generation. He was the natural successor to Mortimer. Richard Abernethie had sent for George, had had him staying in the house for some days. It seemed probable that at the end of the visit the older man had not found George satisfactory. Had he felt instinctively, as Mr Entwhistle felt, that George was not straight? George's father, so the family had thought, had been a poor choice on Laura's part. A stockbroker who had had other rather mysterious activities. George took after his father rather than after the Abernethies.

Perhaps misinterpreting the old lawyer's silence, George said with an uneasy laugh:

"Truth is, I've not been very lucky with my investments lately. I took a bit of a risk and it didn't come off. More or less cleaned me out. But I'll be able to recoup myself now. All one needs is a bit of capital. Ardens Consolidated are pretty good, don't you think?"

Mr Entwhistle neither agreed nor dissented. He was wondering if by any chance George had been speculating with money that belonged to clients and not with his own? If George had been in danger of criminal prosecution—

Mr Entwhistle said precisely:

"I tried to reach you the day after the funeral, but I suppose you weren't in the office."

"Did you? They never told me. As a matter of fact, I thought I was entitled to a day off after the good news!"

"The good news?"

George reddened.

"Oh look here, I didn't mean Uncle Richard's death. But knowing you've come into money does give one a bit of a kick. One feels one must celebrate. As a matter of fact I went to Hurst Park. Backed two winners. It never rains but it pours! If your luck's in, it's in! Only a matter of fifty quid, but it all helps."

"Oh yes," said Mr Entwhistle. "It all helps. And there will now be an additional sum coming to you as a result of your Aunt Cora's death."

George looked concerned.

"Poor old girl," he said. "It does seem rotten luck, doesn't it? Probably just when she was all set to enjoy herself."

"Let us hope the police will find the person responsible for her death," said Mr Entwhistle.

"I expect they'll get him all right. They're good, our police. They round up all the undesirables in the neighbourhood and go through 'em with a tooth comb—make them account for their actions at the time it happened."

"Not so easy if a little time has elapsed," said Mr Entwhistle. He gave a wintry little smile that indicated he was about to make a joke. "I myself was in Hatchard's bookshop at 3.30 on the day in question. Should I remember that if I were questioned by the police in ten days' time? I very much doubt it. And you, George, you were at Hurst Park. Would you remember which day you went to the races in—say—a month's time?"

"Oh I could fix it by the funeral—the day after."

"True—true. And then you backed a couple of winners. Another aid to memory. One seldom forgets the name of a horse on which one has won money. Which were they, by the way?"

"Let me see. Gaymarck and Frogg II. Yes, I shan't forget them in a hurry."

Mr Entwhistle gave his dry little cackle of laughter and took his leave.

### iii

"It's lovely to see you, of course," said Rosamund without any marked enthusiasm. "But it's frightfully early in the morning."

She yawned heavily.

"It's eleven o'clock," said Mr Entwhistle.

Rosamund yawned again. She said apologetically:

"We had the hell of a party last night. Far too much to drink. Michael's got a terrible hangover still."

Michael appeared at this moment, also yawning. He had a cup of black coffee in his hand and was wearing a very smart dressing gown. He looked haggard and attractive—and his smile had the usual charm. Rosamund was wearing a black skirt, a rather dirty yellow pullover, and nothing else as far as Mr Entwhistle could judge.

The precise and fastidious lawyer did not approve at all of the young Shanes' way of living. The rather ramshackle flat on the first floor of a Chelsea house—the bottles and glasses and cigarette ends that lay about in profusion—the stale air, and the general air of dust and dishevelment.

In the midst of this discouraging setting Rosamund and Michael bloomed with their wonderful good looks. They were certainly a very handsome couple and they seemed, Mr Entwhistle thought, very fond of each other. Rosamund was certainly adoringly fond of Michael.

"Darling," she said. "Do you think just a teeny sip of champagne? Just to pull us together and toast the future. Oh, Mr Entwhistle, it really is the most marvellous luck Uncle Richard leaving us all that lovely money just now—"

Mr Entwhistle noted the quick almost scowling frown that Michael gave, but Rosamund went on serenely:

"Because there's the most wonderful chance of a play. Michael's got an option on it. It's a most wonderful part for him and even a small part for me, too. It's about one of these young criminals, you know, that are really saints —it's absolutely full of the latest modern ideas."

"So it would seem," said Mr Entwhistle stiffly.

"He robs, you know, and he kills, and he's hounded by the police and by society—and then in the end, he does a miracle."

Mr Entwhistle sat in outraged silence. Pernicious nonsense these young fools talked! *And* wrote.

Not that Michael Shane was talking much. There was still a faint scowl on his face.

"Mr Entwhistle doesn't want to hear all our rhapsodies, Rosamund," he said. "Shut up for a bit and let him tell us why he's come to see us."

"There are just one or two little matters to straighten out," said Mr Entwhistle. "I have just come back from Lytchett St. Mary."

"Then it *was* Aunt Cora who was murdered? We saw it in the paper. And I said it must be because it's a very uncommon name. Poor old Aunt Cora. I was looking at her at the funeral that day and thinking what a frump she was and that really one might as well be dead if one looked like that—and now she *is* dead. They absolutely wouldn't *believe* it last night when I told them that the murder with the hatchet in the paper was actually *my aunt!* They just laughed, didn't they, Michael?"

Michael Shane did not reply and Rosamund with every appearance of enjoyment said:

"Two murders one after another. It's almost too much, isn't it?"

"Don't be a fool, Rosamund, your Uncle Richard wasn't murdered."

"Well, Cora thought he was."

Mr Entwhistle intervened to ask:

"You came back to London after the funeral, didn't you?"

"Yes, we came by the same train as you did."

"Of course . . . of course. I ask because I tried to get hold of you," he shot a quick glance at the telephone—

"on the following day—several times in fact, and couldn't get an answer."

"Oh dear—I'm so sorry. What were we doing that day? The day before yesterday. We were here until about twelve, weren't we? And then you went round to try and get hold of Rosenheim and you went on to lunch with Oscar and I went out to see if I could get some nylons and round the shops. I was to meet Janet but we missed each other. Yes, I had a lovely afternoon shopping—and then we dined at the *Castile*. We got back here about ten o'clock, I suppose."

"About that," said Michael. He was looking thoughtfully at Mr Entwhistle. "What did you want to get hold of us for, sir?"

"Oh! Just some points that had arisen about Richard Abernethie's estate—papers to sign—all that."

Rosamund asked: "Do we get the money now, or not for ages?"

"I'm afraid," said Mr Entwhistle, "that the law is prone to delays."

"But we can get an advance, can't we?" Rosamund looked alarmed. "Michael said we could. Actually it's terribly important. Because of the play."

Michael said pleasantly:

"Oh, there's no real hurry. It's just a question of deciding whether or not to take up the option."

"It will be quite easy to advance you some money," said Mr Entwhistle. "As much as you need."

"Then that's all right." Rosamund gave a sigh of relief. She added as an afterthought: "Did Aunt Cora leave any money?"

"A little. She left it to your Cousin Susan."

"Why Susan, I should like to know! Is it much?"

"A few hundred pounds and some furniture."

"Nice furniture?"

"No," said Mr Entwhistle.

Rosamund lost interest. "It's all very odd, isn't it?" she said. "There was Cora, after the funeral, suddenly coming out with 'He *was* murdered!' and then, the very next day, *she* goes and gets *herself* murdered! I mean, it is *odd*, isn't it?"

There was a moment's rather uncomfortable silence before Mr Entwhistle said quietly:

"Yes, it is indeed very odd. . . ."

### iv

Mr Entwhistle studied Susan Banks as she leant forward across the table talking in her animated manner.

None of the loveliness of Rosamund here. But it was an attractive face and its attraction lay, Mr Entwhistle decided, in its vitality. The curves of the mouth were rich and full. It was a woman's mouth and her body was very decidedly a woman's—emphatically so. Yet in many ways Susan reminded him of her uncle, Richard Abernethie. The shape of her head, the line of her jaw, the deep set reflective eyes. She had the same kind of dominant personality that Richard had had, the same driving energy, the same foresightedness and forthright judgment. Of the three members of the younger generation she alone seemed to be made of the mettle that had raised up the vast Abernethie fortunes. Had Richard recognised in this niece a kindred spirit to his own? Mr Entwhistle thought he must have done. Richard had always had a keen appreciation of character. Here, surely, were exactly the qualities of which he was in search. And yet, in his will, Richard Abernethie had made no distinction in her favour. Distrustful, as Mr Entwhistle believed, of George, passing over that lovely dimwit, Rosamund—could he not have found in Susan what he was seeking—an heir of his own mettle?

If not, the cause must be—yes, it followed logically—the husband. . . .

Mr Entwhistle's eyes slid gently over Susan's shoulder to where Gregory Banks stood absently whittling at a pencil.

A thin pale nondescript young man with reddish sandy hair. So overshadowed by Susan's colourful personality that it was difficult to realise what he himself was really like. Nothing to take hold of in the fellow—quite pleasant, ready to be agreeable—a yes man, as the modern term went. And yet that did not seem to describe him satisfactorily. There was something vaguely disquieting about the unobtrusiveness of Gregory Banks. He had been an unsuitable match—yet Susan had insisted on marrying him—had overborne all opposition—why? What had she seen in him?

And now, six months after the marriage—"She's crazy about the fellow," Mr Entwhistle said to himself. He knew the signs. A large number of wives with matrimonial troubles had passed through the office of Bollard, Entwhistle, Entwhistle and Bollard. Wives madly devoted to unsatisfactory and often what appeared quite unprepossessing husbands, wives contemptuous of, and bored by, apparently attractive and impeccable husbands. What any woman saw in some particular man was beyond the comprehension of the average intelligent male. It just was so. A woman who could be intelligent about everything else in the world could be a complete fool when it came to some particular man. Susan, thought Mr Entwhistle, was one of those women. For her the world revolved around Greg. And that had its dangers in more ways than one.

Susan was talking with emphasis and indignation.

"—because it *is* disgraceful. You remember that woman who was murdered in Yorkshire last year? Nobody was ever arrested. And the old woman in the sweet shop who was killed with a crowbar. They detained some man, and then they let him go!"

"There has to be evidence, my dear," said Mr Entwhistle.

Susan paid no attention.

"And that other case—a retired Nurse—that was a hatchet or an axe—just like Aunt Cora."

"Dear me, you appear to have made quite a study of these crimes, Susan," said Mr Entwhistle mildly.

"Naturally one remembers these things—and when someone in one's own family is killed—and in very much the same way—well, it shows that there must be a lot of these sort of people going round the countryside, breaking into places and attacking lonely women—and that the police just don't *bother!*"

Mr Entwhistle shook his head.

"Don't belittle the police, Susan. They are a very shrewd and patient body of men—persistent, too. Just because it isn't still mentioned in the newspapers doesn't mean that a case is closed. Far from it."

"And yet there are hundreds of unsolved crimes every year."

"Hundreds?" Mr Entwhistle looked dubious. "A certain number, yes. But there are many occasions when the police know who has committed a crime but where the evidence is insufficient for a prosecution."

"I don't believe it," said Susan. "I believe if you knew definitely *who* committed a crime you could always get the evidence."

"I wonder now." Mr Entwhistle sounded thoughtful. "I very much wonder. . . ."

"Have they any idea *at all*—in Aunt Cora's case—of who it might be?"

"That I couldn't say. Not as far as I know. But they would hardly confide in me—and it's early days yet—the murder took place only the day before yesterday, remember."

"It's definitely got to be a certain kind of person," Susan mused. "A brutal, perhaps slightly half witted type—a discharged soldier or a gaol bird. I mean, using a hatchet like that."

Looking slightly quizzical, Mr Entwhistle raised his eyebrows and murmured

> "Lizzie Borden with an axe
> Gave her father forty whacks
> When she saw what she had done
> She gave her mother forty-one."

"Oh," Susan flushed angrily, "Cora hasn't got any relations living with her—unless you mean the companion. And anyway Lizzie Borden was acquitted. Nobody knows for certain she killed her father and stepmother."

"The rhyme is quite definitely libellous," Mr Entwhistle agreed.

"You mean the companion *did* do it? Did Cora leave her anything?"

"An amethyst brooch of no great value and some sketches of fishing villages of sentimental value only."

"One has to have a motive for murder—unless one is half-witted."

Mr Entwhistle gave a little chuckle.

"As far as one can see, the only person who had a motive is *you,* my dear Susan."

"What's that?" Greg moved forward suddenly. He was like a sleeper coming awake. An ugly light showed in his eyes. He was suddenly no longer a negligible feature in the background. "What's Sue got to do with it? What do you mean—saying things like that?"

Susan said sharply:

"Shut up, Greg. Mr Entwhistle doesn't mean anything—"

"Just my little joke," said Mr Entwhistle apologetically. "Not in the best taste, I'm afraid. Cora left her estate, such as it was, to you, Susan. But to a young lady who has just inherited several hundred thousand pounds, an estate, amounting at the most to a few hundreds, can hardly be said to represent a motive for murder."

"She left her money to me?" Susan sounded surprised. "How extraordinary. She didn't even know me. Why did she do it, do you think?"

"I think she had heard rumours that there had been a little difficulty—er—over your marriage." Greg, back again at sharpening his pencil, scowled. "There had been a certain amount of trouble over her own marriage—and I think she experienced a fellow feeling."

Susan asked with a certain amount of interest:

"She married an artist, didn't she, whom none of the family liked? Was he a good artist?"

Mr Entwhistle shook his head very decidedly.

"Are there any of his paintings in the cottage?"

"Yes."

"Then I shall judge for myself," said Susan.

Mr Entwhistle smiled at the resolute tilt of Susan's chin.

"So be it. Doubtless I am an old fogey and hopelessly old fashioned in matters of art, but I really don't think you will dispute my verdict."

"I suppose I ought to go down there, anyway? And look over what there is. Is there anybody there now?"

"I have arranged with Miss Gilchrist to remain there until further notice."

Greg said: "She must have a pretty good nerve—to stay in a cottage where a murder's been committed."

"Miss Gilchrist is quite a sensible woman, I should say. Besides," added the lawyer drily, "I don't think she has anywhere else to go until she gets another situation."

"So Aunt Cora's death left her high and dry? Did she —were she and Aunt Cora—on intimate terms—"

Mr Entwhistle looked at her rather curiously, wondering just exactly what was in her mind.

"Moderately so, I imagine," he said. "She never treated Miss Gilchrist as a servant."

"Treated her a damned sight worse, I daresay," said Susan. "These wretched so called 'ladies' are the ones who get it taken out of them nowadays. I'll try and find her a decent post somewhere. It won't be difficult. Anyone who's willing to do a bit of housework and cook is worth their weight in gold—she does cook, doesn't she?"

"Oh yes. I gather it is something she called—er—*the rough* that she objected to. I'm afraid I don't quite know what 'the rough' is."

Susan appeared to be a good deal amused.

Mr Entwhistle, glancing at his watch, said:

"Your Aunt left Timothy her executor."

"Timothy," said Susan with scorn. "Uncle Timothy is practically a myth. Nobody ever sees him."

"Quite." Mr Entwhistle glanced at his watch. "I am travelling up to see him this afternoon. I will acquaint him with your decision to go down to the cottage."

"It will only take me a day or two, I imagine. I don't want to be long away from London. I've got various schemes in hand. I'm going into business."

Mr Entwhistle looked round him at the cramped sitting room of the tiny flat. Greg and Susan were evidently hard up. Her father, he knew, had run through most of his money. He had left his daughter badly off.

"What are your plans for the future, if I may ask?"

"I've got my eye on some premises in Cardigan Street. I suppose, if necessary, you can advance me some money? I may have to pay a deposit."

"That can be managed," said Mr Entwhistle. "I rang

you up the day after the funeral several times—but could get no answer. I thought perhaps you might care for an advance. I wondered whether you might perhaps have gone out of town."

"Oh no," said Susan quickly. "We were in all day. Both of us. We didn't go out at all."

Greg said gently:

"You know, Susan, I think our telephone must have been out of order that day. You remember how I couldn't get through to Hard and Co. in the afternoon? I meant to report it, but it was all right the next morning."

"Telephones," said Mr Entwhistle, "can be very unreliable sometimes."

Susan said suddenly:

"How did Aunt Cora know about our marriage? It was at a Registry Office and we didn't tell anyone until afterwards—"

"I fancy Richard may have told her about it. She remade her will about three weeks ago. (It was formerly in favour of the Theosophical Society)—just about the time he had been down to see her."

Susan looked startled.

"Did Uncle Richard go down to see her? I'd no idea of that!"

"I hadn't any idea of it myself," said Mr Entwhistle.

"So that was when—"

"When what?"

"Nothing," said Susan.

# 6

"VERY GOOD of you to come along," said Maude gruffly, as she greeted Mr Entwhistle on the platform of Bayham Compton station. "I can assure you that both Timothy and I much appreciate it. Of course the truth is that Richard's death was the worst thing possible for Timothy."

Mr Entwhistle had not yet considered his friend's death from this particular angle. But it was, he saw, the only angle from which Mrs Timothy Abernethie was likely to regard it.

As they proceeded towards the exit, Maude developed the theme.

"To begin with, it was a *shock*—Timothy was really very attached to Richard. And then unfortunately it put the idea of death into Timothy's head. Being such an invalid has made him rather nervous about himself. He realised that he was the only one of the brothers left alive —and he started saying that he'd be the next to go—and that it wouldn't be long now—all very morbid talk, as I told him."

They emerged from the station and Maude led the way to a dilapidated car of almost fabulous antiquity.

"Sorry about our old rattletrap," she said. "We've wanted a new car for years, but really we couldn't afford it. This has had a new engine twice—and these old cars really stand up to a lot of hard work—

"I hope it will start," she added. "Sometimes one has to wind it."

She pressed the starter several times but only a meaningless whirr resulted. Mr Entwhistle who had never cranked a car in his life, felt rather apprehensive, but Maude herself descended, inserted the starting handle and with a vigorous couple of turns woke the motor to life. It was fortunate, Mr Entwhistle reflected, that Maude was such a powerfully built woman.

"That's that," she said. "The old brute's been playing me up lately. Did it when I was coming back after the funeral. Had to walk a couple of miles to the nearest garage and they weren't good for much—just a village affair. I had to put up at the local Inn while they tinkered at it. Of course *that* upset Timothy too. I had to phone through to him and tell him I couldn't be back till the next day. Fussed him terribly. One tries to keep things from him as much as possible—but some things one can't do anything about —Cora's murder, for instance. I had to send for Dr Barton to give him a sedative. Things like murder are too much for a man in Timothy's state of health. I gather Cora was always a fool."

Mr Entwhistle digested this remark in silence. The inference was not quite clear to him.

"I don't think I'd seen Cora since our marriage," said Maude. "I didn't like to say to Timothy at the time: 'Your youngest sister's batty,' not just like that. But it's what I *thought*. There she was saying the most extraordinary things! One didn't know whether to resent them or whether to laugh. I suppose the truth is she lived in a kind of imaginary world of her own—full of melodrama and fantastic ideas about other people. Well, poor soul, she's paid for it now. She didn't have any protégés, did she?"

"Protégés? What do you mean?"

"I just wondered. Some young cadging artist, or musician—or something of that kind. Someone she might have let in that day, and who killed her for her loose cash. Perhaps an adolescent—they're so queer at that age sometimes—especially if they're the neurotic arty type. I mean, it seems so odd to break in and murder her in the middle of the afternoon. If you break into a house surely you'd do it at night."

"There would have been two women there then."

"Oh yes, the companion. But really I can't believe that anyone would deliberately wait until she was out of the way and then break in and attack Cora. What for? He can't have expected she'd have any cash or stuff to speak of, and there must have been times when both the women were out and the house was empty. That would have been much safer. It seems so stupid to go and commit a murder unless it's absolutely necessary."

"And Cora's murder, you feel, was unnecessary?"

"It all seems so stupid."

Should murder make sense? Mr Entwhistle wondered. Academically the answer was yes. But many pointless crimes were on record. It depended, Mr Entwhistle reflected, on the mentality of the murderer.

What did he really know about murderers and their mental processes? Very little. His firm had never had a criminal practice. He was no student of criminology himself. Murderers, as far as he could judge seemed to be of all sorts and kinds. Some had had over-weening vanity, some had had a lust for power, some, like Seddon, had been mean and avaricious, others, like Smith and Rowse had had an incredible fascination for women; some, like Armstrong, had been pleasant fellows to meet. Edith

Thompson had lived in a world of violent unreality, Nurse Waddington had put her elderly patients out of the way with businesslike cheerfulness.

Maude's voice broke into his meditations.

"If I could only keep the newspapers from Timothy! But he will insist on reading them—and then, of course, it upsets him. You do understand, don't you, Mr Entwhistle, that there can be *no question* of Timothy's attending the inquest? If necessary, Dr Barton can write out a certificate or whatever it is."

"You can set your mind at rest about that."

"Thank goodness!"

They turned in through the gates of Stansfield Grange, and up a neglected drive. It had been an attractive small property once—but had now a doleful and neglected appearance. Maude sighed as she said:

"We had to let this go to seed during the war. Both gardeners called up. And now we've only got one old man —and he's not much good. Wages have gone up so terribly. I must say it's a blessing to realise that we'll be able to spend a little money on the place now. We're both so fond of it. I was really afraid that we might have to sell it. . . . Not that I suggested anything of the kind to Timothy. It would have upset him—dreadfully."

They drew up before the portico of a very lovely old Georgian house which badly needed a coat of paint.

"No servants," said Maude bitterly, as she led the way in. "Just a couple of women who come in. We had a resident maid until a month ago—slightly hunchbacked and terribly adenoidal and in many ways not too bright, but she was *there* which was such a comfort—and quite good at plain cooking. And would you believe it, she gave notice and went to a fool of a woman who keeps six pekinese dogs (it's a larger house than this and more work) because she was 'so fond of little doggies,' she said. Dogs, indeed! Being sick and making messes all the time I've no doubt! Really, these girls are *mental!* So there we are, and if I have to go out any afternoon, Timothy is left quite alone in the house and if anything should happen, how could he get help? Though I do leave the telephone close by his chair so that if he felt faint he could dial Dr Barton immediately."

Maude led the way into the drawing room where tea was laid ready by the fireplace, and establishing Mr Entwhistle there, disappeared, presumably to the back regions. She returned in a few minutes' time with a teapot and silver kettle, and proceeded to minister to Mr Entwhistle's needs. It was a good tea with homemade cake and fresh buns. Mr Entwhistle murmured:

"What about Timothy?" and Maude explained briskly that she had taken Timothy his tray before she set out for the station.

"And now," said Maude, "he will have had his little nap and it will be the best time for him to see you. Do try and not let him excite himself too much."

Mr Entwhistle assured her that he would exercise every precaution.

Studying her in the flickering firelight, he was seized by a feeling of compassion. This big stalwart matter of fact woman, so healthy, so vigorous, so full of common sense, and yet so strangely, almost pitifully, vulnerable in one spot. Her love for her husband was maternal love, Mr Entwhistle decided. Maude Abernethie had borne no child and she was a woman built for motherhood. Her invalid husband had become her child, to be shielded, guarded, watched over. And perhaps, being the stronger character of the two, she had unconsciously imposed on him a state of invalidism greater than might otherwise have been the case.

"Poor Mrs Tim," thought Mr Entwhistle to himself.

ii

"Good of you to come, Entwhistle."

Timothy raised himself up in his chair as he held out a hand.

He was a big man with a marked resemblance to his brother Richard. But what was strength in Richard, in Timothy was weakness. The mouth was irresolute, the chin very slightly receding, the eyes less deepset. Lines of peevish irritability showed on his forehead.

His invalid status was emphasised by the rug across his knees and a positive pharmacopeia of little bottles and boxes on a table at his right hand.

"I mustn't exert myself," he said warningly. "Doctor's forbidden it. Keeps telling me not to worry! Worry! If *he'd* had a murder in his family *he'd* do a bit of worrying, I bet! It's too much for a man—first Richard's death— then hearing all about his funeral and his will—what a will!—and on top of that poor little Cora killed with a hatchet. Hatchet! Ugh! This country's full of gangsters nowadays,—thugs—left over from the war! Going about killing defenseless women. Nobody's got the guts to put these things down—to take a strong hand. What's the country coming to, I'd like to know? What's the damned country coming to?"

Mr Entwhistle was familiar with this gambit. It was a question almost invariably asked sooner or later by his clients for the last twenty years and he had his routine for answering it. The non-committal words he uttered could have been classified under the heading of soothing noises.

"It all began with that damned Labour Government," said Timothy. "Sending the whole Country to blazes. And the Government we've got now is no better. Mealy mouthed milk and water socialists! Look at the state *we're* in! Can't get a decent gardener, can't get servants— poor Maude here has to work herself to a shadow messing about in the kitchen—(by the way I think a custard pudding would go well with the sole tonight, my dear—and perhaps a little clear soup first?) I've got to keep my strength up—Doctor Barton said so—let me see, where was I? Oh yes, *Cora.* It's a shock, I can tell you, to a man, when he hears his sister—his own sister—has been *murdered!* Why, I had palpitations for twenty minutes! You'll have to attend to everything for me, Entwhistle. *I* can't go to the inquest or be bothered by business of any kind connected with Cora's estate. I want to forget the whole thing. What happens, by the way, to Cora's share of Richard's money? Comes to me, I suppose?"

Murmuring something about clearing away tea, Maude left the room.

Timothy lay back in his chair and said:

"Good thing to get rid of the women. Now we can talk business without any silly interruptions."

"The sum left in trust for Cora," said Mr Entwhistle, "goes equally to you and the nieces and nephew."

"But look here," Timothy's cheeks assumed a purplish hue of indignation. "Surely I'm her next of kin? Only surviving brother."

Mr Entwhistle explained with some care the exact provisions of Richard Abernethie's will, reminding Timothy gently that he had had a copy sent him.

"Don't expect me to understand all that legal jargon, do you?" said Timothy ungratefully. "You lawyers! Matter of fact, I couldn't believe it when Maude came home and told me the gist of it. Thought she'd got it wrong. Women are never clear headed. Best woman in the world, Maude—but women don't understand finance. I don't believe Maude even realises that if Richard hadn't died when he did, we might have had to clear out of here. Fact!"

"Surely if you had applied to Richard——"

Timothy gave a short bark of harsh laughter.

"That's not my style. Our father left us all a perfectly reasonable share of his money—that is, if we didn't want to go into the family concern. I didn't. I've a soul above cornplasters, Entwhistle! Richard took my attitude a bit hard. Well, what with taxes, depreciation of income, one thing and another—it hasn't been easy to keep things going. I've had to realise a good deal of capital. Best thing to do these days. I did hint once to Richard that this place was getting a bit hard to run. He took the attitude that we'd be much better off in a smaller place altogether. Easier for Maude, he said, more labour saving—labour saving, what a term! Oh no, I wouldn't have asked Richard for help. But I can tell you, Entwhistle, that the worry affected my health most unfavourably. A man in my state of health oughtn't to have to worry. Then Richard died and though of course naturally I was cut up about it—my brother and all that—I couldn't help feeling relieved about future prospects. Yes, it's all plain sailing now—and a great relief. Get the house painted—get a couple of really good men on the garden—you can get them at a price. Restock the rose garden completely. And —where was I——"

"Detailing your future plans."

"Yes, yes—but I mustn't bother you with all that.

What did hurt me—and hurt me cruelly—were the terms of Richard's will."

"Indeed?" Mr Entwhistle looked enquiring. "They were not—as you expected?"

"I should say they weren't! Naturally, after Mortimer's death, I assumed that Richard would leave everything to *me.*"

"Ah—did he—ever indicate that to you?"

"He never said so—not in so many words. Reticent sort of chap, Richard. But he asked himself here—not long after Mortimer's death. Wanted to talk over family affairs generally. We discussed young George—and the girls and their husbands. Wanted to know my views—not that I could tell him much. I'm an invalid and I don't get about, and Maude and I live out of the world. Rotten silly marriages both of those girls made, if you ask me. Well, I ask you, Entwhistle, naturally I thought he was consulting me as the head of the family after he was gone and naturally I thought the control of the money would be mine. Richard could surely trust me to do the right thing by the younger generation. And to look after poor old Cora. Dash it all, Entwhistle, I'm an Abernethie—the last Abernethie. Full control should have been left in my hands."

In his excitement Timothy had kicked aside his rug and had sat up in his chair. There were no signs of weakness or fragility about him. He looked, Mr Entwhistle thought, a perfectly healthy man, even if a slightly excitable one. Moreover the old lawyer realised very clearly that Timothy Abernethie had probably always been secretly jealous of his brother Richard. They had been sufficiently alike for Timothy to resent his brother's strength of character and firm grasp of affairs. When Richard had died, Timothy had exulted in the prospect of succeeding at this late date to the power to control the destinies of others.

Richard Abernethie had not given him that power. Had he thought of doing so and then decided against it?

A sudden squalling of cats in the garden brought Timothy up out of his chair. Rushing to the window he threw up the sash, bawled out "Stop it, you!" and picking up a large book hurled it out at the marauders.

"Beastly cats," he grumbled, returning to his visitor. "Ruin the flower beds and I can't stand that damned yowling."

He sat down again and asked:

"Have a drink, Entwhistle?"

"Not quite so soon. Maude has just given me an excellent tea."

Timothy grunted.

"Capable woman, Maude. But she does too much. Even has to muck about with the inside of that old car of ours—she's quite a mechanic in her way, you know."

"I hear she had a breakdown coming back from the funeral?"

"Yes. Car conked out. She had the sense to telephone through about it, in case I should be anxious, but that ass of a daily woman of ours wrote down the message in a way that didn't make sense. I was out getting a bit of fresh air—I'm advised by the doctor to take what exercise I can if I feel like it—I got back from my walk to find scrawled on a bit of paper: 'Madam's sorry car gone wrong got to stay night.' Naturally I thought she was still at Enderby. Put a call through and found Maude had left that morning. Might have had the breakdown *anywhere!* Pretty kettle of fish! Fool of a daily woman only left me a lumpy macaroni cheese for supper. I had to go down to the kitchen and warm it up *myself—and* make myself a cup of tea—to say nothing of stoking the boiler. I might have had a heart attack—but does that class of woman care? Not she. With any decent feelings she'd have come back that evening and looked after me properly. No loyalty any more in the lower classes—"

He brooded sadly.

"I don't know how much Maude told you about the funeral and the relatives," said Mr Entwhistle. "Cora produced rather an awkward moment. Said brightly that Richard had been murdered, hadn't he? Perhaps Maude told you."

Timothy chuckled easily.

"Oh yes, I heard about that. Everybody looked down their noses and pretended to be shocked. Just the sort of thing Cora would say! You know how she always managed to put her foot in it when she was a girl, Entwhistle? Said something at our wedding that upset Maude, I remember. Maude never cared for her very much. Yes, Maude rang me up that evening after the funeral to know if I was all right and if Mrs Jones had come in to give me my evening meal and then she told me it had all gone off very well, and I said 'What about the will?' and she tried to hedge a bit, but of course I had the truth out of her. I couldn't believe it, and I said she must have made a mistake, but she stuck to it. It hurt me, Entwhistle—it really *wounded* me, if you know what I mean. If you ask me, it was just *spite* on Richard's part. I know one shouldn't speak ill of the dead, but, upon my word—"

Timothy continued on this theme for some time.

Then Maude came back into the room and said firmly:

"I think, dear, Mr Entwhistle has been with you quite long enough. You really *must* rest. If you have settled everything—"

"Oh, we've settled things. I leave it all to you, Entwhistle. Let me know when they catch the fellow—if they ever do. I've no faith in the police nowadays—the Chief Constables aren't the right type. You'll see to the—er—interment—won't you? We shan't be able to come I'm afraid. But order an expensive wreath—and there must be a proper stone put up in due course—she'll be buried locally, I suppose? No point in bringing her North and I've no idea where Lansquenet is buried, somewhere in France I believe. I don't know what one puts on a stone when it's murder. . . . Can't very well say 'entered into rest' or anything like that. One will have to choose a text—something appropriate. R.I.P.? No, that's only for Catholics."

"O Lord thou hast seen my wrong. Judge thou my case," murmured Mr Entwhistle.

The startled glance Timothy bent on him made Mr Entwhistle smile faintly.

"From Lamentations," he said. "It seemed appropriate if somewhat melodramatic. However, it will be some time before the question of the Memorial stone comes up. The —er—ground has to settle, you know. Now don't worry about anything. We will deal with things and keep you fully informed."

Mr Entwhistle left for London by the breakfast train on the following morning.

When he got home, after a little hesitation, he rang up a friend of his.

# 7

"**I CAN'T TELL** you how much I appreciate your invitation."

Mr Entwhistle pressed his host's hand warmly.

Hercule Poirot gestured hospitably to a chair by the fire.

Mr Entwhistle sighed as he sat down.

On one side of the room a table was laid for two.

"I returned from the country this morning," he said.

"And you have a matter on which you wish to consult me?"

"Yes. It's a long rambling story, I'm afraid."

"Then we will not have it until after we have dined. *Georges?*"

The efficient Georges materialized with some *Pâté de Foie Gras* accompanied by hot toast in a napkin.

"We will have our *Pâté* by the fire," said Poirot. "Afterwards we will move to the table."

It was an hour and a half later that Mr Entwhistle stretched himself comfortably out in his chair and sighed a contented sigh.

"You certainly know how to do yourself well, Poirot. Trust a Frenchman."

"I am a Belgian. But the rest of your remark applies. At my age the chief pleasure, almost the *only* pleasure that still remains, is the pleasure of the table. Mercifully I have an excellent stomach."

"Ah," murmured Mr Entwhistle.

They had dined off a *Sole Veronique,* followed by *Escalope de Veau Milanaise,* proceeding to *Poire Flambée* with ice cream.

They had drunk a *Pouilly Fuissé* followed by a *Corton*

and a very good port now reposed at Mr Entwhistle's elbow. Poirot, who did not care for port, was sipping *Crème de Cacao*.

"I don't know," muttered Mr Entwhistle reminiscently, "how you manage to get hold of an escalope like that! It melted in the mouth!"

"I have a friend who is a Continental butcher. For him I solve a small domestic problem. He is appreciative— and ever since then he is most sympathetic to me in the matters of the stomach."

"A domestic problem." Mr Entwhistle sighed. "I wish you had not reminded me. . . . This is such a perfect moment. . . ."

"Prolong it, my friend. We will have presently the *demi tasse* and the fine brandy, and then, when digestion is peacefully under way, *then* you shall tell why you need my advice."

The clock struck the half hour after nine before Mr Entwhistle stirred in his chair. The psychological moment had come. He no longer felt reluctant to bring forth his perplexities—he was eager to do so.

"I don't know," he said, "whether I'm making the most colossal fool of myself. In any case I don't see that there's anything that can possibly be done. But I'd like to put the facts before you, and I'd like to know what you think."

He paused for a moment or two, then in his dry meticulous way, he told his story. His trained legal brain enabled him to put the facts clearly, to leave nothing out, and to add nothing extraneous. It was a clear succinct account, and as such appreciated by the little elderly man with the egg shaped head who sat listening to him.

When he had finished there was a pause. Mr Entwhistle was prepared to answer questions, but for some few moments no question came. Hercule Poirot was reviewing the evidence.

He said at last:

"It seems very clear. You have in your mind the suspicion that your friend, Richard Abernethie, may have been murdered? That suspicion, or assumption, rests on the basis of one thing only—*the words spoken by Cora Lansquenet at Richard Abernethie's funeral*. Take those away —and there is nothing left. The fact that she herself was

murdered the day afterwards *may* be the purest coincidence. It is true that Richard Abernethie died suddenly,
but he was attended by a reputable doctor who knew him
well, and that doctor had no suspicions and gave a death
certificate. Was Richard buried or cremated?"

"Cremated—according to his own request."

"Yes, that is the law. And it means that a second doctor signed the certificate—but there would be no difficulty
about that. So we come back to the essential point, *what
Cora Lansquenet said.* You were there and you heard her.
She said: 'But he *was* murdered, wasn't he?' "

"Yes."

"And the real point is—that you believe she was
speaking the truth."

The lawyer hesitated for a moment, then he said:

"Yes, I do."

"Why?"

"Why?" Entwhistle repeated the word, slightly puzzled.

"But yes, *why?* Is it because, already, deep down, you
had an uneasiness about the manner of Richard's death?"

The lawyer shook his head. "No, no, not in the least."

"Then it is because of *her*—of Cora herself. You knew
her well?"

"I had not seen her for—oh—over twenty years."

"Would you have known her if you had met her in the
street?"

Mr Entwhistle reflected.

"I might have passed her by in the street without rec-
ognising her. She was a thin slip of a girl when I saw her
last and she had turned into a stout shabby middle-aged
woman. But I think that the moment I spoke to her face
to face I should have recognised her. She wore her hair in
the same way, a bang cut straight across the forehead and
she had a trick of peering up at you through her fringe
like a rather shy animal, and she had a very characteristic
abrupt way of talking, and a way of putting her head on
one side and then coming out with something quite outrageous. She had *character,* you see, and character is always
highly individual."

"She was, in fact, the same Cora you had known years
ago. And she still said outrageous things! The things, the

outrageous things, she had said in the past—were they usually—justified?"

"That was always the awkward thing about Cora. When truth would have been better left unspoken, she spoke it."

"And that characteristic remained unchanged. Richard Abernethie was murdered—so Cora at once mentioned the fact."

Mr Entwhistle stirred.

"You think he *was* murdered?"

"Oh, no, no, my friend, we cannot go so fast. We agree on this—Cora *thought* he had been murdered. She was quite sure he had been murdered. It was, to her, more a certainty than a surmise. And so, we come to this, *she must have had some reason for the belief*. We agree, by your knowledge of her, that it was not just a bit of mischief making. Now tell me—when she said what she did, there was, at once, a kind of chorus of protest—that is right?"

"Quite right."

"And she then became confused, abashed, and retreated from the position—saying—as far as you can remember, something like 'But I thought—from what he told me—' "

The lawyer nodded.

"I wish I could remember more clearly. But I am fairly sure of that. She used the words 'he told me' or 'he said'—"

"And the matter was then smoothed over and everyone spoke of something else. You can remember, looking back, no special expression on anyone's face? Anything that remains in your memory as—shall we say—*unusual?*"

"No."

"And the very next day, *Cora* is killed—and you ask yourself: 'Can it be cause and effect?' "

The lawyer stirred.

"I suppose that seems to you quite fantastic?"

"Not at all," said Poirot. "Given that the original assumption is correct, it is logical. The perfect murder, the murder of Richard Abernethie, had been committed, all

has gone off smoothly—and suddenly it appears that
there is one person who has a knowledge of the truth!
Clearly that person must be silenced *as quickly as possible.*"

"Then you do think that—it was murder?"

Poirot said gravely:

"I think, *mon cher,* exactly as you thought—that there
is a case for investigation. Have you taken any steps? You
have spoken of these matters to the police?"

"No." Mr Entwhistle shook his head. "It did not seem
to me that any good purpose could be achieved. My position is that I represent the family. If Richard Abernethie
was murdered, there seems only one method by which it
could be done."

"By poison?"

"Exactly. *And the body has been cremated.* There is
now no evidence available. But I decided that I, myself,
*must* be satisfied on the point. That is why, Poirot, I have
come to *you.*"

"Who was in the house at the time of his death?"

"An old butler who has been with him for years, a
cook and a housemaid. It would seem, perhaps, as though
it must necessarily be one of them—"

"Ah! do not try to pull the wool upon my eyes. This
Cora, she knows Richard Abernethie was killed, yet she
acquiesces in the hushing up. She says 'I think you are all
quite right.' Therefore it *must* be one of the family who is
concerned, someone whom the victim himself might prefer not to have openly accused. Otherwise, since Cora was
fond of her brother, she would not agree to let the sleeping murderer lie. You agree to that, yes?"

"It was the way I reasoned—yes," confessed Mr Entwhistle. "Though how any of the family could possibly—"

Poirot cut him short.

"Where poison is concerned there are all sorts of possibilities. It must, presumably, have been a narcotic of
some sort if he died in his sleep and if there were no suspicious appearances. Possibly he was already having some
narcotic administered to him."

"In any case," said Mr Entwhistle, "the *how* hardly
matters. We shall never be able to prove anything."

"In the case of Richard Abernethie, no. But the

murder of Cora Lansquenet is different. Once we know
'who' then evidence ought to be possible to get." He
added with a sharp glance, "You have, perhaps, already
done something."

"Very little. My purpose was mainly, I think, *elimina-
tion*. It is distasteful to me to think that one of the Abernethie family is a murderer. I still can't quite believe it. I
hoped that by a few apparently idle questions I could ex-
onerate certain members of the family beyond question.
Perhaps, who knows, *all* of them? In which case, Cora
would have been wrong in her assumption and her own
death could be ascribed to some casual prowler who
broke in. After all, the issue is very simple. What were the
members of the Abernethie family doing on the afternoon
that Cora Lansquenet was killed?"

*"Eh bien,"* said Poirot, "what were they doing?"

"George Crossfield was at Hurst Park races. Rosamund
Shane was out shopping in London. Her husband—for
one must include husbands—"

"Assuredly."

"Her husband was fixing up a deal about an option on
a play, Susan and Gregory Banks were at home all day.
Timothy Abernethie who is an invalid was at his home in
Yorkshire, and his wife was driving herself home from
Enderby."

He stopped.

Hercule Poirot looked at him and nodded comprehend-
ingly.

"Yes, that is what they *say*. And is it all true?"

"I simply don't know, Poirot. Some of the statements
are capable of proof or disproof—but it would be difficult
to do so without showing one's hand pretty plainly. In
fact to do so would be tantamount to an accusation. I will
simply tell you certain conclusions of my own. George
*may* have been at Hurst Park races, but I do not think he
was. He was rash enough to boast that he had backed a
couple of winners. It is my experience that so many of-
fenders against the law ruin their own case by saying too
much. I asked him the name of the winners, and he gave
me the names of two horses without any apparent hesitation. Both of them, I found, had been heavily tipped on
the day in question and one had duly won. The other,

though an odds on favourite, had unaccountably failed even to get a place."

"Interesting. Had this George any urgent need for money at the time of his uncle's death?"

"It is my impression that his need was very urgent. I have no evidence for saying so, but I strongly suspect that he has been speculating with his clients' funds and that he was in danger of prosecution. It is only my impression but I have some experience in these matters. Defaulting solicitors, I regret to say, are not entirely uncommon. I can only tell you that I would not have cared to entrust my own funds to George, and I suspect that Richard Abernethie, a very shrewd judge of men, was dissatisfied with his nephew and placed no reliance on him.

"His mother," the lawyer continued, "was a good looking rather foolish girl and she married a man of what I should call dubious character." He sighed. "The Abernethie girls were not good choosers."

He paused and then went on.

"As for Rosamund she is a lovely nit-wit. I really cannot see her smashing Cora's head in with a hatchet! Her husband, Michael Shane, is something of a dark horse—he's a man with ambition and also a man of overweening vanity I should say—But really I know very little about him. I have no reason to suspect him of a brutal crime or of a carefully planned poisoning, but until I know that he really was doing what he says he was doing I cannot rule him out."

"But you have no doubts about the wife?"

"No—no—there is a certain rather startling callousness . . . but no, I really cannot envisage the hatchet. She is a fragile looking creature."

"And beautiful!" said Poirot with a faint cynical smile. "And the other niece?"

"Susan? She is a very different type from Rosamund—a girl of remarkable ability, I should say. She and her husband were at home together that day. I said (falsely) that I had tried to get them on the telephone on the afternoon in question. Greg said very quickly that the telephone had been out of order all day. He had tried to get someone and failed."

"So again it is not conclusive. . . . You cannot eliminate as you hoped to do. . . . What is the husband like?"

"I find him hard to make out. He has a somewhat unpleasing personality though one cannot say exactly why he makes this impression. As for Susan—"

"Yes?"

"Susan reminds me of her uncle. She has the vigour, the drive, the mental capacity of Richard Abernethie. It may be my fancy that she lacks some of the kindliness and the warmth of my old friend."

"Women are never kind," remarked Poirot. "Though they can sometimes be tender. She loves her husband?"

"Devotedly, I should say. But really, Poirot, I can't believe—I *won't* believe for one moment that Susan—"

"You prefer George?" said Poirot. "It is natural! As for me, I am not so sentimental about beautiful young ladies. Now tell me about your visit to the older generation?"

Mr Entwhistle described his visit to Timothy and Maude at some length. Poirot summarised the result.

"So Mrs Abernethie is a good mechanic. She knows all about the inside of a car. And Mr Abernethie is not the invalid he likes to think himself. He goes out for walks and is according to you, capable of vigorous action. He is also a bit of an ego maniac and he resented his brother's success and superior character."

"He spoke very affectionately of Cora."

"And ridiculed her silly remark after the funeral. What of the sixth beneficiary?"

"Helen? Mrs Leo? I do not suspect her for a moment. In any case, her innocence will be easy to prove. She was at Enderby. With three servants in the house."

"*Eh bien,* my friend," said Poirot. "Let us be practical. What do you want me to do?"

"I want to know the truth, Poirot."

"Yes. Yes, I should feel the same in your place."

"And you're the man to find it out for me. I know you don't take cases any more, but I ask you to take this one. This is a matter of business. I will be responsible for your fees. Come now, money is always useful."

Poirot grinned.

"Not if it all goes in the taxes! But I will admit, your

problem interests me! Because it is not easy. . . . It is all so nebulous. . . . One thing, my friend, had better be done by you. After that, I will occupy myself of everything. But I think it will be best if you yourself seek out the doctor who attended Mr Richard Abernethie. You know him?"

"Slightly."

"What is he like?"

"Middle aged G.P. Quite competent. On very friendly terms with Richard. A thoroughly good fellow."

"Then seek him out. He will speak more freely to you than to me. Ask him about Mr Abernethie's illness. Find out what medicines Mr Abernethie was taking at the time of his death and before. Find out if Richard Abernethie ever said anything to his doctor about fancying himself being poisoned. By the way, this Miss Gilchrist is sure that he used the term *poisoned* in talking to his sister?"

Mr Entwhistle reflected.

"It was the word she used—but she is the type of witness who often changes the actual words used, because she is convinced she is keeping to the sense of them. If Richard had said he was afraid someone wanted to kill him, Miss Gilchrist might have assumed poison because she connected his fears with those of an aunt of hers who thought her food was being tampered with. I can take up the point with her again some time."

"Yes. Or I will do so." He paused and then said in a different voice: "Has it occurred to you, my friend, that your Miss Gilchrist may be in some danger herself?"

Mr Entwhistle looked surprised.

"I can't say that it had."

"But, yes. Cora voiced her suspicions on the day of the funeral. The question in the murderer's mind will be, did she voice them to anybody when she first heard of Richard's death? And the most likely person for her to have spoken to about them will be Miss Gilchrist. I think, *mon cher,* that she had better not remain alone in that cottage."

"I believe Susan is going down."

"Ah, so Mrs Banks is going down?"

"She wants to look through Cora's things."

"I see. . . . I see. . . . Well, my friend, do what I have asked of you. You might also prepare Mrs Abernethie— Mrs Leo Abernethie, for the possibility that I may arrive in the house. We will see. From now on I occupy myself of everything."

And Poirot twirled his moustaches with enormous energy.

# 8

MR ENTWHISTLE looked at Dr Larraby thoughtfully.

He had had a lifetime of experience in summing people up. There had been frequent occasions on which it had been necessary to tackle a difficult situation or a delicate subject. Mr Entwhistle was an adept by now in the art of how exactly to make the proper approach. How would it be best to tackle Dr Larraby on what was certainly a very difficult subject and one which the doctor might very well resent as reflecting upon his own professional skill?

Frankness, Mr Entwhistle thought—or at least a modified frankness. To say that suspicions had arisen because of a haphazard suggestion thrown out by a silly woman would be ill-advised. Dr Larraby had not known Cora.

Mr Entwhistle cleared his throat and plunged bravely.

"I want to consult you on a very delicate matter," he said. "You may be offended, but I sincerely hope not. You are a sensible man and you will realise, I'm sure, that a—er—preposterous suggestion is best dealt with by finding a reasonable answer and not by condemning it out of hand. It concerns my client, the late Mr Abernethie. I'll ask you my question flat out. Are you certain, *absolutely certain,* that he died what is termed a natural death?"

Dr Larraby's good humoured rubicund middle-aged face turned in astonishment on his questioner.

"What on earth—Of course he did. I gave a certificate, didn't I? If I hadn't been satisfied—"

Mr Entwhistle cut in adroitly:

"Naturally, naturally. I assure you that I am not assuming anything to the contrary. But I would be glad to have your positive assurance—in face of the—er—rumours that are flying around."

"Rumours? What rumours?"

"One doesn't know quite how these things start," said Mr Entwhistle mendaciously. "But my feeling is that they should be stopped—authoritatively, if possible."

"Abernethie was a sick man. He was suffering from a disease that would have proved fatal within, I should say, at the earliest, two years. It might have come much sooner. His son's death had weakened his will to live, and his powers of resistance. I admit that I did not expect his death to come so soon, or indeed so suddenly, but there are precedents—plenty of precedents. Any medical man who predicts exactly when a patient will die, or exactly how long he will live, is bound to make a fool of himself. The human factor is always incalculable. The weak have often unexpected powers of resistance, the strong sometimes succumb."

"I understand all that. I am not doubting your diagnosis. Mr Abernethie was, shall we say—(rather melodramatically, I'm afraid)—under sentence of death. All I'm asking you is, is it quite impossible that a man, knowing or suspecting that he is doomed, might of his own accord shorten that period of life? Or that someone else might do it for him?"

Dr Larraby frowned.

"Suicide, you mean? Abernethie wasn't a suicidal type."

"I see. You can assure me, medically speaking, that such a suggestion is impossible."

The doctor stirred uneasily.

"I wouldn't use the word impossible. After his son's death life no longer held the interest for Abernethie that it had done. I certainly don't feel that suicide is likely—but I can't say that it's *impossible*."

"You are speaking from the psychological angle. When I said *medically,* I really meant do the circumstances of his death make such a suggestion impossible?"

"No, oh no. No, I can't say that. He died in his sleep, as people often do. There was no reason to suspect suicide, no evidence of his state of mind. If one were to demand an autopsy every time a man who is seriously ill died in his sleep—"

The doctor's face was getting redder and redder. Mr Entwhistle hastened to interpose.

"Of course. Of course. But if there *had* been evidence —evidence of which you yourself were not aware? If, for instance, he had said something to someone—"

"Indicating that he was contemplating suicide? Did he? I must say it surprises me."

"But if it *were* so—my case is purely hypothetical—could you rule out the possibility?"

Dr Larraby said slowly:

"No—no—I could not do that. But I say again, I should be very much surprised."

Mr Entwhistle hastened to follow up his advantage.

"If, then, we assume that his death was *not* natural— (all this is *purely* hypothetical)—what could have caused it? What kind of a drug, I mean?"

"Several. Some kind of a narcotic would be indicated. There was no sign of cyanosis, the attitude was quite peaceful."

"He had sleeping draughts or pills? Something of that kind."

"Yes. I had prescribed Slumberyl—a very safe and dependable hypnotic. He did not take it every night. And he only had a small bottle of tablets at a time. Three or even four times the prescribed dose would not have caused death. In fact, I remember seeing the bottle on his washstand after his death still nearly full."

"What else had you prescribed for him?"

"Various things—a medicine containing a small quantity of morphia to be taken when he had an attack of pain. Some vitamin capsules. An indigestion mixture."

Mr Entwhistle interrupted.

"Vitamin capsules? I think I was once prescribed a course of those. Small round capsules of gelatin."

"Yes. Containing adexoline."

"Could anything else have been introduced into—say —one of those capsules?"

"Something lethal, you mean?" The doctor was looking more and more surprised. "But surely no man would ever —look here, Entwhistle, what are you getting at? My God, man, are you suggesting *murder?*"

"I don't quite know what I'm suggesting. . . . I just want to know what would be *possible.*"

"But what evidence have you for even suggesting such a thing?"

"I haven't any evidence," said Mr Entwhistle in a tired voice. "Mr Abernethie is dead—and the person to whom he spoke is also dead. The whole thing is rumour—vague, unsatisfactory rumour, and I want to scotch it if I can. If you tell me that no one could possibly have poisoned Abernethie in any way whatsoever, I'll be delighted! It would be a big weight off my mind, I can assure you."

Dr Larraby got up and walked up and down.

"I can't tell you what you want me to tell you," he said at last. "I wish I could. Of course it could have been done. Anybody could have extracted the oil from a capsule and replaced it with—say—pure nicotine or half a dozen other things. Or something could have been put in his food or drink? Isn't that more likely?"

"Possibly. But you see there were only the servants in the house when he died—and I don't think it was any of them—in fact I'm quite sure it wasn't. So I'm looking for some delayed action possibility. There's no drug, I suppose, that you can administer and then the person dies weeks later?"

"A convenient idea—but untenable, I'm afraid," said the doctor drily. "I know you're a responsible person, Entwhistle, but who *is* making this suggestion? It seems to me wildly farfetched."

"Abernethie never said anything to you? Never hinted that one of his relations might be wanting him out of the way?"

The doctor looked at him curiously.

"No, he never said anything to me. Are you sure, Entwhistle, that somebody hasn't been—well, playing up the sensational? Some hysterical subjects can give an appearance of being quite reasonable and normal, you know."

"I hope it was like that. It might well be."

"Let me understand. Someone claims that Abernethie told her—it was a woman, I suppose?"

"Oh yes, it was a woman."

"—told her that someone was trying to kill him?"

Cornered, Mr Entwhistle reluctantly told the tale of Cora's remark at the funeral. Dr Larraby's face lightened.

"My dear fellow. I shouldn't pay any attention! The

explanation is quite simple. The woman's at a certain time of life—craving for sensation, unbalanced, unreliable —might say anything. They do, you know!"

Mr Entwhistle resented the doctor's easy assumption. He himself had had to deal with plenty of sensation-hunting and hysterical women.

"You may be quite right," he said, rising. "Unfortunately we can't tackle her on the subject, as she's been murdered herself."

"What's that—murdered?" Dr Larraby looked as though he had grave suspicions of Mr Entwhistle's own stability of mind.

"You've probably read about it in the paper. Mrs Lansquenet at Lytchett St. Mary in Berkshire."

"Of course—I'd no idea she was a relation of Richard Abernethie's!" Dr Larraby was looking quite shaken.

Feeling that he had revenged himself for the doctor's professional superiority, and unhappily conscious that his own suspicions had not been assuaged as a result of the visit, Mr Entwhistle took his leave.

ii

Back at Enderby, Mr Entwhistle decided to talk to Lanscombe.

He started by asking the old butler what his plans were.

"Mrs Leo has asked me to stay on here until the house is sold, sir, and I'm sure I shall be very pleased to oblige her. We are all very fond of Mrs Leo." He sighed. "I feel it very much, sir, if you will excuse me mentioning it, that the house has to be sold. I've known it for so very many years, and seen all the young ladies and gentlemen grow up in it. I always thought that Mr Mortimer would come after his father and perhaps bring up a family here, too. It was arranged, sir, that I should go to the North Lodge when I got past doing my work here. A very nice little place, the North Lodge—and I looked forward to having it very spick and span. But I suppose that's all over now."

"I'm afraid so, Lanscombe. The estate will all have to be sold together. But with your legacy—"

"Oh I'm not complaining, sir, and I'm very sensible of Mr Abernethie's generosity. I'm well provided for, but it's not so easy to find a little place to buy nowadays and though my married niece has asked me to make my home with them, well, it won't be quite the same thing as living on the estate."

"I know," said Mr Entwhistle. "It's a hard new world for us old fellows. I wish I'd seen more of my old friend before he went. How did he seem those last few months?"

"Well, he wasn't himself, sir. Not since Mr Mortimer's death."

"No, it broke him up. And then he was a sick man—sick men have strange fancies sometimes. I imagine Mr Abernethie suffered from that sort of thing in his last days. He spoke of enemies sometimes, of somebody wishing to do him harm—perhaps? He may even have thought his food was being tampered with?"

Old Lanscombe looked surprised—surprised and offended.

"I cannot recall anything of that kind, sir."

Entwhistle looked at him keenly.

"You're a very loyal servant, Lanscombe, I know that. But such fancies on Mr. Abernethie's part would be quite—er—unimportant—a natural symptom in some—er—diseases."

"Indeed, sir? I can only say Mr Abernethie never said anything like that to me, or in my hearing."

Mr Entwhistle slid gently to another subject.

"He had some of his family down to stay with him, didn't he, before he died. His nephew and his two nieces and their husbands?"

"Yes, sir, that is so."

"Was he satisfied with those visits? Or was he disappointed?"

Lanscombe's eyes became remote, his old back stiffened.

"I really could not say, sir."

"I think you could, you know," said Mr Entwhistle gently. "It's not your place to say anything of that kind—that's what you really mean. But there are times when one has to do violence to one's sense of what is fitting. I was one of your master's oldest friends. I cared for him very much. So did you. That's why I'm asking you for your opinion as a *man,* not as a butler."

Lanscombe was silent for a moment, then he said in a colourless voice:

"Is there anything—wrong, sir?"

Mr Entwhistle replied truthfully.

"I don't know," he said. "I hope not. I would like to make sure. Have you yourself felt that something was—wrong?"

"Only since the funeral, sir. And I couldn't say exactly what it is. But Mrs Leo and Mrs Timothy, too, they didn't seem quite themselves that evening after the others had gone."

"You know the contents of the will?"

"Yes, sir. Mrs Leo thought I would like to know. It seemed to me, if I may permit myself to comment, a very fair will."

"Yes, it was a fair will. Equal benefits. But it is not, I think, the will that Mr Abernethie originally intended to make after his son died. Will you answer now the question that I asked you just now?"

"As a matter of personal opinion—"

"Yes, yes, that is understood."

"The master, sir, was very much disappointed after Mr George had been here. . . . He had hoped, I think, that Mr George might resemble Mr Mortimer. Mr George, if I may say so, did not come up to standard. Miss Laura's husband was always considered unsatisfactory, and I'm afraid Mr George took after him." Lanscombe paused and then went on, "Then the young ladies came with their husbands. Miss Susan he took to at once—a very spirited and handsome young lady, but it's my opinion he couldn't abide her husband. Young ladies make funny choices nowadays, sir."

"And the other couple?"

"I couldn't say much about that. A very pleasant and good-looking young pair. I think the master enjoyed having them here—but I don't think—" the old man hesitated.

"Yes, Lanscombe?"

"Well, the master had never had much truck with the stage. He said to me one day, 'I can't understand why anyone gets stagestruck. It's a foolish kind of life. Seems to deprive people of what little sense they have. I don't know what it does to your moral sense. You certainly lose your sense of proportion.' Of course he wasn't referring directly—"

"No, no, I quite understand. Now after these visits, Mr Abernethie himself went away—first to his brother, and afterwards to his sister Mrs Lansquenet."

"That I did not know, sir. I mean he mentioned to me that he was going to Mr Timothy and afterwards to Something St. Mary."

"That is right. Can you remember anything he said on his return in regard to those visits?"

Lanscombe reflected.

"I really don't know—nothing direct. He was glad to be back. Travelling and staying in strange houses tired him very much—that I do remember his saying."

"Nothing else? Nothing about either of them?"

Lanscombe frowned.

"The master used to—well, to *murmur,* if you get my meaning—speaking to me and yet more to himself— hardly noticing I was there—because he knew me so well. . . ."

"Knew you and trusted you, yes."

"But my recollection is very vague as to what he said —something about he couldn't think what he'd done with his money—that was Mr Timothy, I take it. And then he said something about 'Women can be fools in ninety-nine different ways but be pretty shrewd in the hundredth.' Oh yes, and he said, 'You can only say what you really think to some of your own generation. They don't think you're fancying things as the younger ones do.' And later he said —but I don't know in what connection—'It's not very nice to have set traps for people, but I don't see what else I can do.' But I think it possible, sir, that he may have been thinking of the second gardener—a question of peaches being taken."

But Mr Entwhistle did not think that it was the second gardener who had been in Richard Abernethie's mind. After a few more questions he let Lanscombe go and re-flected on what he had learned. Nothing, really—nothing, that is, that he had not deduced before. Yet there were suggestive points. It was not his sister-in-law, Maude, but his sister Cora of whom he had been thinking when he made the remark about women who were fools and yet shrewd. And it was to her he had confided his "fancies." And he had spoken of setting a trap. For whom?

### iii

Mr Entwhistle had meditated a good deal over how much he should tell Helen. In the end he decided to take her wholly into his confidence.

First he thanked her for sorting out Richard's things and for making various household arrangements. The house had been advertised for sale and there were one or two prospective buyers who would be shortly coming to look over it.

"Private buyers?"

"I'm afraid not. The Y.W.C.A. are considering it, and there is a young people's club, and the Trustees of the Jefferson Trust are looking for a suitable place to house their Collection."

"It seems sad that the house will not be lived in, but of course it is not a practicable proposition nowadays."

"I am going to ask you if it would be possible for you to remain here until the house is sold. Or would it be a great inconvenience?"

"No—actually it would suit me very well. I don't want to go to Cyprus until May, and I much prefer being here than to being in London as I had planned. I love this house, you know, Leo loved it, and we were always happy when we were here together."

"There is another reason why I should be grateful if you would stay on. There is a friend of mine, a man called Hercule Poirot—"

Helen said sharply: "Hercule Poirot? Then you think—"

"You know of him?"

"Yes. Some friends of mine—but I imagined that he was dead long ago."

"He is very much alive. Not young, of course."

"No, he could hardly be young."

She spoke mechanically. Her face was white and strained. She said with an effort:

"You think—that Cora was right? That Richard was—*murdered?*"

Mr Entwhistle unburdened himself. It was a pleasure to unburden himself to Helen with her clear calm mind.

When he had finished she said:

"One ought to feel it's fantastic—but one doesn't. Maude and I, that night after the funeral—it was in both our minds, I'm sure. Saying to ourselves what a silly woman Cora was—and yet being uneasy. And then—Cora was killed—and I told myself it was just coincidence—and of course it may be—but oh! if one can only be sure. It's all so difficult."

"Yes, it's difficult. But Poirot is a man of great originality and he has something really approaching genius. He understands perfectly what we need—assurance that the whole thing is a mare's nest."

"And suppose it isn't?"

"What makes you say that?" asked Mr Entwhistle sharply.

"I don't know. I've been uneasy. . . . Not just about what Cora said that day—something else. Something that I felt at the time to be wrong."

"Wrong? In what way?"

"That's just it. I don't know."

"You mean it was something about one of the people in the room?"

"Yes—yes—something of that kind. But I don't know who or what. . . . Oh, that sounds absurd—"

"Not at all. It is interesting—very interesting. You are not a fool, Helen. If you noticed something that something had significance."

"Yes, but I can't remember what it *was*. The more I think—"

"Don't think. That is the wrong way to bring anything back. Let it go. Sooner or later it will flash into your mind. And when it does—let me know—at once."

"I will."

## 9

Miss Gilchrist pulled her black felt hat down firmly on her head and tucked in a wisp of grey hair. The inquest was set for twelve o'clock and it was not quite twenty past eleven. Her grey coat and skirt looked quite nice, she thought, and she had bought herself a black blouse. She wished she could have been all in black, but that would have been far beyond her means. She looked round the small neat bedroom and at the walls hung with representations of Brixham harbour, Cockington Forge, Anstey's Cove, Kynance Cove, Polflexan harbour, Babbacombe Bay, etc., all signed in a dashing way, Cora Lansquenet. Her eyes rested with particular fondness on Polflexan harbour. On the chest of drawers a faded photograph, carefully framed, represented the Willow Teashop. Miss Gilchrist looked at it lovingly and sighed.

She was disturbed from her reverie by the sound of the door bell below.

"Dear me," murmured Miss Gilchrist, "I wonder who—"

She went out of her room and down the rather rickety stairs. The bell sounded again and there was a sharp knock.

For some reason Miss Gilchrist felt nervous. For a moment or two her steps slowed up, then she went rather unwillingly to the door, adjuring herself not to be so silly.

A young woman dressed smartly in black and carrying a small suitcase was standing on the step. She noticed the alarmed look on Miss Gilchrist's face and said quickly:

"Miss Gilchrist? I am Mrs Lansquenet's niece—Susan Banks."

"Oh dear, yes, of course. I didn't know. Do come in, Mrs Banks. Mind the hall stand—it sticks out a little. In here, yes. I didn't know you were coming down for the inquest. I'd have had something ready—some coffee or something."

Susan Banks said briskly:

"I don't want anything. I'm so sorry if I startled you."

"Well, you know you *did,* in a way. It's very silly of me. I'm not usually nervous. In fact, I told the lawyer that I wasn't nervous, and that I wouldn't be nervous staying on here alone, and really I'm not nervous. Only—perhaps it's just the inquest and—thinking of things, but I have been jumpy all this morning. Just about half an hour ago the bell rang and I could hardly bring myself to open the door—which was really very stupid and so untimely that a murderer would come back—and why should he?—and actually it was only a nun, collecting for an orphanage— and I was so relieved I gave her two shillings although I'm *not* a Roman Catholic, though I believe the Little Sisters of the Poor do really do good work. But do please sit down, Mrs—Mrs—"

"Banks."

"Yes, of course, Banks. Did you come down by train?"

"No, I drove down. The lane seemed so narrow I ran the car on a little way and found a sort of old quarry I backed it into."

"This lane is very narrow, but there's hardly ever any traffic along here. It's rather a lonely road."

Miss Gilchrist gave a little shiver as she said those last words.

Susan Banks was looking round the room.

"Poor old Aunt Cora," she said. "She left what she had to me, you know."

"Yes, I know. Mr Entwhistle told me. I expect you'll be glad of the furniture. You're newly married, I understand, and furnishing is such an expense nowadays. Mrs Lansquenet had some very nice things."

Susan did not agree. Cora had no taste for the antique. The contents varied between "modernistic" pieces and the "arty" type.

"I shan't want any of the furniture," she said. "I've got my own, you know. I shall put it up for auction. Unless— is there any of it you would like? I'd be very glad . . ."

She stopped, a little embarrassed. But Miss Gilchrist was not at all embarrassed. She beamed.

"Now really, that's *very* kind of you, Mrs Banks—yes, very kind indeed. I really do appreciate it. But actually, you know, I have my own things. I put them in store in case—someday—I should need them. There are some pictures my father left, too. I had a small teashop at one time, you know—but then the war came—it was all very unfortunate. But I didn't sell up everything, because I did hope to have my own little home again one day, so I put the best things in store with my father's pictures and some relics of our old home. But I *would* like very much, if you *really* wouldn't mind, to have that little painted tea table of dear Mrs Lansquenet's. Such a pretty thing and we always had tea on it."

Susan, looking with a slight shudder at a small green table painted with large purple clematis, said quickly that she would be delighted for Miss Gilchrist to have it.

"Thank you *very* much, Mrs Banks. I feel a little greedy. I've got all her beautiful pictures, you know, and a lovely amethyst brooch, but I feel that perhaps I ought to give *that* back to you."

"No, no, indeed."

"You'll want to go through her things? After the inquest, perhaps?"

"I thought I'd stay here a couple of days, go through things, and clear everything up."

"Sleep here, you mean?"

"Yes. Is there any difficulty?"

"Oh no, Mrs Banks, of course not. I'll put fresh sheets on my bed, and I can doss down here on the couch quite well."

"But there's Aunt Cora's room, isn't there? I can sleep in that."

"You—you wouldn't mind?"

"You mean because she was murdered there? Oh no, I wouldn't mind. I'm very tough, Miss Gilchrist. It's been—I mean—it's all right again?"

Miss Gilchrist understood the question.

"Oh *yes*, Mrs Banks. All the blankets sent away to the cleaners and Mrs Panter and I scrubbed the whole room out thoroughly. And there are plenty of spare blankets. But come up and see for yourself."

She led the way upstairs and Susan followed her.

The room where Cora Lansquenet had died was clean and fresh and curiously devoid of any sinister atmosphere. Like the sitting room it contained a mixture of modern utility and elaborately painted furniture. It represented Cora's cheerful tasteless personality. Over the mantelpiece an oil painting showed a buxom young woman about to enter her bath.

Susan gave a slight shudder as she looked at it and Miss Gilchrist said:

"That was painted by Mrs Lansquenet's husband. There are a lot more of his pictures in the dining room downstairs."

"How terrible."

"Well, I don't care very much for that style of painting *myself*—but Mrs Lansquenet was very proud of her husband as an artist and thought that his work was sadly unappreciated."

"Where are Aunt Cora's own pictures?"

"In my room. Would you like to see them?"

Miss Gilchrist displayed her treasures proudly.

Susan remarked that Aunt Cora seemed to have been fond of sea coast resorts.

"Oh yes. You see, she lived for many years with Mr Lansquenet at a small fishing village in Brittany. Fishing boats are always so picturesque, are they not?"

"Obviously," Susan murmured. A whole series of picture postcards could, she thought, have been made from Cora Lansquenet's paintings which were faithful to detail and very highly coloured. They gave rise to the suspicion that they might actually have been painted from picture postcards.

But when she hazarded this opinion Miss Gilchrist was indignant. Mrs Lansquenet *always* painted from Nature! Indeed once she had had a touch of the sun from reluctance to leave a subject when the light was just right.

"Mrs Lansquenet was a real artist," said Miss Gilchrist reproachfully.

She glanced at her watch and Susan said quickly:

"Yes, we ought to start for the inquest. Is it far? Shall I get the car?"

It was only five minutes' walk, Miss Gilchrist assured her. So they set out together on foot. Mr Entwhistle who had come down by train met them and shepherded them into the Village Hall.

There seemed to be a large number of strangers present. The inquest was not sensational. There was evidence of identification of the deceased. Medical evidence as to the nature of the wounds that had killed her. There were no signs of a struggle. Deceased was probably under a narcotic at the time she was attacked and would have been taken quite unawares. Death was unlikely to have occurred later than four thirty. Between two and four thirty was the nearest approximation. Miss Gilchrist testified to finding the body. A police constable and Inspector Morton gave their evidence. The Coroner summed up briefly. The jury made no bones about the verdict *"Murder by some person or persons unknown."*

It was over. They came out again into the sunlight. Half a dozen cameras clicked. Mr Entwhistle shepherded Susan and Miss Gilchrist into the King's Arms where he had taken the precaution to arrange for lunch to be served in a private room behind the bar.

"Not a very good lunch, I am afraid," he said apologetically.

But the lunch was not at all bad. Miss Gilchrist sniffed a little and murmured that "it was all so dreadful" but cheered up and tackled the Irish stew with appetite after Mr Entwhistle had insisted on her drinking a glass of sherry. He said to Susan:

"I'd no idea you were coming down today, Susan. We could have come together."

"I know I said I wouldn't. But it seemed rather mean for none of the family to be there. I rang up George but he said he was very busy and couldn't possibly make it, and Rosamund had an audition and Uncle Timothy, of course, is a crock. So it had to be me."

"Your husband didn't come with you?"

"Greg had to settle up with his tiresome shop."

Seeing a startled look in Miss Gilchrist's eye, Susan said: "My husband works in a chemist's shop."

A husband in retail trade did not quite square with Miss Gilchrist's impression of Susan's smartness, but she said valiantly:

"Oh yes, just like Keats."

"Greg's no poet," said Susan.

She added:

"We've got great plans for the future—a double barrelled establishment—Cosmetics and Beauty parlour and a laboratory for special preparations."

"That will be much nicer," said Miss Gilchrist approvingly. "Something like Elizabeth Arden who is really a Countess, so I have been told—or is that Helena Rubinstein? In any case," she added kindly, "a pharmacist's is not in the least like an ordinary shop—a *draper,* for instance, or a *grocer.*"

"You kept a tea shop, you said, didn't you?"

"Yes, indeed," Miss Gilchrist's face lit up. That the Willow Tree had ever been "trade" in the sense that a shop was trade, would never have occurred to her. To keep a tea shop was in her mind the essence of gentility. She started telling Susan about the Willow Tree.

Mr Entwhistle who had heard about it before let his mind drift to other matters. When Susan had spoken to him twice without his answering he hurriedly apologised.

"Forgive me, my dear, I was thinking, as a matter of fact, about your uncle Timothy. I am a little worried."

"About uncle Timothy? I shouldn't be. I don't believe really there's anything the matter with him. He's just a hypochondriac."

"Yes—yes, you may be right. I confess it was not his health that was worrying me. It's Mrs Timothy. Apparently she's fallen downstairs and twisted her ankle. She's laid up and your uncle is in a terrible state."

"Because he'll have to look after her instead of the other way about? Do him a lot of good," said Susan.

"Yes—yes, I daresay. But will your poor aunt *get* any looking after? That is really the question. With no servants in the house."

"Life is really Hell for elderly people," said Susan.

"They live in a kind of Georgian Manor house, don't they?"

Mr Entwhistle nodded.

They came rather warily out of the King's Arms, but the Press seemed to have dispersed.

A couple of reporters were lying in wait for Susan by the cottage door. Shepherded by Mr Entwhistle she said a few necessary and non-committal words. Then she and Miss Gilchrist went into the cottage and Mr Entwhistle returned to the King's Arms where he had booked a room. The funeral was to be on the following day.

"My car's still in the quarry," said Susan. "I'd forgotten about it. I'll drive it along to the village later."

Miss Gilchrist said anxiously:

"Not too late. You won't go out after dark, will you?"

Susan looked at her and laughed.

"You don't think there's a murderer still hanging about, do you?"

"No—no, I suppose not." Miss Gilchrist looked embarrassed.

"But it's exactly what she does think," thought Susan. "How amazing!"

Miss Gilchrist had vanished towards the kitchen.

"I'm sure you'd like tea early. In about half an hour, do you think, Mrs Banks?"

Susan thought that tea at half past three was overdoing it, but she was charitable enough to realise that "a nice cup of tea" was Miss Gilchrist's idea of restoration for the nerves and she had her own reasons for wishing to please Miss Gilchrist, so she said:

"Whenever you like, Miss Gilchrist."

A happy clatter of kitchen implements began and Susan went into the sitting room. She had only been there a few minutes when the bell sounded and was succeeded by a very precise little rat-tat-tat.

Susan came out into the hall and Miss Gilchrist appeared at the kitchen door wearing an apron and wiping floury hands on it.

"Oh dear, who do you think that can be?"

"More reporters, I expect," said Susan.

"Oh dear, how annoying for you, Mrs Banks."

"Oh well, never mind, I'll attend to it."

"I was just going to make a few scones for tea."

Susan went towards the front door and Miss Gilchrist hovered uncertainly. Susan wondered whether she thought a man with a hatchet was waiting outside.

The visitor, however, proved to be an elderly gentleman who raised his hat when Susan opened the door and said, beaming at her in avuncular style,

"Mrs Banks, I think?"

"Yes."

"My name is Guthrie—Alexander Guthrie. I was a friend—a very old friend, of Mrs Lansquenet's. You, I think, are her niece, formerly Miss Susan Abernethie?"

"That's quite right."

"Then since we know who we are, I may come in?"

"Of course."

Mr Guthrie wiped his feet carefully on the mat, stepped inside, divested himself of his overcoat, laid it down with his hat on a small oak chest and followed Susan into the sitting room.

"This is a melancholy occasion," said Mr Guthrie to whom melancholy did not seem to come naturally, his own inclination being to beam. "Yes, a very melancholy occasion. I was in this part of the world and I felt the least I could do was to attend the inquest—and of course the funeral. Poor Cora—poor foolish Cora. I have known her, my dear Mrs Banks, since the early days of her marriage. A high-spirited girl—and she took art very seriously—took Pierre Lansquenet seriously, too—as an artist, I mean. All things considered, he didn't make her too bad a husband. He strayed, if you know what I mean, yes, he strayed—but fortunately Cora took it as part of the artistic temperament. He was an artist and therefore immoral! In fact, I'm not sure she didn't go further: he was immoral and therefore he must be an artist! No kind of sense in artistic matters, poor Cora—though in other ways, mind you, Cora had a lot of sense—yes, a surprising lot of sense."

"That's what everybody seems to say," said Susan. "I didn't really know her."

"No, no, cut herself off from her family because they didn't appreciate her precious Pierre. She was never a pretty girl—but she had *something*. She was good company! You never knew what she'd say next and you never knew if her *naiveté* was genuine or whether she was doing it deliberately. She made us all laugh a good deal. The eternal child—that's what we always felt about her. And really the last time I saw her (I have seen her from time to time since Pierre died) she struck me as still behaving very much like a child."

Susan offered Mr Guthrie a cigarette, but the old gentleman shook his head.

"No thank you, my dear. I don't smoke. You must wonder why I've come? To tell you the truth I was feeling rather conscience-stricken. I promised Cora to come and see her some weeks ago. I usually called upon her once a year, and just lately she'd taken up the hobby of buying pictures at local sales, and wanted me to look at some of them. My profession is that of art critic, you know. Of course most of Cora's purchases were horrible daubs, but take it all in all, it isn't such a bad speculation. Pictures go for next to nothing at these country sales and the frames alone are worth more than you pay for the picture. Naturally any important sale is attended by dealers and one isn't likely to get hold of masterpieces. But only the other day, a small Cuyp was knocked down for a few pounds at a farmhouse sale. The history of it was quite interesting. It had been given to an old nurse by the family she had served faithfully for many years—they had no idea of its value. Old nurse gave it to farmer nephew who liked the horse in it but thought it was a dirty old thing! Yes, yes, these things sometimes happen, and Cora was convinced that she had an eye for pictures. She hadn't, of course. Wanted me to come and look at a Rembrandt she had picked up last year. A Rembrandt! Not even a respectable copy of one! But she had got hold of a quite nice Bartolozzi engraving—damp spotted unfortunately. I sold it for her for thirty pounds and of course that spurred her on. She wrote to me with great gusto about an Italian Primitive she had bought at some sale and I promised I'd come along and see it."

"That's it over there, I expect," said Susan, gesturing to the wall behind him.

Mr Guthrie got up, put on a pair of spectacles, and went over to study the picture.

"Poor dear Cora," he said at last.

"There are a lot more," said Susan.

Mr Guthrie proceeded to a leisurely inspection of the art treasures acquired by the hopeful Mrs Lansquenet. Occasionally he said, "Tchk tchk," occasionally he sighed.

Finally he removed his spectacles.

"Dirt," he said, "is a wonderful thing, Mrs Banks! It gives a patina of romance to the most horrible examples of the painter's art. I'm afraid that Bartolozzi was beginner's luck. Poor Cora. Still it gave her an interest in life. I am really thankful that I did not have to disillusion her."

"There are some pictures in the dining room," said Susan, "but I think they are all her husband's work."

Mr Guthrie shuddered slightly and held up a protesting hand.

"Do not force me to look at those again. Life classes have much to answer for! I always tried to spare Cora's feelings. A devoted wife—a very devoted wife. Well, dear Mrs Banks, I must not take up more of your time."

"Oh, do stay and have some tea. I think it's nearly ready."

"That is very kind of you." Mr Guthrie sat down again promptly.

"I'll just go and see."

In the kitchen, Miss Gilchrist was just lifting a last batch of scones from the oven. The teatray stood ready and the kettle was just gently rattling its lid.

"There's a Mr Guthrie here, and I've asked him to stay for tea."

"Mr Guthrie? Oh yes, he was a great friend of dear Mrs Lansquenet's. He's the celebrated art critic. How fortunate; I've made a nice lot of scones and that's some home made strawberry jam, and I just whipped up some little drop cakes. I'll just make the tea—I've warmed the pot. Oh please, Mrs Banks, don't carry that heavy tray. I can manage *everything*."

However Susan took in the tray and Miss Gilchrist followed with teapot and kettle, greeted Mr Guthrie, and they set to.

"Hot scones, that *is* a treat," said Mr Guthrie, "and what delicious jam! Really, the stuff one buys nowadays."

Miss Gilchrist was flushed and delighted. The little cakes were excellent and so were the scones, and everyone did justice to them. The ghost of the Willow Tree hung over the party. Here, it was clear, Miss Gilchrist was in her element.

"Well, thank you, perhaps I will," said Mr Guthrie as he accepted the last cake, pressed upon him by Miss Gilchrist. "I do feel rather guilty, though—enjoying my tea, here, where poor Cora was so brutally murdered."

Miss Gilchrist displayed an unexpected Victorian reaction to this.

"Oh but Mrs Lansquenet would have wished you to make a good tea. You've got to keep your strength up."

"Yes, yes, perhaps you are right. The fact is, you know, that one cannot really bring oneself to believe that someone you knew—actually knew—*can* have been murdered!"

"I agree," said Susan. "It just seems—fantastic."

"And certainly not by some casual tramp who broke in and attacked her. I *can* imagine, you know, reasons why Cora might have been murdered—"

Susan said quickly, "Can you? What reasons?"

"Well, she wasn't discreet," said Mr Guthrie. "Cora was never discreet. And she enjoyed—how shall I put it —showing how sharp she could be? Like a child who's got hold of somebody's secret. If Cora got hold of a secret she'd want to talk about it. Even if she promised not to, she'd still do it. She wouldn't be able to help herself."

Susan did not speak. Miss Gilchrist did not either. She looked worried. Mr Guthrie went on.

"Yes, a little dose of arsenic in a cup of tea—*that* would not have surprised me, or a box of chocolates by post. But sordid robbery and assault—that seems highly incongruous. I may be wrong but I should have thought she had very little to take that would be worth a burglar's while. She didn't keep much money in the house, did she?"

Miss Gilchrist said, "Very little."

Mr Guthrie sighed and rose to his feet.

"Ah! well, there's a lot of lawlessness about since the war. Times have changed."

Thanking them for tea, he took a polite farewell of the

two women. Miss Gilchrist saw him out and helped him on with his overcoat. From the window of the sitting room, Susan watched him trot briskly down the front path to the gate.

Miss Gilchrist came back into the room with a small parcel in her hand.

"The postman must have been while we were at the inquest. He pushed it through the letter box and it had fallen in the corner behind the door. Now I wonder—why, of course, it must be wedding cake."

Happily Miss Gilchrist ripped off the paper. Inside was a small white box tied with silver ribbon.

"It is!" She pulled off the ribbon; inside was a modest wedge of rich cake with almond paste and white icing. "How nice! Now who—" she consulted the card attached. *"John and Mary*—Now who *can* that be? How silly to put no surname."

Susan, rousing herself from contemplation, said vaguely,

"It's quite difficult sometimes with people just using Christian names. I got a post-card the other day signed Joan. I counted up I knew eight Joans—and with telephoning so much, one often doesn't know their handwriting."

Miss Gilchrist was happily going over the possible Johns or Marys of her acquaintance.

"It might be Dorothy's daughter—*her* name was Mary, but I hadn't heard of an engagement, still less of a marriage. Then there's little John Banfield—I suppose he's grown up and old enough to be married—or the Enfield girl—no, her name was Margaret. No address or anything. Oh well, I daresay it will come to me . . ."

She picked up the tray and went out to the kitchen.

Susan roused herself and said:

"Well—I suppose I'd better go and put the car somewhere."

# 10

Susan retrieved the car from the quarry where she had left it and drove it into the village. There was a petrol pump but no garage and she was advised to take it to the King's Arms. They had room for it there and she left it by a big Daimler which was preparing to go out. It was chauffeur driven and inside it, very much muffled up, was an elderly foreign gentleman with a large moustache.

The boy to whom Susan was talking about the car was staring at her with such rapt attention that he did not seem to be taking in half of what she said.

Finally he said in an awestricken voice:

"You're her niece, aren't you?"

"What?"

"You're the victim's niece," the boy repeated with relish.

"Oh—yes—yes, I am."

"Ar! Wondered where I'd seen you before."

"Ghoul," thought Susan as she retraced her steps to the cottage.

Miss Gilchrist greeted her with:

"Oh you're safely back," in tones of relief which further annoyed her. Miss Gilchrist added anxiously:

"You *can* eat spaghetti, can't you? I thought for to-night—"

"Oh yes, anything. I don't want much."

"I really flatter myself that I can make a very tasty spaghetti *au gratin*."

The boast was not an idle one. Miss Gilchrist, Susan reflected, was really an excellent cook. Susan offered to help wash up but Miss Gilchrist, though clearly gratified by the offer, assured Susan that there was very little to do.

She came in a little while later with coffee. The coffee was less excellent, being decidedly weak. Miss Gilchrist offered Susan a piece of the wedding cake which Susan refused.

"It's really very good cake," Miss Gilchrist insisted, tasting it. She had settled to her own satisfaction that it must have been sent by someone whom she alluded to as "dear Ellen's daughter who I know was engaged to be married but I can't remember her name."

Susan let Miss Gilchrist chirrup away into silence before starting her own subject of conversation. This moment, after supper, sitting before the fire, was a companionable one.

She said at last:

"My uncle Richard came down here before he died, didn't he?"

"Yes, he did."

"When was that exactly?"

"Let me see—it must have been one, two—nearly three weeks before his death was announced."

"Did he seem—ill?"

"Well, no, I wouldn't say he seemed exactly ill. He had a very hearty vigorous manner. Mrs Lansquenet was very surprised to see him. She said, 'Well, really, Richard, after all these years!' And he said, 'I came to see for myself exactly how things are with you.' And Mrs Lansquenet said, '*I*'m all right.' I think you know, she was a teeny bit offended by his turning up so casually—after the long break. Anyway Mr Abernethie said, 'No use keeping up old grievances. You and I and Timothy are the only ones left—and nobody can talk to Timothy except about his own health.' And he said, 'Pierre seems to have made you happy, so it seems I was in the wrong. There, will that content you?' Very nicely he said it. A handsome man, though elderly, of course."

"How long was he here?"

"He stayed for lunch. Beef olives, I made. Fortunately it was the day the butcher called."

Miss Gilchrist's memory seemed to be almost wholly culinary.

"They seemed to be getting on well together?"

"Oh yes."

Susan paused and then said:

"Was Aunt Cora surprised when—he died?"

"Oh yes, it was quite sudden, wasn't it?"

"Yes, it was sudden . . . I meant—she *was* surprised. He hadn't given her any indication how ill he was."

"Oh—I see what you mean." Miss Gilchrist paused a moment. "No, no, I think perhaps you are right. She did say that he had got very old—I think she said senile . . ."

"But *you* didn't think he was senile?"

"Well, not to *look* at. But I didn't talk to him much. Naturally, I left them alone together."

Susan looked at Miss Gilchrist speculatively. Was Miss Gilchrist the kind of woman who listened at doors? She was honest, Susan felt sure, she wouldn't ever pilfer, or cheat over the housekeeping, or open letters. But inquisitiveness can drape itself in a mantle of rectitude. Miss Gilchrist might have found it necessary to garden near an open window, or to dust the hall . . . That would be within the permitted lengths. And then, of course, she could not have helped hearing something . . .

"You didn't hear any of their conversation?" Susan asked.

Too abrupt. Miss Gilchrist flushed angrily.

"No, indeed, Mrs Banks. It has never been my custom to listen at doors!"

That means she does, thought Susan, otherwise she'd just say "No."

Aloud she said: "I'm so sorry, Miss Gilchrist. I didn't mean it that way. But sometimes, in these small flimsily built cottages, one simply can't help hearing everything that goes on, and now that they are both dead, it's really rather important to the family to know just what was said at that meeting between them."

The cottage was anything but flimsily built—it dated from a sturdier era of building, but Miss Gilchrist accepted the bait, and rose to the suggestion held out.

"Of course what you say is quite true, Mrs Banks—this *is* a very small place and I do appreciate that you would want to know what passed between them, but really I'm afraid I can't help very much. I think they were talking about Mr Abernethie's health—and certain—well, *fancies* he had. He didn't look it, but he must have been a sick man and as is so often the case, he put his ill health down to *outside agencies*. A common symptom, I believe. My aunt—"

Miss Gilchrist described her aunt.

Susan, like Mr Entwhistle, sidetracked the aunt.

"Yes," she said. "That is just what we thought. My uncle's servants were all very attached to him and naturally they are upset by his thinking—" She paused.

"Oh of course! Servants are *very* touchy about anything of that kind. I remember that my aunt—"

Again Susan interrupted.

"It *was* the servants he suspected, I suppose? Of poisoning him, I mean?"

"I don't know . . . I—really—"

Susan noted her confusion.

"It wasn't the servants. Was it one particular person?"

"I don't know, Mrs Banks. Really I don't know—"

But her eye avoided Susan's. Susan thought to herself that Miss Gilchrist knew more than she was willing to admit.

It was possible that Miss Gilchrist knew a good deal. . . .

Deciding not to press the point for the moment, Susan said:

"What are your own plans for the future, Miss Gilchrist?"

"Well, really, I was going to speak to you about that, Mrs Banks. I told Mr Entwhistle I would be willing to stay on until everything was cleared up."

"I know. I'm very grateful."

"And I wanted to ask you how long that was likely to be, because, of course, I must start looking about for another post."

Susan considered.

"There's really not very much to be done here. In a couple of days I can get things sorted and notify the auctioneer."

"You have decided to sell up everything, then?"

"Yes. I don't suppose there will be any difficulty in letting the cottage?"

"*Oh no*—people will queue up for it, I'm sure. There

are so few cottages to rent. One nearly always has to buy."

"So it's all very simple, you see." Susan hesitated a moment before saying, "I wanted to tell you—that I hope you'll accept three months' salary."

"That's very generous of you, I'm sure, Mrs Banks. I do appreciate it. And you would be prepared to—I mean I could ask you—if necessary—to—to recommend me? To say that I had been with a relation of yours and that I had—proved satisfactory?"

"Oh, of course."

"I don't know whether I ought to ask it." Miss Gilchrist's hands began to shake and she tried to steady her voice. "But would it be possible not to—to mention the circumstances—or even the *name?*"

Susan stared.

"I don't understand."

"That's because you haven't thought, Mrs Banks. It's *murder.* A murder that's been in the papers and that everybody has read about. Don't you see? People might think. 'Two women living together, and one of them is killed—and *perhaps the companion did it.*' Don't you see, Mrs Banks? I'm sure that if *I* was looking for someone, I'd—well, I'd think twice before engaging myself—if you understand what I mean. Because one never *knows!* It's been worrying me dreadfully, Mrs Banks; I've been lying awake at night thinking that perhaps I'll never get another job—not of this kind. And what else is there that I can do?"

The question came out with unconscious pathos. Susan felt suddenly stricken. She realised the desperation of this pleasant-spoken commonplace woman who was dependent for existence on the fears and whims of employers. And there was a lot of truth in what Miss Gilchrist had said. You wouldn't, if you could help it, engage a woman to share domestic intimacy who had figured, however innocently, in a murder case.

Susan said: "But if they find the man who did it—"

"Oh *then,* of course, it will be quite all right. But will they find him? I don't think, myself, the police have the *least idea.* And if he's *not* caught—well, that leaves me as—as not quite the most likely person, but as a person who *could* have done it."

Susan nodded thoughtfully. It was true that Miss Gilchrist did not benefit from Cora Lansquenet's death—but who was to know that? And besides there were so many tales—ugly tales—of animosity arising between women who lived together—strange pathological motives for sudden violence. Someone who had not known them might imagine that Cora Lansquenet and Miss Gilchrist had lived on those terms. . . .

Susan spoke with her usual decision.

"Don't worry, Miss Gilchrist," she said, speaking briskly and cheerfully. "I'm sure I can find you a post amongst my friends. There won't be the least difficulty."

"I'm afraid," said Miss Gilchrist, regaining some of her customary manner, "that I couldn't undertake any really *rough* work. Just a little plain cooking and housework—"

The telephone rang and Miss Gilchrist jumped.

"Dear me, I wonder who *that* can be."

"I expect it's my husband," said Susan, jumping up. "He said he'd ring me tonight."

She went to the telephone.

"Yes? —yes, this is Mrs Banks speaking personally . . ." There was a pause and then her voice changed. It became soft and warm. "Hullo, darling—yes, it's me. . . . Oh, quite well . . . Murder by someone unknown . . . the usual thing. . . . Only Mr Entwhistle. . . . What? . . . It's difficult to say, but I think so. . . . Yes, just as we thought. . . . Absolutely according to plan. . . . I shall sell the stuff. There's nothing *we'd* want. . . . Not for a day or two. . . . Absolutely frightful. . . . Don't fuss. I know what I'm doing. . . . Greg, you didn't . . . You were careful to . . . No, it's nothing. Nothing at all. Good night, darling."

She rang off. The nearness of Miss Gilchrist had hampered her a little. Miss Gilchrist could probably hear from the kitchen, where she had tactfully retired, exactly what went on. There were things she had wanted to ask Greg, but she hadn't liked to.

She stood by the telephone, frowning abstractedly. Then suddenly an idea came to her.

"Of course," she murmured. "Just the thing."

Lifting the receiver she asked for Trunk Enquiry.

Some quarter of an hour later a weary voice from the exchange was saying:

"I'm afraid there's no reply."

"Please go on ringing them."

Susan spoke autocratically. She listened to the far off buzzing of a telephone bell. Then, suddenly it was interrupted and a man's voice, peevish and slightly indignant, said:

"Yes, yes, what is it?"

"Uncle Timothy?"

"What's that? I can't hear you."

"Uncle Timothy? I'm Susan Banks."

"Susan who?"

"Banks. Formerly Abernethie. Your niece Susan."

"Oh, you're Susan, are you? What's the matter? What are you ringing up for at this time of night?"

"It's quite early still."

"It isn't. I was in bed."

"You must go to bed very early. How's Aunt Maude?"

"Is that all you rang up to ask? Your aunt's in a good deal of pain and she can't do a thing. Not a thing. She's helpless. We're in a nice mess, I can tell you. That fool of a doctor says he can't even get a nurse. He wanted to cart Maude off to hospital. I stood out against *that*. He's trying to get hold of someone for us. *I* can't do anything—I daren't even try. There's a fool from the village staying in the house tonight—but she's murmuring about getting back to her husband. Don't know *what* we're going to do."

"That's what I rang you up about. Would you like Miss Gilchrist?"

"Who's she? Never heard of her."

"Aunt Cora's companion. She's very nice and capable."

"Can she cook?"

"Yes, she cooks very well, and she could look after Aunt Maude."

"That's all very well, but when could she come? Here I am, all on my own, with only these idiots of village women popping in and out at odd hours, and it's not good for me. My heart's playing me up."

"I'll arrange for her to get off to you as soon as possible. The day after tomorrow, perhaps?"

"Well, thanks very much," said the voice rather grudgingly. "You're a good girl, Susan—er—thank you."

Susan rang off and went into the kitchen.

"Would you be willing to go up to Yorkshire and look after my aunt? She fell and broke her ankle and my uncle is quite useless. He's a bit of a pest but Aunt Maude is a very good sort. They have help in from the village, but you could cook and look after Aunt Maude."

Miss Gilchrist dropped the coffee pot in her agitation.

"Oh thank you, thank you—that really is kind. I think I can say of myself that I am really good in the sickroom, and I'm sure I can manage your uncle and cook him nice little meals. It's really very kind of you, Mrs Banks, and I *do* appreciate it."

# 11

Susan lay in bed and waited for sleep to come. It had been a long day and she was tired. She had been quite sure that she would go to sleep at once. She never had any difficulty in going to sleep. And yet here she lay, hour after hour, wide awake, her mind racing.

She had said she did not mind sleeping in this room, in this bed. This bed where Cora Abernethie—

No, no, she must put all that out of her mind. She had always prided herself on having no nerves. Why think of that afternoon less than a week ago? Think ahead—the future. Her future and Greg's. Those premises in Cardigan Street—just what they wanted. The business on the ground floor and a charming flat upstairs. The room out at the back a laboratory for Greg. For purposes of income tax it would be an excellent set up. Greg would get calm and well again. There would be no more of those alarming brain storms. The times when he looked at her without seeming to know who she was. Once or twice she'd been quite frightened . . . And old Mr Cole—he'd hinted—threatened: "If this happens again . . ." And it might have happened again—it *would* have happened again. If Uncle Richard hadn't died just when he did . . .

Uncle Richard—but really why look at it like that? He'd nothing to live for. Old and tired and ill. His son dead. It was a mercy really. To die in his sleep quietly like that. Quietly . . . in his sleep. . . . If only she could sleep. It was so stupid lying awake hour after hour . . . hearing the furniture creak, and the rustling of trees and bushes outside the window and the occasional queer melancholy hoot—an owl, she supposed. How sinister the country was, somehow. So different from the big noisy indifferent town. One felt so safe there—surrounded by people—never alone. Whereas here . . .

Houses where a murder had been committed were sometimes haunted. Perhaps this cottage would come to be known as the haunted cottage. Haunted by the spirit of Cora Lansquenet . . . Aunt Cora. Odd, really, how ever since she had arrived she had felt as though Aunt Cora were quite close to her . . . within reach. All nerves and fancy. Cora Lansquenet was dead, tomorrow she would be buried. There was no one in the cottage except Susan herself and Miss Gilchrist. Then why did she feel that there was someone in this room, someone close beside her. . . .

She had lain on this bed when the hatchet fell . . . Lying there trustingly asleep . . . Knowing nothing till the hatchet fell . . . And now she wouldn't let Susan sleep. . . .

The furniture creaked again . . . was that a stealthy step? . . . Susan switched on the light. Nothing. Nerves, nothing but nerves. Relax . . . close your eyes. . . .

Surely that was a groan—a groan or a faint moan . . . Someone in pain—someone dying. . . .

"I mustn't imagine things, I mustn't, I mustn't," Susan whispered to herself.

Death was the end—there was no existence after death. Under no circumstances could anyone come back. Or was she re-living a scene from the past—a dying woman groaning. . . .

There it was again . . . stronger . . . someone groaning in acute pain. . . .

But—this was real. Once again Susan switched on the light, sat up in bed and listened. The groans were real groans and she was hearing them through the wall. They came from the room next door.

Susan jumped out of bed, flung on a dressing gown and crossed to the door. She went out into the landing, tapped for a moment on Miss Gilchrist's door and then went in. Miss Gilchrist's light was on. She was sitting up in bed. She looked ghastly. Her face was distorted with pain.

"Miss Gilchrist, what's the matter? Are you ill?"

"Yes. I don't know what—I—" she tried to get out of bed, was seized with a fit of vomiting and then collapsed back on the pillows.

She murmured: "Please—ring up doctor. Must have eaten something. . . ."

"I'll get you some bicarbonate. We can get the doctor in the morning if you're not better."

Miss Gilchrist shook her head.

"No, get doctor now. I—I feel dreadful."

"Do you know his number? Or shall I look in the book?"

Miss Gilchrist gave her the number. She was interrupted by another fit of retching.

Susan's call was answered by a sleepy male voice.

"Who? Gilchrist? In Mead's Lane. Yes, I know. I'll be right along."

He was as good as his word. Ten minutes later Susan heard his car draw up outside and she went to open the door to him.

She explained the case as she took him upstairs. "I think," she said, "she must have eaten something that disagreed with her. But she seems pretty bad."

The doctor had had the air of one keeping his temper in leash and who has had some experience of being called out unnecessarily on more than one occasion. But as soon as he examined the moaning woman his manner changed. He gave various curt orders to Susan and presently came down and telephoned. Then he joined Susan in the sitting room.

"I've sent for an ambulance. Must get her into hospital."

"She's really bad then?"

"Yes. I've given her a shot of morphia to ease the pain. But it looks—" he broke off. "What's she eaten?"

"We had macaroni *au gratin* for supper and a custard pudding. Coffee afterwards."

"You have the same things?"

"Yes."

"And you're all right? No pain or discomfort?"

"No."

"She's taken nothing else? No tinned fish? Or sausages?"

"No. We had lunch at the King's Arms—after the inquest."

"Yes, of course. You're Mrs Lansquenet's niece?"

"Yes."

"That was a nasty business. Hope they catch the man who did it."

"Yes, indeed."

The ambulance came. Miss Gilchrist was taken away and the doctor went with her. He told Susan he would ring her up in the morning. When he had left she went upstairs to bed.

This time she fell asleep as soon as her head touched the pillow.

ii

The funeral was well attended. Most of the village had turned out. Susan and Mr Entwhistle were the only mourners, but various wreaths had been sent by the other members of the family. Mr Entwhistle asked where Miss Gilchrist was, and Susan explained the circumstances in a hurried whisper. Mr Entwhistle raised his eyebrows.

"Rather an odd occurrence?"

"Oh, she's better this morning. They rang up from the hospital. People do get these bilious turns. Some make more fuss than others."

Mr Entwhistle said no more. He was returning to London immediately after the funeral.

Susan went back to the cottage. She found some eggs and made herself an omelette. Then she went up to Cora's room and started to sort through the dead woman's things.

She was interrupted by the arrival of the doctor.

The doctor was looking worried. He replied to Susan's inquiry by saying that Miss Gilchrist was much better.

"She'll be out and around in a couple of days," he said. "But it was lucky I got called in so promptly. Otherwise —it might have been a near thing."

Susan stared. "Was she really so bad?"

"Mrs Banks, will you tell me again exactly what Miss Gilchrist had to eat and drink yesterday. Everything."

Susan reflected and gave a meticulous account. The doctor shook his head in a dissatisfied manner.

"There must have been something she had and you didn't?"

"I don't think so . . . Cakes, scones, jam, tea—and then supper. No, I can't remember anything."

The doctor rubbed his nose. He walked up and down the room.

"Was it definitely something she ate? Definitely food poisoning?"

The doctor threw her a sharp glance. Then he seemed to come to a decision.

"It was arsenic," he said.

"Arsenic?" Susan stared. "You mean somebody gave her arsenic?"

"That's what it looks like."

"Could she have taken it herself? Deliberately, I mean?"

"Suicide? She says not and she should know. Besides if she wanted to commit suicide she wouldn't be likely to choose arsenic. There are sleeping pills in this house. She could have taken an overdose of them."

"Could the arsenic have got into something by accident?"

"That's what I am wondering. It seems very unlikely, but such things have been known. But if you and she ate the same things—"

Susan nodded. She said, "It all seems impossible—" then she gave a sudden gasp. "Why, of course, the wedding cake!"

"What's that? Wedding cake?"

Susan explained. The doctor listened with close attention.

"Odd. And you say she wasn't sure who sent it? Any of it left? Or is the box it came in lying around?"

"I don't know. I'll look."

They searched together and finally found the white cardboard box with a few crumbs of cake still in it lying on the kitchen dresser. The doctor packed it away with some care.

"I'll take charge of this. Any idea where the wrapping paper it came in might be?"

Here they were not successful and Susan said that it had probably gone into the Ideal boiler.

"You won't be leaving here just yet, Mrs Banks?"

His tone was genial, but it made Susan feel a little uncomfortable.

"No, I have to go through my aunt's things. I shall be here for a few days."

"Good. You understand the police will probably want to ask some questions. You don't know of anyone who—well, might have had it in for Miss Gilchrist?"

Susan shook her head.

"I don't really know much about her. She was with my aunt for some years—that's all I know."

"Quite, quite. Always seemed a pleasant unassuming woman—quite ordinary. Not the kind, you'd say, to have enemies or anything melodramatic of that kind. Wedding cake through the post. Sounds like some jealous woman —but who'd be jealous of Miss Gilchrist? Doesn't seem to fit."

"No."

"Well, I must be on my way. I don't know what's happening to us in quiet little Lytchett St. Mary. First a brutal murder and now attempted poisoning through the post. Odd, the one following the other."

He went down the path to his car. The cottage felt stuffy and Susan left the door standing open as she went slowly upstairs to resume her task.

Cora Lansquenet had not been a tidy or methodical woman. Her drawers held a miscellaneous assortment of things. There were toilet accessories and letters and old handkerchiefs and paint brushes mixed up together in one drawer. There were a few old letters and bills thrust in amongst a bulging drawer of underclothes. In another drawer under some woollen jumpers was a cardboard box holding two false fringes. There was another drawer full of old photographs and sketching books. Susan lingered over a group taken evidently at some French place many years ago and which showed a younger thinner Cora clinging to the arm of a tall lanky man with a straggling beard dressed in what seemed to be a velveteen coat and whom Susan took to be the late Pierre Lansquenet.

The photographs interested Susan, but she laid them aside, sorted all the papers she had found into a heap and began to go through them methodically. About a quarter way through she came on a letter. She read it through twice and was still staring at it when a voice speaking behind her caused her to give a cry of alarm.

"And what may you have got hold of there, Susan? Hullo, what's the matter?"

Susan reddened with annoyance. Her cry of alarm had been quite involuntary and she felt ashamed and anxious to explain.

"George! How you startled me!"

Her cousin smiled lazily.

"So it seems."

"How did you get here?"

"Well, the door downstairs was open, so I walked in. There seemed to be nobody about on the ground floor, so I came up here. If you mean how did I get to this part of the world, I started down this morning to come to the funeral."

"I didn't see you there?"

"The old bus played me up. The petrol feed seemed choked. I tinkered with it for some time and finally it seemed to clear itself. I was too late for the funeral by then, but I thought I might as well come on down. I knew you were here."

He paused and then went on:

"I rang you up, as a matter of fact—and Greg told me you'd come down to take possession, as it were. I thought I might give you a hand."

Susan said, "Aren't you needed in the office? Or can you take days off whenever you like?"

"A funeral has always been a recognised excuse for absenteeism. And this funeral is indubitably genuine. Besides a murder always fascinates people. Anyway, I shan't be going much to the office in future—not now that I'm a man of means. I shall have better things to do."

He paused and grinned. "Same as Greg," he said.

Susan looked at George thoughtfully. She had never seen much of this cousin of hers and when they did meet she had always found him rather difficult to make out.

She asked, "Why did you really come down here, George?"

"I'm not sure it wasn't to do a little detective work. I've been thinking a good deal about the last funeral we attended. Aunt Cora certainly threw a spanner into the works that day. I've wondered whether it was sheer irresponsibility and aunty *joie de vivre* that prompted her words, or whether she really had something to go upon. What actually is in that letter that you were reading so attentively when I came in?"

Susan said slowly, "It's a letter that Uncle Richard wrote to Cora after he'd been down to see her."

How very black George's eyes were. She'd thought of them as brown but they were black, and there was something curiously impenetrable about black eyes. They concealed the thoughts that lay behind them.

George drawled slowly, "Anything interesting in it?"

"No, not exactly . . ."

"Can I see?"

She hesitated for a moment, then put the letter into his outstretched hand.

He read it, skimming over the contents in a low monotone.

*"Glad to have seen you again after all these years . . . looking very well . . . had a good journey home and arrived back not too tired. . . ."*

His voice changed suddenly, sharpened:

*"Please don't say anything to anyone about what I told you. It may be a mistake. Your loving brother, Richard."*

He looked up at Susan. "What does that mean?"

"It might mean anything. . . . It might be just about his health. Or it might be some gossip about a mutual friend."

"Oh yes, it might be a lot of things. It isn't conclusive

—but it's suggestive. . . . What did he tell Cora? Does anyone know what he told her?"

"Miss Gilchrist might know," said Susan thoughtfully. "I think she listened."

"Oh yes, the companion help. Where is she, by the way?"

"In hospital, suffering from arsenic poisoning."

George stared.

"You don't mean it?"

"I do. Someone sent her some poisoned wedding cake."

George sat down on one of the bedroom chairs and whistled.

"It looks," he said, "as though Uncle Richard was not mistaken."

### iii

On the following morning Inspector Morton called at the cottage.

He was a quiet middle-aged man with a soft country burr in his voice. His manner was quiet and unhurried, but his eyes were shrewd.

"You realise what this is about, Mrs Banks?" he said. "Dr Proctor has already told you about Miss Gilchrist. The few crumbs of wedding cake that he took from here have been analysed and show traces of arsenic."

"So somebody deliberately wanted to poison her?"

"That's what it looks like. Miss Gilchrist herself doesn't seem able to help us. She keeps repeating that it's impossible—that nobody would do such a thing. But somebody did. *You* can't throw any light on the matter?"

Susan shook her head.

"I'm simply dumbfounded," she said. "Can't you find out anything from the postmark? Or the handwriting?"

"You've forgotten—the wrapping paper was presumably burnt. And there's a little doubt whether it came through the post at all. Young Andrews, the driver of the postal van, doesn't seem able to remember delivering it. He's got a big round, and he can't be sure—but there it is —there's a doubt about it."

"But—what's the alternative?"

"The alternative, Mrs Banks, is that an old piece of

brown paper was used that already had Miss Gilchrist's name and address on it and a cancelled stamp, and that the package was pushed through the letter box or deposited inside the door by hand to create the impression that it had come by post."

He added dispassionately:

"It's quite a clever idea, you know, to choose wedding cake. Lonely middle-aged women are sentimental about wedding cake, pleased at having been remembered. A box of sweets, or something of that kind *might* have awakened suspicion."

Susan said slowly:

"Miss Gilchrist speculated a good deal about who could have sent it, but she wasn't at all suspicious—as you say, she was pleased and yes—flattered."

She added: "Was there enough poison in it to—kill?"

"That's difficult to say until we get the quantitative analysis. It rather depends on whether Miss Gilchrist ate the whole of the wedge. She seems to think that she didn't. Can you remember?"

"No—no, I'm not sure. She offered me some and I refused and then she ate some and said it was a very good cake, but I don't remember if she finished it or not."

"I'd like to go upstairs if you don't mind, Mrs Banks."

"Of course."

She followed him up to Miss Gilchrist's room. She said apologetically:

"I'm afraid it's in a rather disgusting state. But I didn't have time to do anything about it with my aunt's funeral and everything, and then after Dr Proctor came I thought perhaps I ought to leave it as it was."

"That was very intelligent of you, Mrs Banks. It's not everyone who would have been so intelligent."

He went to the bed and slipping his hand under the pillow raised it carefully. A slow smile spread over his face.

"There you are," he said.

A piece of wedding cake lay on the sheet looking somewhat the worse for wear.

"How extraordinary," said Susan.

"Oh no, it's not. Perhaps your generation doesn't do it. Young ladies nowadays mayn't set so much store on getting married. But it's an old custom. Put a piece of wedding cake under your pillow and you'll dream of your future husband."

"But surely Miss Gilchrist——"

"She didn't want to tell us about it because she felt foolish doing such a thing at her age. But I had a notion that's what it might be." His face sobered. "And if it hadn't been for an old maid's foolishness, Miss Gilchrist mightn't be alive today."

"But who could have possibly wanted to kill her?"

His eyes met hers, a curious speculative look in them that made Susan feel uncomfortable.

"You don't know?" he asked.

"No—of course I don't."

"It seems then as though we shall have to find out," said Inspector Morton.

## 12

TWO ELDERLY men sat together in a room whose furnishings were of the most modern kind. There were no curves in the room. Everything was square. Almost the only exception was Hercule Poirot himself who was full of curves. His stomach was pleasantly rounded, his head resembled an egg in shape, and his moustaches curved upwards in a flamboyant flourish.

He was sipping a glass of *sirop* and looking thoughtfully at Mr Goby.

Mr Goby was small and spare and shrunken. He had always been refreshingly nondescript in appearance and he was now so nondescript as practically not to be there at all. He was not looking at Poirot because Mr Goby never looked at anybody.

Such remarks as he was now making seemed to be addressed to the left hand corner of the chromium plated fireplace curb.

Mr Goby was famous for the acquiring of information. Very few people knew about him and very few employed his services—but those few were usually extremely rich. They had to be, for Mr Goby was very expensive. His specialty was the acquiring of information quickly. At the flick of Mr Goby's double jointed thumb, hundreds of patient questioning plodding men and women, old and young, of all apparent stations in life, were despatched to question, and probe, and achieve results.

Mr Goby had now practically retired from business. But he occasionally "obliged" a few old patrons. Hercule Poirot was one of these.

"I've got what I could for you," he told the fire curb in a soft confidential whisper. "I sent the boys out. They do what they can—good lads—good lads all of them, but not what they used to be in the old days. They don't come that way nowadays. Not willing to learn, that's what it is. Think they know everything after they've only been a couple of years on the job. And they work to time. Shocking the way they work to time."

He shook his head sadly and shifted his gaze to an electric plug socket.

"It's the Government," he told it. "And all this education racket. It gives them ideas. They come back and tell us what they think. They *can't* think, most of them, anyway. All they know is things out of books. That's no good in our business. Bring in the answers—that's all that's needed—no thinking."

Mr Goby flung himself back in his chair and winked at a lampshade.

"Mustn't crab the Government, though! Don't know really what we'd do without it. I can tell you that nowadays you can walk in most anywhere with a notebook and pencil, dressed right, and speaking B.B.C., and ask people all the most intimate details of their daily lives and all their back history, and what they had for dinner on November 23rd because that was a test day for middle class incomes—or whatever it happens to be, (making it a grade above to butter them up!)—ask 'em any mortal thing you can; and nine times out of ten they'll come up rough, they won't doubt for a minute that you're what you say you are—and that the Government really wants to know—for some completely unfathomable reason! I can tell you, M. Poirot," said Mr Goby still talking to the lampshade, "that it's the best line we've ever had; much better than taking the electric meter or tracing a fault in the telephone—yes, or than calling as nuns, or the Girl Guides or the Boy Scouts asking for subscriptions—though we use all those too. Yes, Government snooping is God's gift to investigators and long may it continue!"

Poirot did not speak. Mr Goby had grown a little garrulous with advancing years, but he would come to the point in his own good time.

"Ar," said Mr Goby and took out a very scrubby little notebook. He licked his finger and flicked over the pages. "Here we are. Mr George Crossfield. We'll take him first. Just the plain facts. You won't want to know how I got them. He's been in Queer Street for quite a while now. Horses, mostly, and gambling—he's not a great one for women. Goes over to France now and then, and Monte too. Spends a lot of time at the Casino. Too downy to cash cheques there, but gets hold of a lot more money than his travelling allowance would account for. I didn't go into that, because it wasn't what you want to know. But he's not scrupulous about evading the law—and being a lawyer he knows how to do it. Some reason to believe that he's been using trust funds entrusted to him to invest. Plunging pretty wildly of late—on the Stock Exchange *and* on the gee-gees. Bad judgment and bad luck. Been off his feed badly for three months. Worried, bad tempered and irritable in the office. *But* since his uncle's death that's all changed. He's like the breakfast eggs (if we had 'em). Sunny side up!

"Now, as to particular information asked for. Statement that he was at Hurst Park races on day in question almost certainly untrue. Almost invariably places bets with one or other of two bookies on the course. They didn't see him that day. Possible that he left Paddington by train for destination unknown. Taxi driver who took fare to Paddington made doubtful identification of his photograph. But I wouldn't bank on it. He's a very common type—nothing outstanding about him. No success with porters etc., at Paddington. Certainly didn't arrive at Cholsey Station—which is nearest for Lytchett St. Mary. Small station, strangers noticeable. Could have gotten out at Reading and taken bus. Buses there crowded, frequent and several routes go within a mile or so of Lytchett St. Mary as well as the bus service that goes right into the village. He wouldn't take that—not if he meant business. All in all, he's a downy card. Wasn't seen in Lytchett St. Mary but he needn't have been. Other ways of approach than through the village. Was in the OUDS at Oxford, by the way. If he went to the cottage that day he mayn't have looked quite like the usual George Crossfield. I'll keep him in my book, shall I? There's a black market angle I'd like to play up."

"You may keep him in," said Hercule Poirot.

Mr Goby licked his finger and turned another page of his notebook.

"Mr Michael Shane. He's thought quite a lot of in the profession. Has an even better idea of himself than other people have. Wants to star and wants to star quickly. Fond of money and doing himself well. Very attractive to women. They fall for him right and left. He's partial to them himself—but business comes first, as you might say. He's been running around with Sorrel Dainton who was playing the lead in the last show he was in. He only had a minor part but made quite a hit in it, and Miss Dainton's husband doesn't like him. His wife doesn't know about him and Miss Dainton. Doesn't know much about anything, it seems. Not much of an actress, I gather, but easy on the eye. Crazy about her husband. Some rumour of a bust up likely between them not long ago, but that seems out now. Out since Mr Richard Abernethie's death."

Mr Goby emphasized the last point by nodding his head significantly at a cushion on the sofa.

"On the day in question, Mr Shane says he was meeting a Mr Rosenheim and a Mr Oscar Lewis to fix up some stage business. He didn't meet them. Sent them a wire to say he was terribly sorry he couldn't make it. What he *did* do was to go to the Emeraldo Car people, who hire out drive yourself cars. He hired a car about twelve o'clock and drove away in it. He returned it about six in the evening. According to the speedometer it had been driven just about the right number of miles for what we're after. No confirmation from Lytchett St. Mary. No strange car seems to have been observed there that day. Lots of places it could be left unnoticed a mile or so away. And there's even a disused quarry a few hundred yards down the lane from the cottage. Three market towns within walking distance where you can park in side streets, without the police bothering about you. All right, we keep Mr Shane in?"

"Most certainly."

"Now Mrs Shane." Mr Goby rubbed his nose and told his left cuff about Mrs Shane. "She says she was shopping. Just shopping . . ." Mr Goby raised his eyes to the ceiling. "Women who are shopping—just scatty, that's what they are. And she'd heard she'd come into money the day before. Naturally there'd be no holding her. She has one or two charge accounts but they're overdrawn and they've been pressing her for payment and she didn't put any more on the sheet. It's quite on the cards that she went in here and there and everywhere, trying on clothes, looking at jewellery, pricing this, that, and the other—and as likely as not, not buying anything! She's easy to approach—I'll say that. I had one of my young ladies who's knowledgeable on the theatrical line do a hook up. Stopped by her table in a restaurant and exclaimed the way they do: "Darling, I haven't seen you since 'Way Down Under.' You were *wonderful* in that! Have you seen Hubert lately?" That was the producer and Mrs Shane was a bit of a flop in the play—but that makes it go all the better. They're chatting theatrical stuff at once, and my girl throws the right names about, and then she says, 'I believe I caught a glimpse of you at so and so, on so and so,' giving the day—and most ladies fall for it and say, 'Oh no, I was—' whatever it may be. But not Mrs Shane. Just looks vacant and says, 'Oh, I daresay.' What can you do with a lady like that?" Mr Goby shook his head severely at the radiator.

"Nothing," said Hercule Poirot with feeling. "Do I not have cause to know it? Never shall I forget the killing of Lord Edgware. I was nearly defeated—yes, I, Hercule Poirot—by the extremely simple cunning of a vacant brain. The very simple minded have often the genius to commit an uncomplicated crime and then leave it alone. Let us hope that our murderer—if there is a murderer in this affair—is intelligent and superior and thoroughly pleased with himself and unable to resist painting the lily. *Enfin*—but continue."

Once more Mr Goby applied himself to his little book.

"Mr and Mrs Banks—who said they were at home all day. *She* wasn't, anyway! Went around to the garage, got out her car, and drove off in it about 1 o'clock. Destination unknown. Back about five. Can't tell about mileage because she's had it out every day since and it's been nobody's business to check.

"As to Mr Banks, we've dug up something curious. To begin with, I'll mention that on the day in question we don't know *what* he did. He didn't go to work. Seems he'd already asked for a couple of days off on account of the funeral. And since then he's chucked his job—with no consideration for the firm. Nice, well established pharmacy, it is. They're not too keen on Master Banks. Seems he used to get into rather queer excitable states.

"Well, as I say, we don't know what he was doing on the day of Mrs L's death. He didn't go with his wife. It *could* be that he stopped in their little flat all day. There's no porter there, and nobody knows whether tenants are in or out. But his back history is interesting. Up till about four months ago—just before he met his wife, he was in a Mental Home. Not certified—just what they call a mental breakdown. Seems he made some slip up in dispensing a medicine. (He was working with a Mayfair firm then.) The woman recovered, and the firm were all over themselves apologising, and there was no prosecution. After all, these accidental slips do occur, and most decent people are sorry for a poor young chap who's done it—so long as there's no permanent harm done, that is. The firm didn't sack him, but he resigned—said it had shaken his nerve. But afterwards, it seems, he got into a very low state and told the doctor he was obsessed by guilt—that it had all been deliberate—the woman had been overbearing and rude to him when she came into the shop, had complained that her last prescription had been badly made up—and that he had resented this and had deliberately added a near lethal dose of some drug or other. He said 'She had to be punished for daring to speak to me like that!' And then wept and said he was too wicked to live and a lot of things like that. The medicos have a long

word for that sort of thing—guilt complex or something
—and don't believe it was deliberate at all, just careless-
ness, but that he wanted to make it important and
serious."

"*Ça se peut,*" said Hercule Poirot.

"Pardon? Anyway, he went into this Sanitarium and
they treated him and discharged him as cured, and he met
Miss Abernethie as she was then. And he got a job in this
respectable but rather obscure little chemist's shop. Told
them he'd been out of England for a year and a half, and
gave them his former reference from some shop in East-
bourne. Nothing against him in that shop, but a fellow
dispenser said he had a very queer temper and was odd in
his manner sometimes. There's a story about a customer
saying once as a joke, 'Wish you'd sell me something to
poison my wife, ha ha!' And Banks says to him, very soft
and quiet: 'I could . . . It would cost you two hundred
pounds.' The man felt uneasy and laughed it off. *May*
have been all a joke, but it doesn't seem to me that Banks
is the joking kind."

"*Mon ami,*" said Hercule Poirot. "It really amazes me
how you get your information! Medical and highly
confidential most of it!"

Mr Goby's eyes swivelled right round the room and he
murmured, looking expectantly at the door, that there
were *ways.* . . .

"Now we come to the country department. Mr and Mrs
Timothy Abernethie. Very nice place they've got, but
sadly needing money spent on it. Very straitened they
seem to be, very straitened. Taxation and unfortunate investments. Mr Abernethie enjoys ill health and the emphasis is on the enjoyment. Complains a lot and has
everyone running and fetching and carrying. Eats hearty
meals, and seems quite strong physically if he likes to
make the effort. There's no one in the house after the
daily woman goes and no one's allowed into Mr Abernethie's room unless he rings his bell. He was in a very
bad temper the morning of the day after the funeral.
Swore at Mrs Jones. Ate only a little of his breakfast and
said he wouldn't have any lunch—he'd had a bad night.
He was in a worse temper still the next day and said the
supper she had left out for him was unfit to eat and a

good deal more. He was alone in the house and unseen by anybody from 9.30 that morning until the following morning."

"And Mrs Abernethie?"

"She started off from Enderby by car at the time you mentioned. Arrived on foot at a small local garage in a place called Cathstone and explained her car had broken down a couple of miles away.

"A mechanic drove her out to it, made an investigation and said they'd have to tow it in and it would be a long job—couldn't promise to finish it that day. The lady was very put out, but went to a small Inn, arranged to stay the night, and asked for some sandwiches as she said she'd like to see something of the countryside—it's on the edge of the moorland country. She didn't come back to the Inn till quite late that evening. My informant said he didn't wonder. It's a sordid little place!"

"And the times?"

"She got the sandwiches at eleven. If she'd walked to the main road, a mile, she could have hitch-hiked into Wallcaster and caught a special South Coast express which stops at Reading West. I won't go into details of buses etcetera. It *could* just have been done if you could make the—er—attack fairly late in the afternoon."

"I understand the doctor stretched the time limit to possibly 4.30."

"Mind you," said Mr Goby, "I shouldn't say it was likely. She seems to be a nice lady, liked by everybody. She's devoted to her husband, treats him like a child."

"Yes, yes, the maternal complex."

"She's strong and hefty, chops the wood and often hauls in great baskets of logs. Pretty good with the inside of a car, too."

"I was coming to that. What exactly *was* wrong with the car?"

"Do you want the exact details, M. Poirot?"

"Heaven forbid. I have no mechanical knowledge."

"It was a difficult thing to spot. And also to put right. And it *could* have been done maliciously by someone without very much trouble. By someone who was familiar with the insides of a car."

"*C'est magnifique!*" said Poirot with bitter enthusiasm.

"All so convenient, all so possible. *Bon dieu,* can we eliminate *nobody?* And Mrs Leo Abernethie?"

"She's a very nice lady, too. Mr Abernethie deceased was very fond of her. She came there to stay about a fortnight before he died."

"After he had been to Lytchett St. Mary to see his sister?"

"No, just before. Her income is a good deal reduced since the war. She gave up her house in England and took a small flat in London. She has a villa in Cyprus and spends part of the year there. She has a young nephew whom she is helping to educate, and there seems to be one or two young artists whom she helps financially from time to time."

"St. Helen of the blameless life," said Poirot shutting his eyes. "And it was quite impossible for her to have left Enderby that day without the servants knowing? Say that that is so, I implore you!"

Mr Goby brought his glance across to rest apologetically on Poirot's polished patent leather shoe, the nearest he had come to a direct encounter, and murmured:

"I'm afraid I can't say that, M. Poirot. Mrs Abernethie went to London to fetch some extra clothes and belongings as she had agreed with Mr Entwhistle to stay on and see to things."

"*Il ne manquait que ça!*" said Poirot with strong feeling.

# 13

WHEN THE card of Inspector Morton of the Berkshire County Police was brought to Hercule Poirot, his eyebrows went up.

"Show him in, Georges, show him in. And bring—what is it that the police prefer?"

"I would suggest beer, sir."

"How horrible! But how British. Bring beer, then."

Inspector Morton came straight to the point.

"I had to come to London," he said. "And I got hold of your address, M. Poirot. I was interested to see you at the inquest on Thursday."

"So you saw me there?"

"Yes. I was surprised—and, as I say, interested. You won't remember me but I remember you very well. In that Pangbourne Case."

"Ah, you were connected with that?"

"Only in a very junior capacity. It's a long time ago but I've never forgotten you."

"And you recognised me at once the other day?"

"That wasn't difficult, sir." Inspector Morton repressed a slight smile. "Your appearance is—rather unusual."

His gaze took in Poirot's sartorial perfection and rested finally on the curving moustaches.

"You stick out in a country place," he said.

"It is possible, it is possible," said Poirot with complacency.

"It interested me *why* you should be there. That sort of crime—robbery—assault—doesn't usually interest you."

"Was it the usual ordinary brutal type of crime?"

"That's what I've been wondering."

"You have wondered from the beginning, have you not?"

"Yes, M. Poirot. There were some unusual features. Since then we've worked along the routine lines. Pulled in one or two people for questioning, but everyone has been able to account quite satisfactorily for his time that afternoon. It wasn't what you'd call an 'ordinary' crime, M. Poirot—we're quite sure of that. The Chief Constable agrees. It was done by someone who wished to make it appear that way. It could have been the Gilchrist woman, but there doesn't seem to be any motive—and there wasn't any emotional background. Mrs Lansquenet was perhaps a bit mental—or 'simple,' if you like to put it that way, but it was a household of mistress and dogsbody with no feverish feminine friendship about it. There are dozens of Miss Gilchrists about, and they're not usually the murdering type."

He paused.

"So it looks as though we'd have to look farther afield.

I came to ask if you could help us at all. *Something* must have brought you down there, M. Poirot."

"Yes, yes, something did. An excellent Daimler car. But not only that."

"You had—information?"

"Hardly in your sense of the word. Nothing that could be used as evidence."

"But something that could be—a pointer?"

"Yes."

"You see, M. Poirot, there have been developments."

Meticulously, in detail, he told of the poisoned wedge of wedding cake.

Poirot took a deep hissing breath.

"Ingenious—yes, ingenious . . . I warned Mr Entwhistle to look after Miss Gilchrist. An attack on her was always a possibility. But I must confess that I did *not* expect poison. I anticipated a repetition of the hatchet *motif*. I merely thought that it would be inadvisable for her to walk alone in unfrequented lanes after dark."

"But *why* did you anticipate an attack on her? I think, M. Poirot, you ought to tell me that."

Poirot nodded his head slowly.

"Yes, I will tell you. Mr Entwhistle will not tell you, because he is a lawyer and lawyers do not like to speak of suppositions, or inferences made from the character of a dead woman, or from a few irresponsible words. But he will not be adverse to *my* telling you—no, he will be relieved. He does not wish to appear foolish or fanciful, but he wants you to know what may—only *may*—be the facts."

Poirot paused as Georges entered with a tall glass of beer.

"Some refreshment, Inspector. No, no, I insist."

"Won't you join me?"

"I do not drink the beer. But I will myself have a glass of *sirop de cassis*—the English they do not care for it, I have noticed."

Inspector Morton looked gratefully at his beer.

Poirot, sipping delicately from his glass of dark purple fluid, said:

"It begins, all this, at a funeral. Or rather, to be exact, *after* the funeral."

Graphically, with many gestures, he set forth the story as Mr Entwhistle had told it to him, but with such embellishments as his exuberant nature suggested. One almost felt that Hercule Poirot had himself been an eye-witness of the scene.

Inspector Morton had an excellent clear cut brain. He seized at once on what were, for his purposes, the salient points.

"This Mr Abernethie may have been poisoned?"

"It is a possibility."

"And the body has been cremated and there is no evidence?"

"Exactly."

Inspector Morton ruminated.

"Interesting. There's nothing in it for *us*. Nothing, that is, to make Richard Abernethie's death worth investigating. It would be waste of time."

"Yes."

"But there are the *people*—the people who were there—the people who heard Cora Lansquenet say what she did, and one of whom *may* have thought that she might say it again and with more detail."

"As she undoubtedly would have. There are, Inspector, as you say, *the people*. And now you see why I was at the inquest, why I interest myself in the case—because it is, always, *people* in whom I interest myself."

"Then the attack on Miss Gilchrist—"

"Was always indicated. Richard Abernethie had been down to the cottage. He had talked to Cora. He had, perhaps, actually mentioned a *name*. The only person who might possibly have known or overheard something was Miss Gilchrist. After Cora is silenced, the murderer might continue to be anxious. Does the other woman know something—anything? Of course, if the murderer is wise he will let well alone, but murderers, Inspector, are seldom wise. Fortunately for us. They brood, they feel uncertain, they desire to make sure—quite sure. They are pleased with their own cleverness. And so, in the end, they protrude their necks as you say."

Inspector Morton smiled faintly.

Poirot went on:

"This attempt to silence Miss Gilchrist, already it is a

mistake. For now there are *two* occasions about which you make enquiry. There is the handwriting on the wedding label also. It is a pity the wrapping paper was burnt."

"Yes, I could have been certain, then, whether it came by post or whether it didn't."

"You have reason for thinking the latter, you say?"

"It's only what the postman thinks—he's not sure. If the parcel had gone through a village post office, it's ten to one the postmistress would have noticed it, but nowadays the mail is delivered by van from Market Keynes and of course the young chap does quite a round and delivers a lot of things. He thinks it was letters only and no parcel at the cottage—but he isn't sure. As a matter of fact he's having a bit of girl trouble and he can't think about anything else. I've tested his memory and he isn't reliable in any way. If he *did* deliver it, it seems to me odd that the parcel shouldn't have been noticed until after this Mr—whatshisname—Guthrie—"

"Ah, Mr Guthrie."

Inspector Morton smiled.

"Yes, M. Poirot. We're checking up on him. After all, it would be easy, wouldn't it, to come along with a plausible tale of having been a friend of Mrs Lansquenet's. Mrs Banks wasn't to know if he was or he wasn't. He could have dropped that little parcel, you know. It's easy to make a thing look as though it's been through the post. Lamp black a little smudged, makes quite a good postmark cancellation mark over a stamp."

He paused and then added:

"And there are other possibilities."

Poirot nodded.

"You think—?"

"Mr George Crossfield was down in that part of the world—but not until the next day. Meant to attend the funeral, but had a little engine trouble on the way. Know anything about him, M. Poirot?"

"A little. But not as much as I would like to know."

"Like that, is it? Quite a little bunch interested in the late Mr Abernethie's will, I understand. I hope it doesn't mean going after all of them."

"I have accumulated a little information. It is at your disposal. Naturally *I* have no authority to ask these people questions. In fact it would not be wise for me to do so."

"I shall go slowly myself. You don't want to fluster your bird too soon. But when you do fluster it, you want to fluster it well."

"A very sound technique. For you then, my friend, the routine—with all the machinery you have at your disposal. It is slow—but sure. For myself—"

"Yes, M. Poirot?"

"For myself, I go North. As I have told you, it is *people* in whom I interest myself. Yes—a little preparatory *camouflage*—and I go North.

"I intend," added Hercule Poirot, "to purchase a country mansion for foreign refugees. I represent U.N.A.R.C.O."

"And what's U.N.A.R.C.O.?"

"United Nations Aid for Refugee Centres Old Age. It sounds well, do you not think?"

Inspector Morton grinned.

# 14

HERCULE POIROT said to a grim-faced Janet:

"Thank you very much. You have been most kind."

Janet, her lips still fixed in a sour line, left the room. These foreigners! The questions they asked. Their impertinence! All very well to say that he was a specialist interested in unsuspected heart conditions such as Mr Abernethie must have suffered from. That was very likely true —gone very sudden the master had, and the doctor had been surprised. But what business was it of some foreign doctor coming along and nosing in?

All very well for Mrs Leo to say: "Please answer Monsieur Pontarlier's questions. He has a good reason for asking."

Questions. Always questions. Sheets of them sometimes to fill in as best you could—and what did the Government or anyone else want to know about your private affairs

for? Asking your age at that census—downright imperti-
nent and she hadn't told them, either! Cut off five years
she had. Why not? If she only felt fifty-four, she'd *call*
herself fifty-four!

At any rate Monsieur Pontarlier hadn't wanted to
know her age. He'd had *some* decency. Just questions
about the medicines the master had taken, and where they
were kept, and if, perhaps, he might have taken too much
of them if he was feeling not quite the thing—or if he'd
been forgetful. As though she could remember all that
rubbish—the master knew what he was doing! And asking if any of the medicines he took were still in the house.
Naturally they'd all been thrown away. Heart condition—
and some long word he'd used. Always thinking of something new they were, these doctors. Look at them telling
old Rogers he had a disc or some such in his spine. Plain
lumbago, that was all that was the matter with him. Her
father had been a gardener and *he*'d suffered from lumbago. Doctors!

The self-appointed medical man sighed and went
downstairs in search of Lanscombe. He had not got very
much out of Janet but he had hardly expected to do so.
All he had really wanted to do was to check such information as could unwillingly be extracted from her with
that given him by Helen Abernethie and which had been
obtained from the same source—but with much less difficulty, since Janet was ready to admit that Mrs Leo had a
perfect right to ask such questions and indeed Janet herself had enjoyed dwelling at length on the last few weeks
of her master's life. Illness and death were congenial subjects to her.

Yes, Poirot thought, he could have relied on the information that Helen had got for him. He had done so really. But by nature and long habit he trusted nobody until
he himself had tried and proved them.

In any case the evidence was slight and unsatisfactory.
It boiled down to the fact that Richard Abernethie had
been prescribed vitamin oil capsules. That these had been
in a large bottle which had been nearly finished at the time
of his death. Anybody who had wanted to, could have
operated on one or more of those capsules with a hypo-
dermic syringe and could have rearranged the bottle so

that the fatal dose would only be taken some weeks after that somebody had left the house. Or someone might have slipped into the house on the day before Richard Abernethie died and have doctored a capsule then—or, which was more likely—have substituted something else for a sleeping tablet in the little bottle that stood beside the bed. Or again might have quite simply tampered with the food or drink.

Hercule Poirot had made his own experiments. The front door was kept locked, but there was a side door giving on the garden which was not locked until evening. At about quarter past one, when the gardeners had gone to lunch and when the household was in the dining room Poirot had entered the grounds, come to the side door, and mounted the stairs to Richard Abernethie's bedroom without meeting anybody. As a variant he had pushed through a baize door and slipped into the larder. He had heard voices from the kitchen at the end of the passage but no one had seen him.

Yes, it could have been done. But had it been done? There was nothing to indicate that that was so. Not that Poirot was really looking for evidence—he wanted only to satisfy himself as to possibilities. The murder of Richard Abernethie could only be a hypothesis. It was Cora Lansquenet's murder for which evidence was needed. What he wanted was to study the people who had been assembled for the funeral that day, and to form his own conclusions about them. He already had his plan, but first he wanted a few more words with old Lanscombe.

Lanscombe was courteous but distant. Less resentful than Janet, he nevertheless regarded this upstart foreigner as the materialization of the Writing on the Wall. This was What We are Coming to!

He put down the leather with which he was lovingly polishing the Georgian teapot and straightened his back.

"Yes, sir?" he said politely.

Poirot sat down gingerly on a pantry stool.

"Mrs Abernethie tells me that you hoped to reside in the lodge by the North gate when you retired from service here?"

"That is so, sir. Naturally all that is changed now. When the property is sold—"

Poirot interrupted deftly:

"It might still be possible. There are cottages for the gardeners. The lodge is not needed for the guests or their attendants. It might be possible to make an arrangement of some kind."

"Well, thank you, sir, for the suggestion. But I hardly think— The majority of the—guests would be foreigners, I presume?"

"Yes, they will be foreigners. Amongst those who fled from Europe to this country are several who are old and infirm. There can be no future for them if they return to their own countries, for these persons, you understand, are those whose relatives there have perished. They cannot earn their living here as an able-bodied man or woman can do. Funds have been raised and are being administered by the organisation which I represent to endow various country homes for them. This place is, I think, eminently suitable. The matter is practically settled."

Lanscombe sighed.

"You'll understand, sir, that it's sad for me to think that this won't be a private dwelling house any longer. But I know how things are nowadays. None of the family could afford to live here—and I don't think the young ladies and gentlemen would even want to do so. Domestic help is too difficult to obtain these days, and even if obtained is expensive and unsatisfactory. I quite realise that these fine mansions have served their turn." Lanscombe sighed again. "If it has to be an—an institution of some kind, I'll be glad to think that it's the kind you're mentioning. We were spared in this country, sir, owing to our Navy and Air Force and our brave young men and being fortunate enough to be an island. If Hitler had landed here we'd all have turned out and given him short shrift. My sight isn't good enough for shooting, but I could have used a pitchfork, sir, and I intended to do so if necessary. We've always welcomed the unfortunate in this country, sir, it's been our pride. We shall continue so to do."

"Thank you, Lanscombe," said Poirot gently. "Your master's death must have been a great blow to you."

"It was, sir. I'd been with the master since he was quite a young man. I've been very fortunate in my life, sir. No one could have had a better master."

"I have been conversing with my friend and—er—colleague, Dr Larraby. We were wondering if your master could have had any extra worry—any unpleasant interview—on the day before he died? You do not remember if any visitors came to the house that day?"

"I think not, sir. I do not recall any."

"No one called at all just about that time?"

"The vicar was here to tea the day before. Otherwise—some nuns called for a subscription—and a young man came to the back door and wanted to sell Marjorie some brushes and saucepan cleaners. Very persistent he was. Nobody else."

A worried expression had appeared on Lanscombe's face. Poirot did not press him further. Lanscombe had already unburdened himself to Mr Entwhistle. He would be far less forthcoming with Hercule Poirot.

With Marjorie, on the other hand, Poirot had had instant success. Marjorie had none of the conventions of "good service." Marjorie was a first class cook and the way to her heart lay through her cooking. Poirot had visited her in the kitchen, praised certain dishes with discernment, and Marjorie, realising that here was someone who knew what he was talking about, hailed him immediately as a fellow spirit. He had no difficulty in finding out exactly what had been served the night before Richard Abernethie had died. Marjorie, indeed, was inclined to view the matter as "It was the night I made that chocolate soufflé that Mr Abernethie died. Six eggs I'd saved up for it. The dairyman he's a friend of mine. Got hold of some cream too. Better not ask how. Enjoyed it, Mr Abernethie did." The rest of the meal was likewise detailed. What had come out from the dining room had been finished in the kitchen. Ready as Marjorie was to talk, Poirot had learned nothing of value from her.

He went now to fetch his overcoat and a couple of scarves, and thus padded against the North Country air he went out on the terrace and joined Helen Abernethie who was clipping some late roses.

"Have you found out anything fresh?" she asked.

"Nothing. But I hardly expected to do so."

"I know. Ever since Mr Entwhistle told me you were

coming, I've been ferreting round, but there's really been nothing."

She paused and said hopefully:

"Perhaps it *is* all a mare's nest?"

"To be attacked with a hatchet?"

"I wasn't thinking of Cora."

"But it is of Cora that I think. Why was it necessary for someone to kill her? Mr Entwhistle has told me that on that_day, at the moment that she came out suddenly with her *gaffe,* you yourself felt that something was wrong. That is so?"

"Well—yes, but I don't know—"

Poirot swept on.

"How 'wrong'? Unexpected? Surprising? Or—what shall we say—uneasy? Sinister?"

"Oh no, not sinister. Just something that wasn't—oh, I don't know. I can't remember and it wasn't important."

"But why cannot you remember—because something else put it out of your head—something more important?"

"Yes—yes—I think you're right there. It was the mention of murder, I suppose. That swept away everything else."

"It was, perhaps, the reaction of some particular person to the word 'murder'?"

"Perhaps . . . But I don't remember looking at anyone in particular. We were all staring at Cora."

"It may have been something you heard—something dropped perhaps . . . or broken . . ."

Helen frowned in an effort of remembrance.

"No . . . I don't think so. . . ."

"Ah well, someday it will come back. And it may be of no consequence. Now tell me, Madame, of those here, who knew Cora best?"

Helen considered.

"Lanscombe, I suppose. He remembers her from a child. The housemaid, Janet, only came after she had married and gone away."

"And next to Lanscombe?"

Helen said thoughtfully: "I suppose—*I* did. Maude hardly knew her at all."

"Then, taking you as the person who knew her best, why do you think she asked that question as she did?"

Helen smiled.

"It was very characteristic of Cora!"

"What I mean is, was it a *bêtise* pure and simple? Did she just blurt out what was in her mind without thinking? Or was she being malicious—amusing herself by upsetting everyone?"

Helen reflected.

"One can't ever be quite sure about a person, can you? I never have known whether Cora was just ingenuous—or whether she counted, childishly, on making an effect. That's what you mean, isn't it?"

"Yes. I was thinking: Suppose this Mrs Cora says to herself, 'What fun it would be to ask if Richard was murdered and see how they all look!' That would be like her, yes?"

Helen looked doubtful.

"It might be. She certainly had an impish sense of humour as a child. But what difference does it make?"

"It would underline the point that it is unwise to make jokes about murder," said Poirot drily.

Helen shivered.

"Poor Cora."

Poirot changed the subject.

"Mrs Timothy Abernethie stayed the night after the funeral?"

"Yes."

"Did she talk to you at all about what Cora had said?"

"Yes, she said it was outrageous and just like Cora!"

"She didn't take it seriously?"

"Oh no. No, I'm sure she didn't. . . ."

The second "no," Poirot thought, had sounded suddenly doubtful. But was not that almost always the case when you went back over something in your mind?"

"And you, Madame, did you take it seriously?"

Helen Abernethie, her eyes looking very blue and strangely young under the sideways sweep of crisp grey hair, said thoughtfully:

"Yes, M. Poirot, I think I did."

"Because of your feeling that something was wrong?"

"Perhaps."

He waited—but as she said nothing more, he went on:

"There has been an estrangement, lasting many years, between Mrs Lansquenet and her family?"

"Yes. None of us liked her husband and she was offended about it, and so the estrangement grew."

"And then, suddenly, your brother-in-law went to see her. Why?"

"I don't know—I suppose he knew, or guessed, that he hadn't very long to live and wanted to be reconciled—but I really don't know."

"He didn't tell you?"

"Tell *me?*"

"Yes. You were here, staying with him, just before he went there. He didn't even mention his intention to you?"

He thought a slight reserve came into her manner.

"He told me that he was going to see his brother Timothy—which he did. He never mentioned Cora at all. Shall we go in? It must be nearly lunchtime."

She walked beside him carrying the flowers she had picked. As they went in by the side door, Poirot said:

"You are sure, quite sure, that during your visit, Mr Abernethie said nothing to you about any member of the family which might be relevant?"

A faint resentment in her manner, Helen said:

"You are speaking like a policeman."

"I *was* a policeman—once. I have no status—no right to question you. But you want the truth—or so I have been led to believe?"

They entered the green drawing room. Helen said with a sigh:

"Richard was disappointed in the younger generation. Old men usually are. He disparaged them in various ways —but there was nothing—*nothing,* do you understand— that could possibly suggest a motive for murder."

"Ah," said Poirot. She reached for a Chinese bowl and began to arrange the roses in it. When they were disposed to her satisfaction she looked round for a place to put it.

"You arrange flowers admirably, Madame," said Hercule. "I think that anything you undertook you would manage to do with perfection."

"Thank you. I am fond of flowers. I think this would look well on that green malachite table."

There was a bouquet of wax flowers under a glass shade on the malachite table. As she lifted it off, Poirot said casually:

"Did anyone tell Mr Abernethie that his niece Susan's husband had come near to poisoning a customer when making up a prescription? Ah, *pardon!*"

He sprang forward.

The Victorian ornament had slipped from Helen's fingers. Poirot's spring forward was not quick enough. It dropped on the floor and the glass shade broke. Helen gave an expression of annoyance.

"How careless of me. However, the flowers are not damaged. I can get a new glass shade made for it. I'll put it away in the big cupboard under the stairs."

It was not until Poirot had helped her to lift it onto a shelf in the dark cupboard and had followed her back to the drawing room that he said:

"It was my fault. I should not have startled you."

"What was it that you asked me? I have forgotten."

"Oh, there is no need to repeat my question. Indeed—I have forgotten what it was."

Helen came up to him. She laid her hand on his arm.

"M. Poirot, is there anyone whose life would really bear close investigation? *Must* people's lives be dragged into this when they have nothing to do with—with—"

"With the death of Cora Lansquenet? Yes. Because one has to examine *everything*. Oh! it is true enough—it is an old maxim—*everyone has something to hide*. It is true of all of us—it is perhaps true of you, too, Madame. But I say to you, nothing can be ignored. That is why your friend, Mr Entwhistle, he has come to me. For I am not the police. I am discreet and what I learn does not concern me. But I have to *know*. And since in this matter is not so much *evidence* as *people*—then it is *people* with whom I occupy myself. I need, Madame, to meet everyone who was here on the day of the funeral. And it would be a great convenience—yes, it would be strategically satisfactory—if I could meet them *here*."

"I'm afraid," Helen said slowly, "that that would be too difficult—"

"Not so difficult as you think. Already I have devised a means. The house, it is sold. So Mr Entwhistle will declare. (*Entendu*, sometimes these things fall through!) He will invite the various members of the family to assemble here and to choose what they will from the furnishings before it is all put up to auction. A suitable weekend can be selected for that purpose."

He paused and then said:

"You see, it is easy, is it not?"

Helen looked at him. The blue eyes were cold—almost frosty.

"Are you laying a trap for someone, M. Poirot?"

"Alas! I wish I knew enough. No. I have still the open mind.

"There may," Hercule Poirot added thoughtfully, "be certain tests . . ."

"Tests? What kind of tests?"

"I have not yet formulated them to myself. And in any case, Madame, it would be better that you should not know them."

"So that I can be tested too?"

"You, Madame, have been taken behind the scenes. Now there is one thing that is doubtful. The young people will, I think, come readily. But it may be difficult, may it not, to secure the presence here of Mr Timothy Abernethie. I hear that he never leaves home."

Helen smiled suddenly.

"I believe you may be lucky there, M. Poirot. I heard from Maude yesterday. The workmen are in painting the house and Timothy is suffering terribly from the smell of the paint. He says that it is seriously affecting his health. I think that he and Maude would both be pleased to come here—perhaps for a week or two. Maude is still not able to get about very well—you know she broke her ankle?"

"I had not heard. How unfortunate."

"Luckily they have got Cora's companion, Miss Gilchrist. It seems that she has turned out a perfect treasure."

"What is that?" Poirot turned sharply on Helen. "Did *they* ask for Miss Gilchrist to go to them? Who suggested it?"

"I think Susan fixed it up. Susan Banks."

"Aha," said Poirot in a curious voice. "So it was the

little Susan who suggested it. She is fond of making the arrangements."

"Susan struck me as being a very competent girl."

"Yes. She is competent. Did you hear that Miss Gilchrist had a narrow escape from death with a piece of poisoned wedding cake?"

"No!" Helen looked startled. "I do remember now that Maude said over the telephone that Miss Gilchrist had just come out of hospital but I'd no idea why she had been in hospital. Poisoned? But, M. Poirot—*why?*"

"Do you really ask that?"

Helen said with sudden vehemence:

"Oh! get them all here! Find out the truth! There mustn't be any more murders."

"So you will co-operate?"

"Yes—I will co-operate."


# 15


"THAT LINOLEUM does look nice, Mrs Jones. What a hand you have with lino. The teapot's on the kitchen table, so go and help yourself. I'll be there as soon as I've taken up Mr Abernethie's elevenses."

Miss Gilchrist trotted up the staircase, carrying a daintily set out tray. She tapped on Timothy's door, interpreted a growl from within as an invitation to enter, and tripped briskly in.

"Morning coffee and biscuits, Mr Abernethie. I do hope you're feeling brighter today. Such a lovely day."

Timothy grunted and said suspiciously:

"Is there skim on that milk?"

"Oh no, Mr Abernethie. I took it off very carefully, and anyway I've brought up the little strainer in case it should form again. Some people like it, you know, they say it's the *cream*—and so it is really."

"Idiots!" said Timothy. "What kind of biscuits are those?"

"They're those nice digestive biscuits."

"Digestive tripe. Ginger nuts are the only biscuits worth eating."

"I'm afraid the grocer hadn't got any this week. But those are really *very* nice. You try them and see."

"I know what they're like, thank you. Leave those curtains alone, can't you?"

"I thought you might like a little sunshine. It's such a nice sunny day."

"I want the room kept dark. My head's terrible. It's this paint. I've always been sensitive to paint. It's poisoning me."

Miss Gilchrist sniffed experimentally and said brightly:

"One really can't smell it much in here. The workmen are over on the other side."

"You're not sensitive like I am. Must I have *all* the books I'm reading taken out of my reach?"

"I'm so sorry, Mr Abernethie, I didn't know you were reading all of them."

"Where's my wife? I haven't seen her for over an hour."

"Mrs Abernethie's resting on the sofa."

"Tell her to come and rest up here."

"I'll tell her, Mr Abernethie. But she may have dropped off to sleep. Shall we say in about a quarter of an hour?"

"No, tell her I want her now. Don't monkey about with that rug. It's arranged the way I like it."

"I'm so sorry. I thought it was slipping off the far side."

"I like it slipping off. Go and get Maude. I want her."

Miss Gilchrist departed downstairs and tiptoed into the drawing room where Maude Abernethie was sitting with her leg up reading a novel.

"I'm so sorry, Mrs Abernethie," she said apologetically. "Mr Abernethie is asking for you."

Maude thrust aside her novel with a guilty expression.

"Oh dear," she said, "I'll go up at once."

She reached for her stick.

Timothy burst out as soon as his wife entered the room:

"So there you are at last!"

"I'm so sorry, dear, I didn't know you wanted me."

"That woman you've got into the house will drive me mad. Twittering and fluttering round like a demented hen. Real typical old maid, that's what she is."

"I'm sorry she annoys you. She tries to be kind, that's all."

"I don't want anybody kind. I don't want a blasted old maid always chirruping over me. She's so damned arch, too——"

"Just a little, perhaps."

"Treats me as though I was a confounded kid! It's maddening."

"I'm sure it must be. But please, *please,* Timothy, do try not to be rude to her. I'm really very helpless still—and you yourself say she cooks well."

"Her cooking's all right," Mr Abernethie admitted grudgingly. "Yes, she's a decent enough cook. But keep her in the kitchen, that's all I ask. Don't let her come fussing round me."

"No, dear, of course not. How are you feeling?"

"Not at all well. I think you'd better send for Barton to come and have a look at me. This paint affects my heart. Feel my pulse—the irregular way it's beating."

Maude felt it without comment.

"Timothy, shall we go to a hotel until the house painting is finished?"

"It would be a great waste of money."

"Does that matter so much—now?"

"You're just like all women—hopelessly extravagant! Just because we've come into a ridiculously small part of my brother's estate, you think we can go and live indefinitely at the Ritz."

"I didn't quite say that, dear."

"I can tell you that the difference Richard's money will make will be hardly appreciable. This bloodsucking Government will see to that. You mark my words, the whole lot will go in taxation."

Mrs Abernethie shook her head sadly.

"This coffee's cold," said the invalid, looking with distaste at the cup which he had not as yet tasted. "Why can't I ever get a cup of really hot coffee?"

"I'll take it down and warm it up."

In the kitchen Miss Gilchrist was drinking tea and conversing affably, though with slight condescension, with Mrs Jones.

"I'm so anxious to spare Mrs Abernethie all I can," she said. "All this running up and down stairs is so painful for her."

"Waits on him hand and foot, she does," said Mrs Jones, stirring the sugar in her cup.

"It's very sad his being such an invalid."

"Not such an invalid either," Mrs Jones said darkly. "Suits him very well to lie up and ring bells and have trays brought up and down. But he's well able to get up and go about. Even seen him out in the village, I have, when *she's* been away. Walking as hearty as you please. Anything he *really* needs—like his tobacco or a stamp— he can come and get. And that's why when *she* was off at that funeral and got held up on the way back, and *he* told me I'd got to come in and stay the night again, I refused. 'I'm sorry, sir,' I said, 'but I've got my husband to think of. Going out to oblige in the mornings is all very well, but I've got to be there to see to him when he comes back from work.' Nor I wouldn't budge, I wouldn't. Do him good, I thought, to get about the house and look after himself for once. Might make him see what a lot he gets done for him. So I stood firm, I did. He didn't half create."

Mrs Jones drew a deep breath and took a long satisfying drink of sweet inky tea.

"Ar," she said.

Though deeply suspicious of Miss Gilchrist, and considering her as a finicky thing, and a "regular fussy old maid" Mrs Jones approved of the lavish way in which Miss Gilchrist dispensed her employer's tea and sugar ration.

She set down the cup and said affably:

"I'll give the kitchen floor a nice scrub down and then I'll be getting along. The potatoes is all ready peeled, dear, you'll find them by the sink."

Though slightly affronted by the "dear," Miss Gilchrist was appreciative of the good will which had divested an enormous quantity of potatoes of their outer coverings.

Before she could say anything the telephone rang and she hurried out in the hall to answer it. The telephone, in the style of fifty-odd years ago was situated inconveniently in a draughty passage behind the staircase.

Maude Abernethie appeared at the top of the stairs, while Miss Gilchrist was still speaking. The latter looked up and said:

"It's Mrs—Leo—is it?—Abernethie speaking."

"Tell her I'm just coming."

Maude descended the stairs slowly and painfully.

Miss Gilchrist murmured, "I'm so sorry you've had to come down again, Mrs Abernethie. Has Mr Abernethie finished his elevenses? I'll just nip up and get the tray."

She trotted up the stairs as Mrs Abernethie said into the receiver:

"Helen? This is Maude here."

The invalid received Miss Gilchrist with a baleful glare. As she picked up the tray he asked fretfully:

"Who's that on the telephone?"

"Mrs Leo Abernethie."

"Oh? Suppose they'll go gossiping for about an hour. Women have no sense of time when they get on the phone. Never think of the money they're wasting."

Miss Gilchrist said brightly that it would be Mrs Leo who had to pay, and Timothy grunted.

"Just pull that curtain aside, will you? No, not that one, the *other* one. I don't want the light slap in my eyes. That's better. No reason because I'm an invalid that I should have to sit in the dark all day."

He went on:

"And you might look in that book case over there for a green— What's the matter now? What are you rushing off for?"

"It's the front door, Mr Abernethie."

"*I* didn't hear anything. You've got that woman downstairs, haven't you? Let her go and answer it."

"Yes, Mr Abernethie. What was the book you wanted me to find?"

The invalid closed his eyes.

"I can't remember now. You've put it out of my head. You'd better go."

Miss Gilchrist seized the tray and hurriedly departed. Putting the tray on the pantry table she hurried into the front hall, passing Mrs Abernethie who was still at the telephone.

She returned in a moment to ask in a muted voice:

"I'm so sorry to interrupt. It's a Nun. Collecting. The Heart of Mary Fund, I think she said. She has a book. Half a crown or five shillings most people seem to have given."

Maude Abernethie said:

"Just a moment, Helen," into the telephone, and to Miss Gilchrist, "We have our own Church charities."

Miss Gilchrist hurried away again.

Maude terminated her conversation after a few minutes with the phrase, "I'll talk to Timothy about it."

She replaced the receiver and came into the front hall. Miss Gilchrist was standing quite still by the drawing room door. She was frowning in a puzzled way and jumped when Maude Abernethie spoke to her.

"There's nothing the matter, is there, Miss Gilchrist?"

"Oh no, Mrs Abernethie, I'm afraid I was just wool gathering. So stupid of me when there's so much to be done."

Miss Gilchrist resumed her imitation of a busy ant and Maude Abernethie climbed the stairs slowly and painfully to her husband's room.

"That was Helen on the telephone. It seems that the place is definitely sold—some Institution for Foreign Refugees—"

She paused whilst Timothy expressed himself forcefully on the subject of Foreign Refugees, with side issues as to the house in which he had been born and brought up. "No decent standards left in this country. My old home! I can hardly bear to think of it."

Maude went on.

"Helen quite appreciates what you—we—will feel about it. She suggests that we might like to come there for a visit before it goes. She was very distressed about your health and the way the painting is affecting it. She thought you might prefer coming to Enderby to going to a hotel. The servants are there still, so you could be looked after comfortably."

Timothy, whose mouth had been open in outraged

protests half way through this, had closed it again. His
eyes had become suddenly shrewd. He now nodded his
head approvingly.

"Thoughtful of Helen," he said. "Very thoughtful. I
don't know, I'm sure, I'll have to think it over. . . .
There's no doubt that this paint is poisoning me—there's
arsenic in paint, I believe. I seem to have heard something of the kind. On the other hand the exertion of moving might be too much for me. It's difficult to know what
would be the best."

"Perhaps you'd prefer a hotel, dear," said Maude. "A
good hotel is very expensive, but where your health is
concerned—"

Timothy interrupted.

"I wish I could make you understand, Maude, that we
*are not millionaires*. Why go to a hotel when Helen has
very kindly suggested that we should go to Enderby? Not
that it's really for her to suggest! The house isn't hers. I
don't understand legal subtleties, but I presume it belongs
to us equally until it's sold and the proceeds divided.
Foreign Refugees! It would have made old Cornelius turn
in his grave. Yes," he sighed, "I should like to see the old
place again before I die."

Maude played her last card adroitly.

"I understand that Mr Entwhistle has suggested that
the members of the family might like to choose certain
pieces of furniture or china or something—before the
contents are put up for auction."

Timothy heaved himself briskly upright.

"We must certainly go. There must be a very exact
valuation of what is chosen by each person. Those men
the girls have married—I wouldn't trust either of them
from what I've heard. There might be some sharp practice. Helen is far too amiable. As the head of the family,
it is my duty to be present!"

He got up and walked up and down the room with a
brisk vigorous tread.

"Yes, it is an excellent plan. Write to Helen and accept. What I am really thinking about is you, my dear. It
will be a nice rest and change for you. You have been
doing far too much lately. The decorators can get on with

the painting while we are away and that Gillespie woman can stay here and look after the house."

"Gilchrist," said Maude.

Timothy waved a hand and said that it was all the same.


## ii


"I can't do it," said Miss Gilchrist.

Maude looked at her in surprise.

Miss Gilchrist was trembling. Her eyes looked pleadingly into Maude's.

"It's stupid of me, I know . . . But I simply can't. Not stay here all alone in the house. If there was anyone who could come and—and sleep here, too?"

She looked hopefully at the other woman, but Maude shook her head. Maude Abernethie knew only too well how difficult it was to get anyone in the neighbourhood to "live in."

Miss Gilchrist went on, a kind of desperation in her voice.

"I know you'll think it nervy and foolish—and I wouldn't have dreamed once that I'd ever feel like this. I've never been a nervous woman—or fanciful. But now it all seems different. I'd be terrified—yes, literally terrified—to be all alone here."

"Of course," said Maude. "It's stupid of me. After what happened at Lytchett St. Mary."

"I suppose that's it. . . . It's not logical, I know. And I didn't feel it at first. I didn't mind being alone in the cottage after—after it had happened. The feeling's grown up gradually. You'll have no opinion of me at all, Mrs Abernethie, but even since I've been here I've been feeling it—*frightened,* you know. Not of anything in particular—but just *frightened* . . . It's so silly and I really am ashamed. It's just as though all the time I was expecting something awful to happen. . . . Even that nun coming to the door startled me. Oh dear, I *am* in a bad way. . . ."

"I suppose it's what they call delayed shock," said Maude vaguely.

"Is it? I don't know. Oh dear, I'm so sorry to appear

so—so ungrateful, and after all your kindness. What you will think—"

Maude soothed her.

"We must think of some other arrangement," she said.

# 16

GEORGE CROSSFIELD paused irresolutely for a moment as he watched a particular feminine back disappear through a doorway. Then he nodded to himself and went in pursuit.

The doorway in question was that of a double fronted shop—a shop that had gone out of business. The plate glass windows showed a disconcerting emptiness within. The door was closed, but George rapped on it. A vacuous faced young man with spectacles opened it and stared at George.

"Excuse me," said George. "But I think my cousin just came in here."

The young man drew back and George walked in.

"Hullo, Susan," he said.

Susan who was standing on a packing case and using a footrule turned her head in some surprise.

"Hullo, George. Where did you spring from?"

"I saw your back. I was sure it was yours."

"How clever of you. I suppose backs are distinctive."

"Much more so than faces. Add a beard and pads in your cheeks and do a few things to your hair and nobody will know you when you come face to face with them—but beware of the moment when you walk away."

"I'll remember. Can you remember seven feet fifteen inches until I've got time to write it down?"

"Certainly. What is this, book shelves?"

"No, cubicle space. Eight feet nineteen—and three twelve . . ."

The young man with the spectacles who had been fidgeting from one foot to the other, coughed apologetically.

"Excuse me, Mrs Banks, but if you want to be here for some time—"

"I do, rather," said Susan. "If you leave the keys, I'll lock the door and return them to the office when I go past. Will that be all right?"

"Yes, thank you. If it weren't that we're short staffed this morning—"

Susan accepted the apologetic intent of the half finished sentence and the young man removed himself to the outer world of the street.

"I'm glad we've got rid of him," said Susan. "House agents are a bother. They will keep talking just when I want to do sums."

"Ah," said George. "Murder in an empty shop. How exciting it would be for the passersby to see the dead body of a beautiful young woman displayed behind plate glass. How they would goggle. Like goldfish."

"There wouldn't be any reason for you to murder me, George."

"Well, I should get a fourth part of your share of our esteemed uncle's estate. If one were sufficiently fond of money that should be a reason."

Susan stopped taking measurements and turned to look at him. Her eyes opened a little.

"You look a different person, George. It's really—extraordinary."

"Different? How different?"

"Like an advertisement. *This is the same man that you saw overleaf, but now he has taken Uppington's Health Salts.*"

She sat down on another packing case and lit a cigarette.

"You must have wanted your share of old Richard's money pretty badly, George?"

"Nobody could honestly say that money isn't welcome these days."

George's tone was light.

Susan said: "You were in a jam, weren't you?"

"Hardly your business, is it, Susan?"

"I was just interested."

"Are you renting this shop as a place of business?"

"I'm buying the whole house."

"With possession?"

"Yes. The two upper floors were flats. One's empty and went with the shop. The other I'm buying the people out."

"Nice to have money, isn't it, Susan?"

There was a malicious tone in George's voice. But Susan merely took a deep breath and said:

"As far as I'm concerned, it's wonderful. An answer to prayer."

"Does prayer kill off elderly relatives?"

Susan paid no attention.

"This place is exactly *right*. To begin with it's a very good piece of period architecture. I can make the living part upstairs something quite unique. There are two lovely moulded ceilings and the rooms are a beautiful shape. This part down here which has already been hacked about I shall have completely modern."

"What is this? A dress business?"

"No. Beauty culture. Herbal preparations. Face creams!"

"The full racket?"

"The racket as before. It pays. It always pays. What you need to put it over is personality. I can do it."

George looked at his cousin appreciatively. He admired the slanting planes of her face, the generous mouth, the radiant colouring. Altogether an unusual and vivid face. And he recognised in Susan that odd, indefinable quality, the quality of success.

"Yes," he said, "I think you've got what it takes, Susan. You'll get back your outlay on this scheme and you'll get places with it."

"It's the right neighbourhood, just off a main shopping street *and* you can park a car right in front of the door."

Again George nodded.

"Yes, Susan, you're going to succeed. Have you had this in mind for a long time?"

"Over a year."

"Why didn't you put it up to old Richard? He might have staked you?"

"I did put it up to him."

"And he didn't see his way? I wonder why. I should

ave thought he'd have recognised the same mettle that
e himself was made of."

Susan did not answer, and into George's mind there
eapt a swift bird's eye view of another figure. A thin nervous suspicious eyed young man.

"Where does—what's his name—Greg—come in on all
his?" he asked. "He'll give up dishing out pills and
owders, I take it?"

"Of course. There will be a laboratory built out at the
ack. We shall have our own formulas for face creams
nd beauty preparations."

George suppressed a grin. He wanted to say: "So baby
s to have his play pen," but he did not say it. As a cousin
e did not mind being spiteful, but he had an uneasy
ense that Susan's feeling for her husband was a thing to
e treated with care. It had all the qualities of a danger-
us explosive. He wondered, as he had wondered on the
ay of the funeral, about that queer fish, Gregory. Some-
hing odd about the fellow. So nondescript in appear-
nce—and yet, in some way, not nondescript . . .

He looked again at Susan, calmly and radiantly trium-
hant.

"You've got the true Abernethie touch," he said. "The
nly one of the family who has. Pity as far as old Richard
vas concerned that you're a woman. If you'd been a boy,
bet he'd have left you the whole caboodle."

Susan said slowly: "Yes, I think he would."

She paused and then went on:

"He didn't like Greg, you know. . . ."

"Ah." George raised his eyebrows. "His mistake."

"Yes."

"Oh well. Anyway things are going well now—all going
ccording to plan."

As he said the words he was struck by the fact that
hey seemed particularly applicable to Susan.

The idea made him, just for a moment, a shade un-
omfortable.

He didn't really like a woman who was so cold blood-
dly efficient.

Changing the subject he said:

"By the way, did you get a letter from Helen? About
nderby?"

"Yes, I did. This morning. Did you?"

"Yes. What are you going to do about it?"

"Greg and I thought of going up the weekend afte
next—if that suits everyone else. Helen seemed to wan
us all together."

George laughed shrewdly.

"Or somebody might choose a more valuable piece o
furniture than somebody else?"

Susan laughed.

"Oh, I suppose there is a proper valuation. But a valu
ation for probate will be much lower than the thing
would be in the open market. And besides I'd quite lik
to have a few relics of the founder of the family fortunes
Then I think it would be amusing to have one or two re
ally absurd and charming specimens of the Victorian ag
in this place. Make a kind of *thing* of them! That period
coming in now. There was a green malachite table in th
drawing room. You could build quite a colour schem
around it. And perhaps a case of stuffed humming bird
—or one of those crowns made of waxed flowers. Some
thing like that—just as a key note can be very effective."

"I trust your judgement."

"You'll be there I suppose?"

"Oh, I shall be there—to see fair play if nothing else."

Susan laughed.

"What do you bet there will be a grand family row?"
she asked.

"Rosamund will probably want your green malachit
table for a stage set!"

Susan did not laugh. Instead she frowned.

"Have you seen Rosamund lately?"

"I have not seen beautiful Cousin Rosamund since w
all came back third class from the funeral."

"I've seen her once or twice. . . . She—she seeme
rather odd—"

"What was the matter with her? Trying to think?"

"No. She seemed—well—upset."

"Upset about coming into a lot of money and bein
able to put on some perfectly frightful play in which Mi
chael can make an ass of himself?"

"Oh, that's going ahead. And it *does* sound frightful—
but all the same it may be a success. Michael's good, yo

know. He can put himself across the footlights—or whatever the term is. He's not like Rosamund who's just beautiful and ham."

"Poor beautiful ham Rosamund."

"All the same Rosamund is not quite so dumb as one might think. She says things that are quite shrewd, sometimes. Things that you wouldn't have imagined she'd even noticed. It's—it's quite disconcerting."

"Quite like our Aunt Cora—"

"Yes . . ."

A momentary uneasiness descended on them both—conjured up, it seemed, by the mention of Cora Lansquenet.

Then George said with a rather elaborate air of unconcern:

"Talking of Cora—what about that companion woman of hers? I rather think something ought to be done about her."

"Done about her? What do you mean?"

"Well, it's up to the family so to speak. I mean I've been thinking Cora was our Aunt—and it occurred to me that this woman mayn't find it easy to get another post."

"That occurred to you, did it?"

"Yes. People are so careful of their skins. I don't say they'd actually think that this Gilchrist female would take a hatchet to them—but at the back of their minds they feel that it might be unlucky. People are superstitious."

"How odd that you should have thought of all that, George? How would you know about things like that?"

George said drily:

"You forget that I'm a lawyer. I see a lot of the queer illogical side of people. What I'm getting at is, that I think we might do something about the woman, give her a small allowance or something, to tide her over, or find some office post for her if she's capable of that sort of thing. I feel rather as though we ought to keep in touch with her."

"You needn't worry," said Susan. Her voice was dry and ironic. "I've seen to things. She's gone to Timothy and Maude."

George looked startled.

"I say, Susan—is that wise?"

"It was the best thing I could think of—at the moment."

George looked at her curiously.

"You're very sure of yourself, aren't you, Susan? You know what you're doing and you don't have—regrets."

Susan said lightly:

"It's a waste of time—having regrets."

# 17

MICHAEL TOSSED the letter across the table to Rosamund.

"What about it?"

"Oh, we'll go. Don't you think so?"

Michael said slowly:

"It might be as well."

"There might be some jewellery . . . Of course all the things in the house are quite hideous—stuffed birds and wax flowers—ugh!"

"Yes. Bit of a mausoleum. As a matter of fact I'd like to make a sketch or two—particularly in that drawing room. The mantelpiece, for instance, and that very odd shaped couch. They'd be just right for 'The Baronet's Progress'—if we revive it."

He got up and looked at his watch.

"That reminds me. I must go round and see Rosenheim. Don't expect me until rather late this evening. I'm dining with Oscar and we're going into the question of taking up that option and how it fits in with the American offer."

"Darling Oscar. He'll be pleased to see you after all this time. Give him my love."

Michael looked at her sharply. He no longer smiled and his face had an alert predatory look.

"What do you mean—after all this time? Anyone would think I hadn't seen him for months."

"Well, you haven't, have you?" murmured Rosamund.

"Yes, I have. We lunched together only a week ago."

"How funny. He must have forgotten about it. He rang up yesterday and said he hadn't seen you since the first night of 'Tilly Looks West.'"

"The old fool must be off his head."

Michael laughed. Rosamund, her eyes wide and blue, looked at him without emotion.

"You think I'm a fool, don't you, Mick?"

Michael protested.

"Darling, of course I don't."

"Yes, you do. But I'm not an absolute nit-wit. You didn't go near Oscar that day. I know where you did go."

"Rosamund darling—what do you mean?"

"I mean I know where you really were. . . ."

Michael, his attractive face uncertain, stared at his wife. She stared back at him, placid, unruffled.

How very disconcerting, he suddenly thought, a really empty stare could be.

He said rather unsuccessfully:

"I don't know what you're driving at. . . ."

"I just meant it's rather silly telling me a lot of lies."

"Look here, Rosamund—"

He had started to bluster—but he stopped, taken aback as his wife said softly:

"We do want to take up this option and put this play on, don't we?"

"Want to? It's the part I've always dreamed must exist somewhere."

"Yes—that's what I mean."

"Just what do you mean?"

"Well—it's worth a good deal, isn't it? But one mustn't take *too* many risks."

He stared at her and said slowly:

"It's your money—I know that. If you don't want to risk it—"

"It's *our* money, darling." Rosamund stressed it. "I think that's rather important."

"Listen, darling. The part of Eileen—it would bear writing up."

Rosamund smiled.

"I don't think—really—I want to play it."

"My dear girl." Michael was aghast. "What's come over you?"

"Nothing."

"Yes, there is, you've been different lately—moody—nervous, what is it?"

"Nothing. I only want you to be—careful, Mick."

"Careful about what? I'm always careful."

"No, I don't think you are. You always think you can get away with things and that everyone will believe whatever you want them to. You were stupid about Oscar that day."

Michael flushed angrily.

"And what about you? You said you were going shopping with Jane. You didn't. Jane's in America, has been for weeks."

"Yes," said Rosamund. "That was stupid, too. I really just went for a walk—in Regent's Park."

Michael looked at her curiously.

"Regent's Park? You never went for a walk in Regent's Park in your life. What's it all about? Have you got a boy friend? You may say what you like, Rosamund, you *have* been different lately. Why?"

"I've been thinking about things. About what to do . . ."

Michael came round the table to her in a satisfying spontaneous rush. His voice held fervour as he cried:

"Darling—you know I love you madly!"

She responded satisfactorily to the embrace, but as they drew apart he was struck again disagreeably by the odd calculation in those beautiful eyes.

"Whatever I'd done, you'd always forgive me, wouldn't you?" he demanded.

"I suppose so," said Rosamund vaguely. "That's not the point. You see, it's all different now. We've got to think and plan."

"Think and plan—what?"

Rosamund, frowning, said:

"Things aren't over when you've done them. It's really a sort of beginning and then one's got to arrange what to do next, and what's important and what is not."

"Rosamund . . ."

She sat, her face perplexed, her wide gaze on a middle distance in which Michael, apparently, did not feature.

At the third repetition of her name, she started slightly and came out of her reverie.

"What did you say?"

"I asked you what you were thinking about. . . ."

"Oh? Oh yes, I was wondering if I'd go down to—what

is it?—Lytchett St. Mary, and see that Miss Somebody—
the one who was with Aunt Cora."

"But why?"

"Well, she'll be going away soon, won't she? To relatives or someone. I don't think we ought to let her go
away until we've asked her."

"Asked her what?"

"Asked her who killed Aunt Cora."

Michael stared.

"You mean—you think she *knows?*"

Rosamund said rather absently:

"Oh yes, I expect so. . . . She lived there, you see."

"But she'd have told the police."

"Oh, I don't mean she knows *that* way—I just mean
that she's probably quite sure. Because of what Uncle
Richard said when he went down there."

"But she wouldn't have heard what he said."

"Oh yes, she would, darling." Rosamund sounded like
someone arguing with an unreasonable child.

"Nonsense, I can hardly see old Richard Abernethie
discussing his suspicions of his family before an outsider."

"Well, of course. She'd have heard it through the
door."

"Eavesdropping, you mean?"

"I expect so—in fact I'm sure. It must be so deadly
dull shut up, two women in a cottage and nothing ever
happening except washing up and the sink and putting the
cat out and things like that. Of course she listened and
read letters—anyone would."

Michael looked at her with something faintly approaching dismay.

"Would you?" he demanded bluntly.

"I wouldn't go and be a companion in the country."
Rosamund shuddered. "I'd rather die."

"I meant—would you read letters and—and all that?"

Rosamund said calmly:

"If I wanted to know, yes. Everybody does, don't you
think so?"

The limpid gaze met his.

"One just wants to know," said Rosamund. "One
doesn't want to do anything about it. I expect that's how

*she* feels—Miss Gilchrist, I mean. But I'm certain she *knows.*"

Michael said in a stifled voice:

"Rosamund, who do you think killed Cora? And old Richard?"

Once again that limpid blue gaze met his.

"Darling—don't be absurd. . . . You know as well as I do. But it's much better *never* to mention it. So we won't."


# 18


FROM HIS seat by the fireplace in the library, Hercule Poirot looked at the assembled company.

His eyes passed thoughtfully over Susan, sitting upright, looking vivid and animated, over her husband, sitting near her, his expression rather vacant and his fingers twisting a loop of string; they went on to George Crossfield, debonair and distinctly pleased with himself, talking about card sharpers on Atlantic Cruises to Rosamund, who said mechanically, "How extraordinary, darling. But why?" in a completely uninterested voice; went on to Michael with his very individual type of haggard good looks and his very apparent charm; to Helen, poised and slightly remote, to Timothy comfortably settled in the best armchair with an extra cushion at his back and Maude, sturdy and thick-set, in devoted attendance, and finally to the figure sitting with a tinge of apology just beyond the range of the family circle—the figure of Miss Gilchrist wearing a rather peculiar "dressy" blouse. Presently, he judged, she would get up, murmur an excuse and leave the family gathering and go up to her room. Miss Gilchrist, he thought, knew her place. She had learned it the hard way.

Hercule Poirot sipped his after dinner coffee and between half closed lids made his appraisal.

He had wanted them there—all together, and he had got them. And what, he thought to himself, was he going to do with them now? He felt a sudden weary distaste for going on with the business. Why was that, he wondered? Was it the influence of Helen Abernethie? There was a quality of passive resistance about her that seemed unexpectedly strong. Had she, while apparently graceful and unconcerned, managed to impress her own reluctance upon him? She was averse to this raking up of the details of old Richard's death, he knew that. She wanted it left alone, left to die out into oblivion. Poirot was not surprised by that. What did surprise him was his own disposition to agree with her.

Mr Entwhistle's account of the family had, he realised, been admirable. He had described all these people shrewdly and well. With the old lawyer's knowledge and appraisal to guide him, Poirot had wanted to see for himself. He had fancied that, meeting these people intimately, he would have a very shrewd idea not of *how* and *when* —(those were questions with which he did not propose to concern himself. Murder had been possible—that was all he needed to know!)—but of *who*. For Hercule Poirot had a lifetime of experience behind him, and as a man who deals with pictures can recognise the artist, so Poirot believed he could recognise a likely type of the amateur criminal who will—if his own particular need arises—be prepared to kill.

But it was not to be so easy.

Because he could visualise almost all of these people as a possible—though not a probable—murderer. George might kill—as the cornered rat kills. Susan calmly—efficiently—to further a plan. Gregory because he had that queer morbid streak which discounts and invites, almost craves, punishment. Michael because he was ambitious and had a murderer's cock-sure vanity. Rosamund because she was frighteningly simple in outlook. Timothy because he had hated and resented his brother and had craved the power his brother's money would give. Maude because Timothy was her child and where her child was concerned she would be ruthless. Even Miss Gilchrist, he thought, might have contemplated murder if it could have restored to her The Willow Tree in its ladylike glory!

And Helen? He could not see Helen as committing murder. She was too civilised—too removed from vio-

lence. And she and her husband had surely loved Richard
Abernethie.

Poirot sighed to himself. There were to be no short cuts
to the truth. Instead he would have to adopt a longer, but
a reasonably sure method. There would have to be conversation. Much conversation. For in the long run, either
through a lie, or through truth, people were bound to give
themselves away. . . .

He had been introduced by Helen to the gathering, and
had set to work to overcome the almost universal annoyance caused by his presence—a foreign stranger!—in
this family gathering. He had used his eyes and his ears.
He had watched and listened—openly and behind doors!
He had noticed affinities, antagonisms, the unguarded
words that arose as always when property was to be divided. He had engineered adroitly tête-à-têtes, walks upon
the terrace, and had made his deductions and observa-
tions. He had talked with Miss Gilchrist about the vanished glories of her teashop and about the correct com-
position of *brioches* and chocolate *éclairs* and had visited
the kitchen garden with her to discuss the proper use of
herbs in cooking. He had spent some long half hours listening to Timothy talking about his own health and about
the effect upon it of paint.

Paint? Poirot frowned. Somebody else had said something about paint—Mr Entwhistle?

There had also been discussion of a different kind of
painting. Pierre Lansquenet as a painter. Cora Lansquenet's paintings, rapturized over by Miss Gilchrist, dismissed
scornfully by Susan. "Just like picture postcards," she had
said. "She did them from postcards, too."

Miss Gilchrist had been quite upset by that and had
said sharply that dear Mrs Lansquenet always painted
from Nature.

"But I bet she cheated," said Susan to Poirot when
Miss Gilchrist had gone out of the room. "In fact I know
she did, though I won't upset the old pussy by saying so."

"And how do you know?"

Poirot watched the strong confident line of Susan's
chin.

"She will always be sure, this one," he thought. "And
perhaps sometime, she will be too sure. . . ."

Susan was going on.

"I'll tell you, but don't pass it on to the Gilchrist. One picture is of Polflexan, the cove and the lighthouse and the pier—the usual aspect that all amateur artists sit down and sketch. But the pier was blown up in the war, and since Aunt Cora's sketch was done a couple of years ago, it can't very well be from Nature, can it? But the postcards they sell there still show the pier as it used to be. There was one in her bedroom drawer. So Aunt Cora started her 'rough sketch' down there, I expect, and then finished it surreptitiously later at home from a postcard! It's funny, isn't it, the way people get caught out?"

"Yes, it is, as you say, funny." He paused, and then thought that the opening was a good one.

"You do not remember me, Madame," he said, "but I remember you. This is not the first time that I have seen you."

She stared at him. Poirot nodded with great gusto.

"Yes, yes, it is so. I was inside an automobile, well wrapped up and from the window I saw you. You were talking to one of the mechanics in the garage. You do not notice me—it is natural—I am inside the car—an elderly muffled-up foreigner! But *I* notice *you,* for you are young and agreeable to look at and you stand there in the sun. So when I arrive here, I say to myself, '*Tiens!* what a coincidence!' "

"A garage? Where? When was this?"

"Oh a little time ago—a week—no, more. For the moment," said Poirot disingenuously and with a full recollection of the King's Arms Garage in his mind, "I cannot remember where. I travel so much all over this country."

"Looking for a suitable house to buy for your refugees?"

"Yes. There is so much to take into consideration, you see. Price—neighbourhood—suitability for conversion."

"I suppose you'll have to pull the house about a lot? Lots of horrible partitions."

"In the bedrooms, yes, certainly. But most of the ground floor rooms we shall not touch." He paused before going on. "Does it sadden you, Madame, that this old family mansion of yours should go this way—to strangers?"

"Of course not." Susan looked amused. "I think it's an excellent idea. It's an impossible place for anybody to think of living in as it is. And I've nothing to be sentimental about. It's not *my* old home. My mother and father lived in London. We just came here for Christmas sometimes. Actually I've always thought it quite hideous —an almost indecent temple to wealth."

"The altars are different now. There is the building in, and the concealed lighting and the expensive simplicity. But wealth still has its temples, Madame. I understand—I am not, I hope, indiscreet—that you yourself are planning such an edifice? Everything *de luxe*—and no expense spared."

Susan laughed.

"Hardly a temple—it's just a place of business."

"Perhaps the name does not matter. . . . But it will cost much money—that is true, is it not?"

"Everything's wickedly expensive nowadays. But the initial outlay will be worthwhile, I think."

"Tell me something about these plans of yours. It amazes me to find a beautiful young woman so practical, so competent. In my young days—a long time ago, I admit—beautiful women thought only of their pleasures, of cosmetics, of *la toilette.*"

"Women still think a great deal about their faces— that's where I come in."

"Tell me."

And she had told him. Told him with a wealth of detail and with a great deal of unconscious self-revelation. He appreciated her business acumen, her boldness of planning and her grasp of detail. A good bold planner, sweeping all side issues away. Perhaps a little ruthless as all those who plan boldly must be. . . .

Watching her, he had said:

"Yes, you will succeed. You will go ahead. How fortunate that you are not restricted, as so many are, by poverty. One cannot go far without the capital outlay. To have had these creative ideas and to have been frustrated by lack of means—that would have been unbearable."

"I couldn't have borne it! But I'd have raised money somehow or other—got someone to back me."

"Ah! of course. Your uncle, whose house this was, was

rich. Even if he had not died, he would, as you express it, have 'staked' you."

"Oh no, he wouldn't. Uncle Richard was a bit of a stick-in-the-mud where women were concerned. If I'd been a man——" A quick flash of anger swept across her face. "He made me very angry."

"I see—yes, I see. . . ."

"The old shouldn't stand in the way of the young. I—oh, I beg your pardon."

Hercule Poirot laughed easily and twirled his moustache.

"I am old, yes. But I do not impede youth. There is no one who needs to wait for my death."

"What a horrid idea."

"But you are a realist, Madame. Let us admit without more ado that the world is full of the young—or even the middle-aged—who wait, patiently or impatiently, for the death of someone whose decease will give them, if not affluence—then opportunity."

"Opportunity!" Susan said, taking a deep breath. "That's what one needs."

Poirot who had been looking beyond her, said gaily:

"And here is your husband come to join our little discussion. . . . We talk, Mr Banks, of opportunity. Opportunity the golden—opportunity who must be grasped with both hands. How far in conscience can one go? Let us hear your views?"

But he was not destined to hear the views of Gregory Banks on opportunity or on anything else. In fact he had found it next to impossible to talk to Gregory Banks at all. Banks had a curious fluid quality. Whether by his own wish, or by that of his wife, he seemed to have no liking for tête-à-têtes or quiet discussions. No, "conversation" with Gregory had failed.

Poirot had talked with Maude Abernethie—also about paint (the smell of) and how fortunate it had been that Timothy had been able to come to Enderby, and how kind it had been of Helen to extend an invitation to Miss Gilchrist also.

"For really she is *most* useful. Timothy so often feels like a snack—and one cannot ask too much of other people's servants but there is a gas ring in a little room off the pantry, so that Miss Gilchrist can warm up Ovaltine or Benger's there without disturbing anybody. And she's so willing about fetching things, she's quite willing to run up and down stairs a dozen times a day. Oh yes, I feel that it was really quite Providential that she should have lost her nerve about staying alone in the house as she did, though I admit it vexed me at the time."

"Lost her nerve?" Poirot was interested.

He listened whilst Maude gave him an account of Miss Gilchrist's sudden collapse.

"She was frightened, you say? And yet could not exactly say why? That is interesting. Very interesting."

"I put it down myself to delayed shock."

"Perhaps."

"Once, during the war, when a bomb dropped about a mile away from us, I remember Timothy——"

Poirot abstracted his mind from Timothy.

"Had anything particular happened that day?" he asked.

"On what day?" Maude looked blank.

"The day that Miss Gilchrist was upset."

"Oh, *that*—no, I don't think so. It seems to have been coming on ever since she left Lytchett St. Mary, or so she said. She didn't seem to mind when she was there."

And the result, Poirot thought, had been a piece of poisoned wedding cake. Not so very surprising that Miss Gilchrist was frightened after that. . . . And even when she had removed herself to the peaceful country round Stansfield Grange, the fear had lingered. More than lingered. Grown. Why grown? Surely attending on an exacting hypochondriac like Timothy must be so exhausting that nervous fears would be likely to be swallowed up in exasperation?

But something in that house had made Miss Gilchrist afraid. What? Did she know herself?

Finding himself alone with Miss Gilchrist for a brief space before dinner, Poirot had sailed into the subject with an exaggerated foreign curiosity.

"Impossible, you comprehend, for me to mention the matter of murder to members of the family. But I am intrigued. Who would not be? A brutal crime—a sensitive artist attacked in a lonely cottage. Terrible for her family.

But terrible, also, I imagine, for *you*. Since Mrs Timothy Abernethie gives me to understand that you were there at the time?"

"Yes, I was. And if you'll excuse me, M. Pontarlier, I don't want to talk about it."

"I understand—oh yes, I completely understand."

Having said this, Poirot waited. And, as he had thought, Miss Gilchrist immediately *did* begin to talk about it.

He heard nothing from her that he had not heard before, but he played his part with perfect sympathy, uttering little cries of comprehension and listening with an absorbed interest which Miss Gilchrist could not but help enjoy.

Not until she had exhausted the subject of what she herself had felt, and what the doctor had said, and how kind Mr Entwhistle had been, did Poirot proceed cautiously to the next point.

"You were wise, I think, not to remain alone down in that cottage."

"I couldn't have done it, M. Pontarlier. I really couldn't have done it."

"No. I understand even that you were afraid to remain alone in the house of Mr Timothy Abernethie whilst they came here?"

Miss Gilchrist looked guilty.

"I'm terribly ashamed about that. So foolish really. It was just a kind of panic I had—I really don't know *why*."

"But of course one knows why. You had just recovered frm a dastardly attempt to poison you—"

Miss Gilchrist here sighed and said she simply couldn't understand it. Why should anyone try to poison her?

"But obviously, my dear lady, because this criminal, this assassin, thought that you knew something that might lead to his apprehension by the police."

"But what could *I* know? Some dreadful tramp, or semi-crazed creature."

"If it *was* a tramp. It seems to me unlikely—"

"Oh please, M. Pontarlier—" Miss Gilchrist became suddenly very upset. "Don't suggest such things. I don't want to believe it."

"You do not want to believe what?"

"I don't want to believe that it wasn't—I mean—that it was—"

She paused, confused.

"And yet," said Poirot shrewdly, "you *do* believe."

"Oh I don't. I *don't!*"

"But I think you do. That is why you are frightened. ... You are still frightened, are you not?"

"Oh no, not since I came here. So many people. And such a nice family atmosphere. Oh no, everything seems quite all right here."

"It seems to me—you must excuse my interest—I am an old man, somewhat infirm, and a great part of my time is given to idle speculation on matters which interest me—it seems to me that there must have been some definite occurrence at Stansfield Grange which, so to speak, brought your fears to a *head*. Doctors recognize nowadays how much takes place in our subconscious."

"Yes, yes—I know they say so."

"And I think your subconscious fears might have been brought to a point by some small concrete happening, something, perhaps, quite extraneous, serving, shall we say, as a focal point."

Miss Gilchrist seemed to lap this up eagerly.

"I'm sure you are right," she said.

"Now what, should you think, was this—er—extraneous circumstance?"

Miss Gilchrist pondered a moment, and then said, unexpectedly:

"I think, you know, M. Pontarlier, it was the *nun*."

Before Poirot could take this up, Susan and her husband came in, closely followed by Helen.

"A nun," thought Poirot. . . . "Now where, in all this, have I heard something about a nun?"

He resolved to lead the conversation to nuns sometime in the course of the evening.

## 19

THE FAMILY had all been polite to M. Pontarlier, the representative of U.N.A.R.C.O. And how right he had been to have chosen to designate himself by initials. Everyone had accepted U.N.A.R.C.O. as a matter of course—had even pretended to know all about it! How averse human beings were ever to admit ignorance! An exception had been Rosamund who had asked him wonderingly: "But what *is* it? I never heard of it." Fortunately no one else had been there at the time. Poirot had explained the organisation in such a way that anyone but Rosamund would have felt abashed at having displayed ignorance of such a well-known, world wide institution. Rosamund, however, had only said vaguely, "Oh! refugees all over *again*. I'm so *tired* of refugees." Thus voicing the unspoken reaction of many, who were usually too conventional to express themselves so frankly.

M. Pontarlier was, therefore, now accepted—as a nuisance but also as a nonentity. He had become, as it were, a piece of foreign *décor*. The general opinion was that Helen should have avoided having him here this particular weekend, but as he was here they must make the best of it. Fortunately this queer little foreigner did not seem to know much English. Quite often he did not understand what you said to him, and when everyone was speaking more or less at once he seemed completely at sea. He appeared to be interested only in refugees and post war conditions, and his vocabulary only included those subjects. Ordinary chit chat appeared to bewilder him. More or less forgotten by all, Hercule Poirot leant back in his chair, sipped his coffee and observed, as a cat may observe, the twitterings, and comings and goings of a flock of birds. The cat is not ready yet to make its spring.

After twenty-four hours of prowling round the house and examining its contents, the heirs of Richard Abernethie were ready to state their preferences, and, if need be, to fight for them.

The subject of conversation was, first, a certain Spode dinner dessert service off which they had just been eating dessert.

"I don't suppose I have long to live," said Timothy in a faint melancholy voice. "And Maude and I have no children. It is hardly worth while burdening ourselves with useless possessions. But for sentiment's sake I *should* like to have the old dessert service. I remember it in the dear old days. It's out of fashion, of course, and I understand dessert services have very little value nowadays—but there it is. I shall be *quite* content with that—and perhaps the Boule Cabinet in the White Boudoir."

"You're too late, Uncle," George spoke with debonair insouciance. "I asked Helen to mark off the Spode service to me this morning."

Timothy became purple in the face.

"Mark it off—mark it off? What do you mean? Nothing's been settled yet. And what do *you* want with a dessert service? You're not married."

"As a matter of fact I collect Spode. And this is really a splendid specimen. But it's quite all right about the Boule Cabinet, Uncle. I wouldn't have that as a gift."

Timothy waved aside the Boule Cabinet.

"Now look here, young George. You can't go butting in, in this way. I'm an older man than you are—and I'm Richard's only surviving brother. That dessert service is *mine.*"

"Why not take the Dresden service, Uncle? A very fine example and I'm sure just as full of sentimental memories. Anyway, the Spode's mine. First come, first served."

"Nonsense—nothing of the kind!" Timothy spluttered.

Maude said sharply:

"Please don't upset your uncle, George. It's very bad for him. Naturally he will take the Spode if he wants to! The first choice is *his,* and you young people must come afterwards. He was Richard's brother, as he says, and you are only a nephew."

"And I can tell you this, young man." Timothy was seething with fury. "If Richard had made a proper will, the disposal of the contents of this place would have been entirely in my hands. That's the way the property *should* have been left, and if it wasn't, I can only suspect *undue influence.* Yes—and I repeat it—*undue influence.*"

Timothy glared at his nephew.

"A preposterous will," he said. "Preposterous!"

He leant back, placed a hand to his heart, and groaned:

"This is very bad for me. If I could have—a little brandy."

Miss Gilchrist hurried to get it and returned with the restorative in a small glass.

"Here you are, Mr Abernethie. Please—please don't excite yourself. Are you sure you oughtn't to go up to bed?"

"Don't be a fool." Timothy swallowed the brandy. "Go to bed? I intend to protect my interests."

"Really, George, I'm surprised at you," said, Maude. "What your uncle says is perfectly true. His wishes come first. If he wants the Spode dessert service he shall have it!"

"It's quite hideous anyway," said Susan.

"Hold your tongue, Susan," said Timothy.

The thin young man who sat beside Susan raised his head. In a voice that was a little shriller than his ordinary tones, he said:

"Don't speak like that to my wife!"

He half rose from his seat.

Susan said quickly: "It's all right, Greg. I don't mind."

"But *I* do."

Helen said: "I think it would be graceful on your part, George, to let your uncle have the dessert service."

Timothy spluttered indignantly: "There's no 'letting' about it!"

But George, with a slight bow to Helen said, "Your wish is law, Aunt Helen. I abandon my claim."

"You didn't really want it, anyway, did you?" said Helen.

He cast a sharp glance at her, then grinned:

"The trouble with you, Aunt Helen, is that you're too sharp by half! You see more than you're meant to see. Don't worry, Uncle Timothy, the Spode is yours. Just my idea of fun."

"Fun, indeed." Maude Abernethie was indignant. "Your uncle might have had a heart attack!"

"Don't you believe it," said George cheerfully. "Uncle Timothy will probably outlive us all. He's what is known as a creaking gate."

Timothy leaned forward balefully.

"I don't wonder," he said, "that Richard was disappointed in *you*."

"What's that?" The good humour went out of George's face.

"You came up here after Mortimer died, expecting to step into his shoes—expecting that Richard would make you his heir, didn't you? But my poor brother soon took *your* measure. He knew where the money would go if you had control of it. I'm surprised that he even left you a part of his fortune. He knew where it would go. Horses, Gambling, Monte Carlo, foreign Casinos. Perhaps worse. He suspected you of not being straight, didn't he?"

George, a white dint appearing each side of his nose, said quietly:

"Hadn't you better be careful of what you are saying?"

"I wasn't well enough to come here for the funeral," said Timothy slowly, "but Maude told me what *Cora said*. Cora always was a fool—but there *may* have been something in it! And if so, I know who *I'd* suspect—"

"Timothy!" Maude stood up, solid, calm, a tower of forcefulness. "You have had a very trying evening. You must consider your health. I can't have you getting ill again. Come up with me. You must take a sedative and go straight to bed. Timothy and I, Helen, will take the Spode dessert service and the Boule Cabinet as mementos of Richard. There is no objection to that, I hope?"

Her glance swept round the company. Nobody spoke, and she marched out of the room supporting Timothy with a hand under his elbow, waving aside Miss Gilchrist who was hovering half heartedly by the door.

George broke the silence after they had departed.

*"Femme formidable!"* he said. "That describes Aunt Maude exactly. I should hate ever to impede her triumphal progress."

Miss Gilchrist sat down again rather uncomfortably and murmured:

"Mrs Abernethie is always so kind."

The remark fell rather flat.

Michael Shane laughed suddenly and said: "You know, I'm enjoying all this! 'The Voysey Inheritance' to the life. By the way, Rosamund and I want that malachite table in the drawing room."

"Oh no," cried Susan. *"I* want that."

"Here we go again," said George, raising his eyes to the ceiling.

"Well, we needn't get angry about it," said Susan. "The reason I want it is for my new Beauty shop. Just a note of colour—and I shall put a great bouquet of wax flowers on it. It would look wonderful. I can find wax flowers easily enough, but a green malachite table isn't so common."

"But, darling," said Rosamund, "that's just why *we* want it. For the new set. As you say, a note of colour—and so *absolutely* period. And either wax flowers or stuffed humming birds. It will be absolutely *right."*

"I see what you mean, Rosamund," said Susan. "But I don't think you've got as good a case as I have. You could easily have a painted malachite table for the stage —it would look just the same. But for my *salon* I've *got* to have the genuine thing."

"Now, ladies," said George. "What about a sporting decision? Why not toss for it? Or cut the cards? All quite in keeping with the period of the table."

Susan smiled pleasantly.

"Rosamund and I will talk about it tomorrow," she said.

She seemed, as usual, quite sure of herself. George looked with some interest from her face to that of Rosamund. Rosamund's face had a vague, rather far away expression.

"Which one will you back, Aunt Helen?" he asked. "An even money chance, I'd say. Susan has determination, but Rosamund is so wonderfully single minded."

"Or perhaps *not* humming birds," said Rosamund.

"One of those big Chinese vases would make a lovely lamp, with a gold shade."

Miss Gilchrist hurried into placating speech.

"This house is full of so many beautiful things," she said. "That green table would look wonderful in your new establishment, I'm sure, Mrs Banks. I've never seen one like it. It must be worth a lot of money."

"It will be deducted from my share of the estate, of course," said Susan.

"I'm so sorry—I didn't mean—" Miss Gilchrist was covered with confusion.

"It may be deducted from *our* share of the estate," Michael pointed out. "With the wax flowers thrown in."

"They look so right on that table," Miss Gilchrist murmured. "Really artistic. Sweetly pretty."

But nobody was paying any attention to Miss Gilchrist's well meant trivialities.

Greg said, speaking again in that high nervous voice:

"Susan *wants* that table."

There was a momentary stir of unease, as though, by his words, Greg had set a different musical key.

Helen said quickly:

"And what do you really want, George? Leaving out the Spode service."

George grinned and the tension relaxed.

"Rather a shame to bait old Timothy," he said. "But he really is quite unbelievable. He's had his own way in everything so long that he's become quite pathological about it."

"You have to humour an invalid, Mr Crossfield," said Miss Gilchrist.

"Ruddy old hypochondriac, that's what he is," said George.

"Of course he is," Susan agreed. "I don't believe there's anything whatever the matter with him, do you, Rosamund?"

"What?"

"Anything the matter with Uncle Timothy."

"No—no, I shouldn't think so." Rosamund was vague. She apologised. "I'm sorry. I was thinking about what lighting would be right for the table."

"You see?" said George. "A woman of one idea. Your

wife's a dangerous woman, Michael. I hope you realise it."

"I realise it," said Michael rather grimly.

George went on with every appearance of enjoyment.

"The Battle of the Table! To be fought tomorrow—politely—but with grim determination. We ought all to take sides. I back Rosamund who looks so sweet and yielding and isn't. Husbands presumably back their own wives. Miss Gilchrist? On Susan's side, obviously."

"Oh really, Mr Crossfield, I wouldn't venture to—"

"Aunt Helen?" George paid no attention to Miss Gilchrist's flutterings. "You have the casting vote. Oh, er—I forgot. M. Pontarlier?"

*"Pardon?"* Hercule Poirot looked blank.

George considered explanations, but decided against it. The poor old boy hadn't understood a word of what was going on. He said: "Just a family joke."

"Yes, yes, I comprehend." Poirot smiled amiably.

"So yours is the casting vote, Aunt Helen. Whose side are you on?"

Helen smiled.

"Perhaps I want it myself, George."

She changed the subject deliberately, turning to her foreign guest.

"I'm afraid this is all very dull for you, M. Pontarlier?"

"Not at all, Madame. I consider myself privileged to be admitted to your family life—" he bowed. "I would like to say—I cannot quite express my meaning—my regret that this house has to pass out of your hands into the hands of strangers. It is, without doubt—a great sorrow."

"No, indeed, we don't regret at all," Susan assured him.

"You are very amiable, Madame. It will be, let me tell you, perfection here for my elderly sufferers of persecution. What a haven! What peace! I beg you to remember that, when the harsh feelings come to you as assuredly they must. I hear that there was also the question of a school coming here—not a regular school, a convent—run by *religieuses*—by 'nuns,' I think you say? You would have preferred that, perhaps?"

"Not at all," said George.

"The Sacred Heart of Mary," continued Poirot. "Fortunately, owing to the kindness of an unknown benefactor we were able to make a slightly higher offer." He addressed Miss Gilchrist directly. "You do not like nuns, I think?"

Miss Gilchrist flushed and looked embarrassed.

"Oh really, Mr Pontarlier, you mustn't—I mean, it's nothing *personal*. But I never do see that it's right to shut yourself up from the world in that way—not necessary, I mean, and really almost selfish, though not teaching ones, of course, or the ones that go about amongst the poor—because I'm sure they're thoroughly unselfish women and do a lot of good."

"I simply can't imagine wanting to be a nun," said Susan.

"It's very becoming," said Rosamund. "You remember —when they revived 'The Miracle' last year. Sonia Wells looked absolutely too glamorous for *words*."

"What beats me," said George, "is why it should be pleasing to the Almighty to dress oneself up in mediaeval dress. For after all, that's all a nun's dress is. Thoroughly cumbersome, unhygienic and impractical."

"And it makes them look so alike, doesn't it?" said Miss Gilchrist. "It's silly, you know, but I got quite a turn when I was at Mrs Abernethie's and a nun came to the door, collecting. I got it into my head she was the same as a nun who came to the door on the day of the inquest on poor Mrs Lansquenet at Lytchett St. Mary. I felt, you know, almost as though she had been following me round!"

"I thought nuns always collected in couples," said George. "Surely a detective story hinged on that point once?"

"There was only one this time," said Miss Gilchrist. "Perhaps they've got to economise," she added vaguely. "And anyway it couldn't have been the same nun, for the other one was collecting for an organ for St.—Barnabas, I think—and this one was for something quite different—something to do with children."

"But they both had the same type of features?" Hercule Poirot asked. He sounded interested. Miss Gilchrist turned to him.

"I suppose that must be it. . . . The upper lip—almost

as though she had a moustache. I think, you know, that *that* is really what alarmed me—being in a rather nervous state at the time, and remembering those stories during the war of nuns who were really men and in the Fifth Column and landed by parachute. Of course it was very foolish of me. I knew that afterwards."

"A nun would be a good disguise," said Susan thoughtfully. "It hides your feet."

"The truth is," said George, "that one very seldom looks properly at anyone. That's why one gets such wildly differing accounts of a person from different witnesses in court. You'd be surprised. A man is often described as tall—short; thin—stout; fair—dark; dressed in a dark— light—suit; and so on. There's usually *one* reliable observer, but one has to make up one's mind who that is."

"Another queer thing," said Susan, "is that you sometimes catch sight of yourself in a mirror unexpectedly and don't know who it is. It just looks vaguely familiar. And you say to yourself, 'That's somebody I know quite well....' and then suddenly realise it's yourself!"

George said: "It would be more difficult still if you could really see yourself—and not a mirror image."

"Why?" asked Rosamund, looking puzzled.

"Because, don't you see, nobody ever sees themselves —*as they appear to other people.* They always see themselves in a *glass*—that is—as a reversed image."

"But does that look any different?"

"Oh yes," said Susan quickly. "It must. Because people's faces aren't the same both sides. Their eyebrows are different, and their mouths go up one side, and their noses aren't really straight. You can see with a pencil—who's got a pencil?"

Somebody produced a pencil, and they experimented, holding a pencil each side of the nose and laughing to see the ridiculous variation in angle.

The atmosphere now had lightened a good deal. Everybody was in a good humour. They were no longer the heirs of Richard Abernethie gathered together for a division of property. They were a cheerful and normal set of people gathered together for a weekend in the country.

Only Helen Abernethie remained silent and abstracted.

With a sigh, Hercule Poirot rose to his feet and bade his hostess a polite good night.

"And perhaps, Madame, I had better say goodbye. My train departs itself at nine o'clock tomorrow morning. That is very early. So I will thank you now for all your kindness and hospitality. The date of possession—that will be arranged with the good Mr Entwhistle. To suit your convenience, of course."

"It can be any time you please, M. Pontarlier. I—I have finished all that I came here to do."

"You will return now to your villa at Cyprus?"

"Yes." A little smile curved Helen Abernethie's lips.

Poirot said:

"You are glad, yes. You have no regrets?"

"At leaving England? Or leaving here, do you mean?"

"I meant—leaving here?"

"No—no. It's no good, is it, to cling on to the past? One must leave that behind one."

"If one can." Blinking his eyes innocently Poirot smiled apologetically round on the group of polite faces that surrounded him.

"Sometimes, is it not, the Past will not be left, will not suffer itself to pass into oblivion? It stands at one's elbow —it says *'I am not done with yet.'*"

Susan gave a rather doubtful laugh. Poirot said:

"But I am serious—yes."

"You mean," said Michael, "that your refugees when they come here will not be able to put their past sufferings completely behind them?"

"I did not mean my refugees."

"He meant us, darling," said Rosamund. "He means Uncle Richard and Aunt Cora and the hatchet, and all that."

She turned to Poirot.

"Didn't you?"

Poirot looked at her with a blank face. Then he said:

"Why do you think that, Madame?"

"Because you're a detective, aren't you? That's why you're here. U.N.A.R.C.O., or whatever you call it, is just nonsense, isn't it?"

## 20

THERE WAS a moment of extraordinary tenseness. Poirot felt it, though he himself did not remove his eyes from Rosamund's lovely placid face.

He said with a little bow, "You have great perspicacity, Madame."

"Not really," said Rosamund. "You were pointed out to me once in a restaurant. I remembered."

"But you have not mentioned it—until now?"

"I thought it would be more fun not to," said Rosamund.

Michael said in an imperfectly controlled voice:

"My—dear girl."

Poirot shifted his gaze then to look at him.

Michael was angry. Angry and something else—apprehensive?

Poirot's eyes went slowly round all the faces. Susan's, angry and watchful; Gregory's, dead and shut in; Miss Gilchrist's, foolish, her mouth wide open; George, wary; Helen, dismayed and nervous. . . .

All those expressions were normal ones under the circumstances. He wished he could have seen their faces a split second earlier, when the words "a detective" fell from Rosamund's lips. For now, inevitably, it could not be quite the same. . . .

He squared his shoulders and bowed to them. His language and his accent became less foreign.

"Yes," he said. "I am a detective."

George Crossfield said, the white dints showing once more each side of his nose:

"Who sent you here?"

"I was commissioned to enquire into the circumstances of Richard Abernethie's death."

"By whom?"

"For the moment, that does not concern you. But it would be an advantage, would it not, if you could be assured *beyond any possible doubt* that Richard Abernethie died a natural death?"

"Of course he died a natural death. Who says anything else?"

"Cora Lansquenet said so. And Cora Lansquenet is dead herself."

A little wave of uneasiness seemed to sigh through the room like an evil breeze.

"She said it here—in this room," said Susan. "But I didn't really think—"

"Didn't you, Susan?" George Crossfield turned his sardonic glance upon her. "Why pretend any more? You won't take M. Pontarlier in?"

"We all thought so really," said Rosamund. "And his name isn't Pontarlier—it's Hercules something."

"Hercule Poirot—at your service."

Poirot bowed.

There were no gasps of astonishment or of apprehension. His name seemed to mean nothing at all to them.

They were less alarmed by it than they had been by the single word *'detective.'*

"May I ask what conclusions you have come to?" asked George.

"He won't tell you, darling," said Rosamund. "Or if he does tell you, what he says won't be true."

Alone of the company she appeared to be amused.

Hercule Poirot looked at her thoughtfully.

ii

Hercule Poirot did not sleep well that night. He was perturbed, and he was not quite sure *why* he was perturbed. Elusive snatches of conversation, various glances, odd movements—all seemed fraught with a tantalising significance in the loneliness of the night. He was on the threshold of sleep, but sleep would not come. Just as he was about to drop off, something flashed into his mind and woke him up again. Paint—Timothy and paint. Oil paint—the smell of oil paint—connected somehow with Mr Entwhistle. Paint and Cora. Cora's paintings—picture postcards . . . Cora was deceitful about her painting. . . . No, back to Mr Entwhistle—something Mr Entwhistle had said—or was it Lanscombe? A nun who came to the house on the day that Richard Abernethie died. A nun with a moustache. A nun at Stansfield Grange—and at Lychett St. Mary. Altogether too many nuns! Rosamund looking glamorous as a nun on the stage. Rosamund —saying that he was a detective—and everyone staring at her when she said it. That was the way they must all have stared at Cora that day when she said "But he was murdered, wasn't he?" What was it Helen Abernethie had felt to be "wrong" on that occasion? Helen Abernethie— leaving the past behind—going to Cyprus . . . Helen dropping the wax flowers with a crash when he had said—*what* was it he had said? He couldn't quite remember. . . .

He slept then, and as he slept he dreamed. . . .

He dreamed of the green malachite table. On it was the glass covered stand of wax flowers—only the whole thing had been painted over with thick crimson oil paint. Paint the colour of blood. He could smell the paint, and Timothy was groaning, was saying "I'm dying—dying . . . this is the end." And Maude, standing by, tall and stern, with a large knife in her hand was echoing him, saying "Yes, it's the end. . . ." The end—a deathbed, with candles and a nun praying. If he could just see the nun's face, he would know. . . .

Hercule Poirot woke up—and he did know!

Yes, it *was* the end. . . .

Though there was still a long way to go.

He sorted out the various bits of the mosaic.

Mr Entwhistle, the smell of paint, Timothy's house and something that must be in it—or might be in it . . . the wax flowers . . . Helen . . . Broken glass . . .

### iii

Helen Abernethie, in her room, took some time in going to bed. She was thinking.

Sitting in front of her dressing table, she stared at herself unseeingly in the glass.

She had been forced into having Hercule Poirot in the house. She had not wanted it. But Mr Entwhistle had made it hard for her to refuse. And now the whole thing had come out into the open. No question any more of letting Richard Abernethie lie quiet in his grave. All started by those few words of Cora's. . . .

That day after the funeral . . . How had they all looked, she wondered? How had they looked to Cora? How had she herself looked?

What was it George had said? About seeing oneself?

There was some quotation, too. *To see ourselves as others see us* . . . As others see us.

The eyes that were staring into the glass unseeingly suddenly focussed. She was seeing herself—but not really herself—not herself as others saw her—not as Cora had seen her that day.

Her right—no, her left eyebrow was arched a little higher than the right. The mouth? No, the curve of the mouth was symmetrical. If she met herself she would surely not see much difference from this mirror image. Not like Cora.

Cora—the picture came quite clearly . . . Cora, on the day of the funeral, her head tilted sideways—asking her question—looking at Helen . . .

Suddenly Helen raised her hands to her face. She said to herself. *"It doesn't make sense . . . It can't make sense . . ."*

### iv

Miss Entwhistle was aroused from a delightful dream, in which she was playing Piquet with Queen Mary, by the ringing of the telephone.

She tried to ignore it—but it persisted. Sleepily she raised her head from the pillow and looked at the watch beside her bed. Five minutes to seven—who on earth could be ringing up at that hour? It must be a wrong number.

The irritating ding-ding continued. Miss Entwhistle

sighed, snatched up a dressing gown and marched into the sitting room.

"This is Kensington 675498," she said with asperity as she picked up the receiver.

"This is Mrs Abernethie speaking. Mrs *Leo* Aberneth-ie. Can I speak to Mr Entwhistle?"

"Oh, good morning, Mrs Abernethie." The 'good morning' was not cordial. "This is Miss Entwhistle. My brother is still asleep I'm afraid. I was asleep myself."

"I'm so sorry," Helen was forced to the apology. "But it's very important that I should speak to your brother at once."

"Wouldn't it do later?"

"I'm afraid not."

"Oh, very well then."

Miss Entwhistle was tart.

She tapped at her brother's door and went in.

"Those Abernethies again!" she said bitterly.

"Eh! The Abernethies?"

"Mrs Leo Abernethie. Ringing up before seven in the morning! Really!"

"Mrs Leo is it? Dear me. How remarkable. Where is my dressing gown? Ah, thank you."

Presently he was saying:

"Entwhistle speaking. Is that you, Helen?"

"Yes. I'm terribly sorry to get you out of bed like this. But you did tell me once to ring you up at once if I remembered what it was that struck me as having been wrong somehow on the day of the funeral when Cora electrified us all by suggesting that Richard had been murdered."

"Ah! You *have* remembered?"

Helen said in a puzzled voice:

"Yes, but it doesn't make sense."

"You must allow me to be the judge of that. Was it something you noticed about one of the people?"

"Yes."

"Tell me."

"It seems absurd." Helen's voice sounded apologetic. "But I'm quite sure of it. It came to me when I was look-ing at myself in the glass last night. Oh . . ."

The little startled half cry was succeeded by a sound

that came oddly through the wires—a dull heavy sound that Mr Entwhistle couldn't place at all—

He said urgently:

"Hullo—hullo—are you there? Helen, are you there? . . . Helen . . ."

## 21

IT WAS NOT until an hour later that Mr Entwhistle after a great deal of conversation with supervisors and others found himself at last speaking to Hercule Poirot.

"Thank heaven!" said Mr Entwhistle with pardonable exasperation. "The Exchange seems to have had the greatest difficulty in getting the number."

"That is not surprising. The receiver was off the hook."

There was a grim quality in Poirot's voice which carried through to the listener.

Mr Entwhistle said sharply:

"Has something happened?"

"Yes. Mrs Leo Abernethie was found by the housemaid about twenty minutes ago lying by the telephone extension in the study. She was unconscious. A serious concussion."

"Do you mean she was struck on the head?"

"I think so. It is *just* possible that she fell and struck her head on a marble doorstop, but me I do not think so, and the doctor, he does not think so either."

"She was telephoning to me at the time. I wondered when we were cut off so suddenly."

"So it was to you she was telephoning. What did she say?"

"She mentioned to me some time ago that on the occasion when Cora Lansquenet suggested her brother had been murdered, she herself had a feeling of something being wrong—odd—she did not quite know how to put it —unfortunately she could not remember *why* she had that impression."

"And suddenly, she did remember?"

"Yes."

"And rang you up to tell you?"

"Yes."

*"Eh bien?"*

"There's no *eh bien* about it," said Mr Entwhistle testily. "She started to tell me, but was interrupted."

"How much had she said?"

"Nothing pertinent."

"You will excuse me, *mon ami,* but *I* am the judge of that, not you. What exactly did she say?"

"She reminded me that I had asked her to let me know at once if she remembered what it was that had struck her as peculiar. She said she had remembered—but that it 'didn't make sense.'"

"I asked her if it was something about one of the people who were there that day, and she said, yes, it was. She said it had come to her when she was looking in the glass—"

"Yes?"

"That was all."

"She gave no hint as to—which of the people concerned it was?"

"I should hardly fail to tell you if she had told me *that,*" said Mr Entwhistle acidly.

"I apologise, *mon ami.* Of course you would have told me."

Mr Entwhistle said:

"We shall have to wait until she recovers consciousness before we know."

Poirot said gravely:

"That may not be for a very long time. Perhaps—never."

"Is it as bad as that?" Mr Entwhistle's voice shook a little.

"Yes, it is as bad as that."

"But—that's terrible, Poirot."

"Yes, it is terrible. And it is why we cannot afford to wait! For it shows that we have to deal with someone who is either completely ruthless or so frightened that it comes to the same thing."

"But look here, Poirot, what about Helen? I feel worried. Are you sure she will be safe at Enderby?"

"No, she would not be safe. So she is not at Enderby.

Already the ambulance has come and is taking her to a nursing home where she will have special nurses and where *no one,* family or otherwise, will be allowed in to see her."

Mr Entwhistle sighed.

"You relieve my mind. She might have been in danger."

"She assuredly would have been in danger!"

Mr Entwhistle's voice sounded deeply moved.

"I have a great regard for Helen Abernethie. I always have had. A woman of very exceptional character. She may have had certain—what shall I say?—reticences in her life?"

"Ah, there were reticences?"

"I have always had an idea that such was the case."

"Hence the villa in Cyprus. Yes, that explains a good deal. . . ."

"I don't want you to begin thinking—"

"You cannot stop me thinking. But now, there is a little commission that I have for you. One moment."

There was a pause, then Poirot's voice spoke again.

"I had to make sure that nobody was listening. All is well. Now here is what I want you to do for me. You must prepare to make a journey."

"A journey?" Mr Entwhistle sounded faintly dismayed. "Oh, I see—you want me to come down to Enderby?"

"Not at all. *I* am in charge here. No, you will not have to travel so far. Your journey will not take you very far from London. You will travel to Bury St. Edmunds— (*Ma foi!* what names your English towns have!) and there you will hire a car and drive to Forsdyke House. It is a Mental Home. Ask for Dr Penrith and inquire of him particulars about a patient who was recently discharged."

"What patient? Anyway, surely—"

Poirot broke in:

"The name of the patient is Gregory Banks. Find out for what form of insanity he was being treated."

"Do you mean that Gregory Banks is insane?"

"Sh. Be careful what you say. And now—I have not yet breakfasted and you, too, I suspect have not breakfasted?"

"Not yet. I was too anxious—"

"Quite so. Then, I pray you, eat your breakfast, repose yourself. There is a good train to Bury St. Edmunds at twelve o'clock. If I have any more news I will telephone you before you start."

"Be careful of *yourself,* Poirot," said Mr Entwhistle with some concern.

"Ah that, yes! Me, I do not want to be hit on the head with a marble doorstop. You may be assured that I will take every precaution. And now—for the moment—goodbye."

Poirot heard the sound of the receiver being replaced at the other end, then he heard a very faint second click—and smiled to himself. Somebody had replaced the receiver on the telephone in the hall.

He went out there. There was no one about. He tiptoed to the cupboard at the back of the stairs and looked inside. At that moment Lanscombe came through the service door carrying a tray with toast and a silver coffee pot. He looked slightly surprised to see Poirot emerge from the cupboard.

"Breakfast is ready in the dining room, sir," he said.

Poirot surveyed him thoughtfully.

The old butler looked white and shaken.

"Courage," said Poirot, clapping him on the shoulder. "All will yet be well. Would it be too much trouble to serve me a cup of coffee in my bedroom?"

"Certainly, sir. I will send Janet up with it, sir."

Lanscombe looked disapprovingly at Hercule Poirot's back as the latter climbed the stairs. Poirot was attired in an exotic silk dressing gown with a pattern of triangles and squares.

"Foreigners!" thought Lanscombe bitterly. "Foreigners in the house! And Mrs Leo with concussion! I don't know what we're coming to. Nothing's the same since Mr Richard died."

Hercule Poirot was dressed by the time he received his coffee from Janet. His murmurs of sympathy were well received, since he stressed the shock her discovery must have given her.

"Yes, indeed, sir, what I felt when I opened the door of the study and came in with the Hoover and saw Mrs Leo lying there I never shall forget. There she lay—and I made sure she wasn't dead. She must have been taken faint as she stood at the phone—and fancy her being up at that time in the morning! I've never known her to do such a thing before."

"Fancy, indeed!" He added casually: "No one else was up, I suppose?"

"As it happens, sir, Mrs Timothy was up and about. She's a very early riser always—often goes for a walk before breakfast."

"She is of the generation that rises early," said Poirot nodding his head. "The younger ones, now—*they* do not get up so early?"

"No, indeed, sir, all fast asleep when I brought them their tea—and very late I was, too, what with the shock and getting the doctor to come and having to have a cup first to steady myself."

She went off and Poirot reflected on what she had said.

Maude Abernethie had been up and about, and the younger generation had been in bed—but that, Poirot reflected, meant nothing at all. Anyone could have heard Helen's door open and close, and have followed her down to listen—and would afterwards have made a point of being fast asleep in bed.

"But if I am right," thought Poirot. "And after all, it is natural to me to be right—it is a habit I have!—then there is no need to go into who was here and who was there. First, I must seek a proof where I have deduced the proof may be. And then—I make my little speech. And I sit back and see what happens . . ."

As soon as Janet had left the room, Poirot drained his coffee cup, put on his overcoat and his hat, left his room, ran nimbly down the back stairs and left the house by the side door. He walked briskly the quarter mile to the post office where he demanded a trunk call. Presently he was once more speaking to Mr Entwhistle.

"Yes, it is I yet again! Pay no attention to the commission with which I entrusted you. *C'était une blague!* Someone was listening. Now, *mon vieux,* to the real commission. You must, as I said, take a train. But not to Bury St. Edmunds. I want you to proceed to the house of Mr Timothy Abernethie."

"But Timothy and Maude are at Enderby."

"Exactly. There is no one in the house but a woman by the name of Jones who has been persuaded by the offer of considerable *largesse* to guard the house whilst they are absent. What I want you to do is to take something out of that house!"

"My dear Poirot! I really can't stoop to burglary!"

"It will not seem like burglary. You will say to the excellent Mrs Jones who knows you, that you have been asked by Mr or Mrs Abernethie to fetch this particular object and take it to London. She will not suspect anything amiss."

"No, no, probably not. But I don't like it." Mr Entwhistle sounded most reluctant. "Why can't you go and get whatever it is yourself."

"Because, my friend, I should be a stranger of foreign appearance and as such a suspicious character, and Mrs Jones would at once raise the difficulties! With you, she will not."

"No, no—I see that. But what on earth are Timothy and Maude going to think when they hear about it? I have known them for forty-odd years."

"And you knew Richard Abernethie for that time also! And you knew Cora Lansquenet when she was a little girl!"

In a martyred voice Mr Entwhistle asked:

"You're sure this is really *necessary,* Poirot?"

"The old question they asked in the war time on the posters. *Is your journey really necessary?* I say to you, it *is* necessary. It is vital!"

"And what is this object I've got to get hold of?"

Poirot told him.

"But really, Poirot, I don't see—"

"It is not necessary for *you* to see. *I* am doing the seeing."

"And what do you want me to do with the damned thing?"

"You will take it to London, to an address in Elm Park Gardens. If you have a pencil, note it down."

Having done so, Mr Entwhistle said, still in his martyred voice:

"I hope you know what you are doing, Poirot?"

He sounded very doubtful—but Poirot's reply was not doubtful at all.

"Of course I know what I am doing. We are nearing the end."

Mr Entwhistle sighed.

"If we could only guess what Helen was going to tell me."

"No need to guess. I *know*."

"You know? But my dear Poirot—"

"Explanations must wait. But let me assure you of this. *I know what Helen Abernethie saw when she looked in her mirror.*"

ii

Breakfast had been an uneasy meal. Neither Rosamund nor Timothy had appeared, but the others were there and had talked in rather subdued tones, and eaten a little less than they normally would have done.

George was the first one to recover his spirits. His temperament was mercurial and optimistic.

"I expect Aunt Helen will be all right," he said. "Doctors always like to pull a long face. After all, what's concussion? Often clears up completely in a couple of days."

"A woman I knew had concussion during the war," said Miss Gilchrist conversationally. "A brick or something hit her as she was walking down Tottenham Court Road—it was during fly bomb time—and she never felt *anything* at all. Just went on with what she was doing—and collapsed in a train to Liverpool twelve hours later. And would you believe it, she had no recollection at all of going to the station and catching the train or *anything*. She just couldn't understand it when she woke up in hospital. She was there for nearly three weeks."

"What I can't make out," said Susan, "is what Helen was doing telephoning at that unearthly hour, and who she was telephoning to?"

"Felt ill," said Maude with decision. "Probably woke up feeling queer and came down to ring up the doctor. Then had a giddy fit and fell. That's the only thing that makes sense."

"Bad luck hitting her head on that doorstop," said Mi-

chael. "If she'd just pitched over onto that thick pile car-
pet she'd have been all right."

The door opened and Rosamund came in, frowning.

"I can't find those wax flowers," she said. "I mean the
ones that were standing on the malachite table the day of
Uncle Richard's funeral." She looked accusingly at Susan.
"*You* haven't taken them?"

"Of course I haven't! Really, Rosamund, you're not
*still* thinking about malachite tables with poor old Helen
carted off to hospital with concussion?"

"I don't see why I shouldn't think about them. If
you've got concussion you don't know what's happening
and it doesn't matter to you. We can't do anything for
Aunt Helen, and Michael and I have got to get back to
London by tomorrow lunch-time because we're seeing
Jackie Lygo about opening dates for 'The Baronet's Progress.' So I'd like to fix up definitely about the table. But
I'd like to have a look at those wax flowers again. There's
a kind of Chinese vase on the table now—nice—but not
nearly so period. I do wonder where they are—perhaps
Lanscombe knows."

Lanscombe had just looked in to see if they had finished breakfast.

"We're all through, Lanscombe," said George getting
up. "What's happened to our foreign friend?"

"He is having his coffee and toast served upstairs."

*"Petit déjeuner* for U.N.A.R.C.O."

"Lanscombe, do you know where those wax flowers
are that used to be on that green table in the drawing
room?" asked Rosamund.

"I understand Mrs Leo had an accident with them,
ma'am. She was going to have a new glass shade made,
but I don't think she has seen about it yet."

"Then where is the thing?"

"It would probably be in the cupboard behind the
staircase, m'am. That is where things are usually placed
when awaiting repair. Shall I ascertain for you?"

"I'll go and look myself. Come with me, Michael sweet-
ie. It's dark there, and I'm not going in any dark corners
by myself after what happened to Aunt Helen."

Everybody showed a sharp reaction. Maude demanded
in her deep voice:

"What *do* you mean, Rosamund?"

"Well, she was coshed by someone, wasn't she?"

Gregory Banks said sharply:

"She was taken suddenly faint and fell."

Rosamund laughed.

"Did she tell you so? Don't be silly, Greg, of course she was coshed."

George said sharply:

"You shouldn't say things like that, Rosamund."

"Nonsense," said Rosamund. "She *must* have been. I mean, it all adds up. A detective in the house looking for clues, and Uncle Richard poisoned, and Aunt Cora killed with a hatchet, and Miss Gilchrist given poisoned wedding cake, and now Aunt Helen struck down with a blunt instrument. You'll see, it will go on like that. One after another of us will be killed and the one that's left will be It—the murderer, I mean. But it's not going to be *me*— who's killed, I mean."

"And why should anyone want to kill you, beautiful Rosamund?" asked George lightly.

Rosamund opened her eyes very wide.

"Oh," she said. "Because I know too much, of course."

"What do you know?" Maude Abernethie and Gregory Banks spoke almost in unison.

Rosamund gave her vacant and angelic smile.

"Wouldn't you all like to know?" she said agreeably. "Come on, Michael."

# 22

At eleven o'clock, Hercule Poirot called an informal meeting in the library. Everyone was there and Poirot looked thoughtfully round the semi-circle of faces.

"Last night," he said, "Mrs Shane announced to you that I was a private detective. For myself, I hoped to retain my—*camouflage,* shall we say?—a little longer. But no matter! Today—or at most the day after—I would have told you the truth. Please listen carefully now to what I have to say.

"I am in my own line a celebrated person—I may say a *most* celebrated person. My gifts, in fact, are unequalled!"

George Crossfield grinned and said:

"That's the stuff, M. Pont—no, it's M. Poirot, isn't it? Funny, isn't it, that I've never even heard of you?"

"It is not funny," said Poirot severely. "It is lamentable! Alas, there is no proper education nowadays. Apparently one learns nothing but economics—and how to set Intelligence Tests! But to continue. I have been a friend for many years of Mr Entwhistle's—"

"So *he's* the nigger in the wood pile!"

"If you like to put it that way, Mr Crossfield. Mr Entwhistle was greatly upset by the death of his old friend, Mr Richard Abernethie. He was particularly perturbed by some words spoken on the day of the funeral by Mr Abernethie's sister, Mrs Lansquenet. Words spoken in this very room."

"Very silly—and just like Cora," said Maude. "Mr Entwhistle should have had more sense than to pay attention to them!"

Poirot went on:

"Mr Entwhistle was even more perturbed after the—the coincidence, shall I say?—of Mrs Lansquenet's death. He wanted one thing only—to be assured that that death *was* a coincidence. In other words he wanted to feel assured that Richard Abernethie had died a natural death. To that end he commissioned me to make the necessary investigations."

There was a pause.

"I have made them. . . ."

Again there was a pause. No one spoke.

Poirot threw back his head.

*"Eh bien,* you will all be delighted to hear that as a result of my investigations—*there is absolutely no reason to believe that Mr Abernethie died anything but a natural death.* There is no reason *at all* to believe that he was murdered!" He smiled. He threw out his hands in a triumphant gesture.

"That is good news, is it not?"

It hardly seemed to be, the way they took it. They stared at him and in all but the eyes of one person there still seemed to be doubt and suspicion.

The exception was Timothy Abernethie who was nodding his head in violent agreement.

"Of course Richard wasn't murdered," he said angrily. "Never could understand why anybody ever even thought of such a thing for a moment! Just Cora up to her tricks, that was all. Wanting to give you all a scare. Her idea of being funny. Truth is that although she was my own sister, she was always a bit mental, poor girl. Well, Mr whatever your name is, I'm glad you've had the sense to come to the right conclusion, though if you ask me, I call it damned cheek of Entwhistle to go commissioning you to come prying and poking about. And if he thinks he's going to charge the estate with your fee, I can tell you he won't get away with it! Damned cheek, and most uncalled for! Who's Entwhistle to set himself up? If the family's satisfied—"

"But the family wasn't, Uncle Timothy," said Rosamund.

"Hey—what's that?"

Timothy peered at her under beetling brows of displeasure.

"We weren't satisfied. And what about Aunt Helen this morning?"

Maude said sharply:

"Helen's just the age when you're liable to get a stroke. That's all there is to that."

"I see," said Rosamund. "Another coincidence, you think?"

She looked at Poirot.

"Aren't there rather too many coincidences?"

"Coincidences," said Hercule Poirot, "do happen."

"Nonsense," said Maude. "Helen felt ill, came down and rang up the doctor, and then—"

"But she didn't ring up the doctor," said Rosamund. "I asked him—"

Susan said sharply:

"Who did she ring up?"

"I don't know," said Rosamund, a shade of vexation passing over her face. "But I daresay I can find out," she added hopefully.

ii

Hercule Poirot was sitting in the Victorian summer-house. He drew his large watch from his pocket and laid it on the table in front of him.

He had announced that he was leaving by the twelve o'clock train. There was still half an hour to go. Half an hour for someone to make up their minds and come to him. Perhaps more than one person . . .

The summerhouse was clearly visible from most of the windows of the house. Surely, soon, someone would come?

If not, his knowledge of human nature was deficient, and his main premises incorrect.

He waited—and above his head a spider in its web waited for a fly.

It was Miss Gilchrist who came first. She was flustered and upset and rather incoherent.

"Oh, Mr Pontarlier—I can't remember your other name," she said. "I had to come and speak to you although I *don't* like doing it—but really I feel I *ought* to. I mean, after what happened to poor Mrs Leo this morning —and I think myself Mrs Shane was *quite right*—and *not* coincidence, and certainly not a *stroke*—as Mrs Timothy suggested, because my own father had a stroke and it was quite a different appearance, and anyway the doctor *said* concussion quite clearly!"

She paused, took breath and looked at Poirot with appealing eyes.

"Yes," said Poirot gently and encouragingly. "You want to tell me something?"

"As I say, I don't like doing it—because she's been so kind. She found me the position with Mrs Timothy and everything. She's been really *very* kind. That's why I feel so ungrateful. And even gave me Mrs Lansquenet's mus-quash jacket which is really *most* handsome and fits beautifully because it never matters if fur is a little on the large side. And when I wanted to return her the amethyst brooch she wouldn't *hear* of it—"

"You are referring," said Poirot gently, "to Mrs Banks?"

"Yes, you see—" Miss Gilchrist looked down, twisting her fingers unhappily. She looked up and said with a sudden gulp:

"You see, I *listened!*"

"You mean you happened to overhear a conversation—"

"No." Miss Gilchrist shook her head with an air of heroic determination. "I'd rather speak the truth. And it's not so bad telling you because you're not English."

Hercule Poirot understood her without taking offense.

"You mean that to a foreigner it is natural that people should listen at doors and open letters, or read letters that are left about?"

"Oh, I'd never open anybody else's letters," said Miss Gilchrist in a shocked tone. "Not *that.* But I *did* listen that day—the day that Mr Richard Abernethie came down to see his sister. I was curious, you know, about his turning up suddenly after all those years. And I did wonder why—and—and—you see when you haven't much life of your own or very many friends, you do tend to get interested—when you're living *with* anybody, I mean."

"Most natural," said Poirot.

"Yes, I do think it was natural. . . . Though not, of course, at all *right.* But I did it! And I heard what he said!"

"You heard what Mr Abernethie said to Mrs Lansquenet?"

"Yes. He said something like—'It's no good talking to Timothy. He pooh-poohs everything. Simply won't listen. But I thought I'd like to get it off my chest to you, Cora. We three are the only ones left. And though you've always liked to play the simpleton you've got a lot of common sense. So what would *you* do about it, if you were me?'

"I couldn't quite hear what Mrs Lansquenet said, but I caught the word *police*—and then Mr Abernethie burst out quite loud, and said, 'I can't do that. Not when it's a question of *my own niece.*' And then I had to run in the kitchen for something boiling over and when I got back Mr Abernethie was saying, 'Even if I die an unnatural death I don't want the police called in, if it can possibly be avoided. You understand that, don't you, my dear girl? But don't worry. Now that I *know,* I shall take all possible precautions.' And he went on, saying he'd made a new will, and that she, Cora, would be quite all right. And then he said about her having been happy with her husband and how perhaps he'd made a mistake over that in the past."

Miss Gilchrist stopped.

Poirot said: "I see—I see . . ."

"But I never wanted to say—to tell. I didn't think Mrs Lansquenet would have wanted me to. . . . But now—after Mrs Leo being attacked this morning—and then you saying so calmly it was coincidence. But, oh, M. Pontarlier, it *wasn't* coincidence!"

Poirot smiled. He said:

"No, it wasn't coincidence. . . . Thank you, Miss Gilchrist, for coming to me. It was very necessary that you should."

### iii

He had a little difficulty in getting rid of Miss Gilchrist, and it was urgent that he should, for he hoped for further confidences.

His instinct was right. Miss Gilchrist had hardly gone before Gregory Banks, striding across the lawn, came impetuously into the summerhouse. His face was pale and there were beads of perspiration on his forehead. His eyes were curiously excited.

"At last!" he said. "I thought that stupid woman would never go. You're all wrong in what you said this morning. You're wrong about everything. Richard Abernethie *was* killed. *I* killed him."

Hercule Poirot let his eyes move up and down over the excited young man. He showed no surprise.

"So you killed him, did you? How?"

Gregory Banks smiled.

"It wasn't difficult for *me*. You can surely realise that. There were fifteen or twenty different drugs I could lay my hands on that would do it. The method of administration took rather more thinking out, but I hit on a very ingenious idea in the end. The beauty of it was that *I* didn't need to be anywhere near at the time."

"Clever," said Poirot.

"Yes." Gregory Banks cast his eyes down modestly. He seemed pleased. "Yes—I *do* think it was ingenious."

Poirot asked with interest:

"Why did you kill him? For the money that would come to your wife?"

"No. No, of course not." Greg was suddenly excitedly indignant. "I'm not a money grubber. I didn't marry Susan for her *money!*"

"Didn't you, Mr Banks?"

"That's what *he* thought," Greg said with sudden venom. "Richard Abernethie! He liked Susan, he admired her, he was proud of her as an example of Abernethie blood! But he thought she'd married beneath her—he thought *I* was no good—he despised me! I daresay I hadn't the right accent—I didn't wear my clothes the right way. He was a snob—a filthy snob!"

"I don't think so," said Poirot mildly. "From all I have heard, Richard Abernethie was no snob."

"He was. He was." The young man spoke with something approaching hysteria. "He thought nothing of me. He sneered at me—always very polite but underneath I could *see* that he didn't like me!"

"Possibly."

"People can't treat me like that and get away with it! They've tried it before! A woman who used to come and have her medicines made up. She was rude to me. Do you know what I did?"

"Yes," said Poirot.

Gregory looked startled.

"So you know that?"

"Yes."

"She nearly died." He spoke in a satisfied manner. "That shows you I'm not the sort of person to be trifled with! Richard Abernethie despised me—and what happened to him? He died."

"A most successful murder," said Poirot with grave congratulation.

He added: "But why come and give yourself away—to me?"

"Because you said you were through with it all! You said he *hadn't* been murdered. I had to show you that you're not as clever as you think you are—and besides—besides—"

"Yes," said Poirot. "And besides?"

Greg collapsed suddenly onto the bench. His face changed. It took on a sudden ecstatic quality.

"It was wrong—wicked. . . . I must be punished. . . . I must go back there—to the place of punishment . . . to atone . . . Yes, to *atone!* Repentance! Retribution!"

His face was alight now with a kind of glowing ecstasy. Poirot studied him for a moment or two curiously.

Then he asked:

"How badly do you want to get away from your wife?"

Gregory's face changed.

"Susan? Susan is wonderful—wonderful!"

"Yes. Susan is wonderful. That is a grave burden. Susan loves you devotedly. That is a burden, too?"

Gregory sat looking in front of him. Then he said, rather in the manner of a sulky child:

"Why couldn't she let me alone?"

He sprang up.

"She's coming now—across the lawn. I'll go now. But you'll tell her what I told you? Tell her I've gone to the police station. To confess."

### iv

Susan came in breathlessly.

"Where's Greg? He was here! I saw him."

"Yes." Poirot paused a moment—before saying: "He came to tell me that it was he who poisoned Richard Abernethie . . ."

"What absolute *nonsense!* You didn't believe him, I hope?"

"Why should I not believe him?"

"He wasn't even near this place when Uncle Richard died!"

"Perhaps not. Where was he when Cora Lansquenet died?"

'   "In London. We both were."

Hercule Poirot shook his head.

"No, no, that will not do. You, for instance, took out your car that day and were away all afternoon. I think I know where you went. You went to Lytchett St. Mary."

"I did no such thing!"

Poirot smiled.

"When I met you here, Madame, it was not, as I told you, the first time I had seen you. After the inquest on Mrs. Lansquenet you were in the garage of the King's Arms. You talk there to a mechanic and close by you is a car containing an elderly foreign gentleman. You did not notice him, but he noticed you."

"I don't see what you mean. That was the day of the inquest."

"Ah, but remember what that mechanic said to you! He asked you if you were a relative of the victim, and you said you were her niece."

"He was just being a ghoul. They're all ghouls."

"And his next words were, 'Ah, I wondered where I'd seen you before.' Where did he see you before, Madame? It must have been in Lytchett St. Mary, since in his mind his seeing you before was accounted for by your being Mrs Lansquenet's niece. Had he seen you near her cottage? And when? It was a matter, was it not, that demands inquiry. And the result of the inquiry is, that you were there—in Lytchett St. Mary—on the afternoon Cora Lansquenet died. You parked your car in the same quarry where you left it the morning of the inquest. The car was seen and the number was noted. By this time Inspector Morton knows whose car it was."

Susan stared at him. Her breath came rather fast, but she showed no signs of discomposure.

"You're talking nonsense, M. Poirot. And you're making me forget what I came here to say—I wanted to try and find you alone—"

"To confess to me that it was you and not your husband who committed the murder?"

"No, of course not. What kind of fool do you think I am? And I've already told you that Gregory never left London that day."

"A fact which you cannot possibly know since you

were away yourself. Why did you go down to Lytchett St. Mary, Mrs Banks?"

Susan drew a deep breath.

"All right, if you must have it! What Cora said at the funeral worried me. I kept on thinking about it. Finally I decided to run down in the car and see her, and ask her what had put the idea into her head. Greg thought it a silly idea, so I didn't even tell him where I was going. I got there about three o'clock, knocked and rang, but there was no answer, so I thought she must be out or gone away. That's all there is to it. I didn't go round to the back of the cottage. If I had, I might have seen the broken window. I just went back to London without the faintest idea there was anything wrong."

Poirot's face was non-committal. He said:

"Why does your husband accuse himself of the crime?"

"Because he's—" a word trembled on Susan's tongue and was rejected. Poirot seized on it.

"You were going to say 'because he is batty' speaking in jest—but the jest was too near the truth, was it not?"

"Greg's all right. He is. He *is*."

"I know something of his history," said Poirot. "He was for some months in Forsdyke House Mental Home before you met him."

"He was never certified. He was a voluntary patient."

"That is true. He is not, I agree, to be classed as insane. But he is, very definitely, unbalanced. He has a punishment complex—has had it, I suspect, since infancy."

Susan spoke quickly and eagerly:

"You don't understand, M. Poirot. Greg has never had a *chance*. That's why I wanted Uncle Richard's money so badly. Uncle Richard was so matter of fact. He couldn't understand. I knew Greg had got to set up for himself. He had got to feel he was *someone*—not just a chemist's assistant, being pushed around. Everything will be different now. He will have his own laboratory. He can work out his own formulas."

"Yes, yes—you will give him the earth—because you love him. Love him too much for safety or for happiness. But you cannot give to people what they are incapable of receiving. At the end of it all, he will still be something that he does not want to be. . . ."

"What's that?"

*"Susan's husband."*

"How cruel you are! And what nonsense you talk!"

"Where Gregory Banks is concerned you are unscrupulous. You wanted your uncle's money—not for yourself —but for your husband. *How badly did you want it?"*

Angrily, Susan turned and dashed away.

v

"I thought," said Michael Shane lightly, "that I'd just come along and say goodbye."

He smiled, and his smile had a singularly intoxicating quality.

Poirot was aware of the man's vital charm.

He studied Michael Shane for some moments in silence. He felt as though he knew this man least well of all the house party, for Michael Shane only showed the side of himself that he wanted to show.

"Your wife," said Poirot conversationally, "is a very unusual woman."

Michael raised his eyebrows.

"Do you think so? She's lovely, I agree. But not, or so I've found, conspicuous for brains."

"She will never try to be too clever," Poirot agreed. "But she knows what she wants." He sighed. "So few people do."

"Ah!" Michael's smile broke out again. "Thinking of the malachite table?"

"Perhaps," Poirot paused and added: *"And of what was on it."*

"The wax flowers, you mean?"

"The wax flowers."

Michael frowned.

"I don't always quite understand you, M. Poirot. However," the smile was switched on again. "I'm more thankful than I can say that we're all out of the wood. It's unpleasant, to say the least of it, to go around with the suspicion that somehow or other one of us murdered poor old Uncle Richard."

"That is how he seemed to you when you met him?" Poirot inquired. "Poor old Uncle Richard?"

"Of course he was very well preserved and all that—"

"And in full possession of his faculties—"

"Oh yes."

"And in fact, quite *shrewd?*"

"I daresay."

"A shrewd judge of character."

The smile remained unaltered.

"You can't expect me to agree with *that,* M. Poirot. He didn't approve of *me.*"

"He thought you, perhaps, the unfaithful type?" Poirot suggested.

Michael laughed.

"What an old-fashioned idea!"

"But it is true, isn't it?"

"Now I wonder what you mean by *that?*"

Poirot placed the tips of his fingers together.

"There have been inquiries made, you know," he murmured.

"By you?"

"Not only by me."

Michael Shane gave him a quick searching glance. His reactions, Poirot noted, were quick. Michael Shane was no fool.

"You mean—the police are interested?"

"They have never been quite satisfied, you know, to regard the murder of Cora Lansquenet as a casual crime."

"And they've been making inquiries about me?"

Poirot said primly:

"They are interested in the movements of Mrs Lansquenet's relations on the day that she was killed."

"That's extremely awkward." Michael spoke with a charming, confidential, rueful air.

"Is it, Mr Shane?"

"More so than you can imagine! I told Rosamund, you see, that I was lunching with a certain Oscar Lewis on that day."

"When, in actual fact, you were not?"

"No. Actually I motored down to see a woman called Sorrel Dainton—quite a well-known actress. I was with her in her last show. Rather awkward, you see—for though it's quite satisfactory as far as the police are concerned, it won't go down very well with Rosamund."

"Ah!" Poirot looked discreet. "There has been a little trouble over this friendship of yours?"

"Yes . . . In fact—Rosamund made me promise I wouldn't see her any more."

"Yes, I can see that may be awkward. . . . *Entre nous,* you had an affair with the lady?"

"Oh, just one of those things! It's not as though I cared for the woman at all."

"But she cares for you?"

"Well, she's been rather tiresome. . . . Women do cling so. However, as you say, the police at any rate will be satisfied."

"You think so?"

"Well, I could hardly be taking a hatchet to Cora if I was dallying with Sorrel miles and miles away. She's got a cottage in Kent."

"I see—I see—and this Miss Dainton, she will testify for you?"

"She won't like it—but as it's murder, I suppose she'll have to do it."

"She will do it, perhaps, even if you were *not* dallying with her."

"What do you mean?" Michael looked suddenly black as thunder.

"The lady is fond of you. When they are fond, women will swear to what is true—and also to what is untrue."

"Do you mean to say that you don't believe me?"

"It does not matter if *I* believe you or not. It is not *I* you have to satisfy."

"Who then?"

Poirot smiled.

"Inspector Morton—who has just come out on the terrace through the side door."

Michael Shane wheeled round sharply.

## 23

"I HEARD YOU were here, M. Poirot," said Inspector Morton.

The two men were pacing the terrace together.

"I came over with Superintendent Parwell from Matchfield. Dr Larraby rang him up about Mrs Leo Abernethie and he's come over here to make a few inquiries. The doctor wasn't satisfied."

"And you, my friend," inquired Poirot, "where do you come in? You are a long way from your native Berkshire."

"I wanted to ask a few questions—and the people I wanted to ask them of seemed very conveniently assembled here." He paused before adding, "Your doing?"

"Yes, my doing."

"And as a result Mrs Leo Abernethie gets knocked out."

"You must not blame me for that. If she had come to *me* . . . But she did not. Instead she rang up her lawyer in London."

"And was in process of spilling the beans to him when —Wonk!"

"When—as you say—Wonk!"

"And what had she managed to tell him?"

"Very little. She had only got as far as telling him that she was looking at herself in the glass."

"Ah! well," said Inspector Morton philosophically. "Women will do it." He looked sharply at Poirot. "That suggests something to you?"

"Yes, I think I know what it was she was going to tell him."

"Wonderful guesser, aren't you? You always were. Well, what was it?"

"Excuse me, are you inquiring into the death of Richard Abernethie?"

"Officially, no. Actually, of course, if it has a bearing on the murder of Mrs Lansquenet—"

"It has a bearing on that, yes. But I will ask you, my friend, to give me a few more hours. I shall know by then if what I have imagined—imagined only, you comprehend —is correct. If it *is*—"

"Well, if it is?"

"Then I may be able to place in your hands a piece of concrete evidence."

"We could certainly do with it," said Inspector Morton with feeling. He looked askance at Poirot. "What have you been holding back?"

"Nothing. Absolutely nothing. Since the piece of evidence I have imagined may not in fact exist. I have only deduced its existence from various scraps of conversation. I may," said Poirot in a completely unconvinced tone, "be wrong."

Morton smiled.

"But that doesn't often happen to you?"

"No. Though I will admit—yes, I am forced to admit —that it *has* happened to me."

"I must say I'm glad to hear it! To be always right must be sometimes monotonous."

"I do not find it so," Poirot assured him.

Inspector Morton laughed.

"And you're asking me to hold off with my questioning?"

"No, no, not at all. Proceed as you had planned to do. I suppose you were not actually contemplating an arrest?"

Morton shook his head.

"Much too flimsy for that. We'd have to get a decision from the Public Prosecutor first—and we're a long way from that. No, just statements from certain parties of their movements on the day in question—in one case with a caution, perhaps."

"I see. Mrs Banks?"

"Smart, aren't you? Yes. She was there that day. Her car was parked in that quarry."

"She was not seen actually *driving* the car?"

"No."

The Inspector added, "It's bad, you know, that she's never said a word about being down there that day. She's got to explain that satisfactorily."

"She is quite skilful at explanations," said Poirot drily.

"Yes. Clever young lady. Perhaps a thought too clever."

"It is never wise to be too clever. That is how murderers get caught. Has anything more come up about George Crossfield?"

"Nothing definite. He's a very ordinary type. There are a lot of young men like him going about the country in trains and buses or on bicycles. People find it hard to remember when a week or so has gone by if it was Wednesday or Thursday when they were at a certain place or noticed a certain person."

He paused and went on: "We've had one piece of rather curious information—from the Mother Superior of some convent or other. Two of her nuns had been out collecting from door to door. It seems that they went to Mrs Lansquenet's cottage on the day *before* she was murdered, but couldn't make anyone hear when they knocked and rang. That's natural enough—she was up North at the Abernethie funeral and Gilchrist had been given the day off and had gone on an excursion to Bournemouth. The point is that they say *there was someone in the cottage*. They say they heard sighs and groans. I've queried whether it wasn't a day later but the Mother Superior is quite definite that that couldn't be so. It's all entered up in some book. Was there someone searching for something in the cottage that day, who seized the opportunity of both the women being away? And did that somebody not find what he or she was looking for and come back the next day? I don't set much store on the sighs and still less on the groans. Even nuns are suggestible and a cottage where murder has occurred positively *asks* for groans. The point is, was there someone in the cottage who shouldn't have been there? And if so, who was it? All the Abernethie crowd were at the funeral."

Poirot asked a seemingly irrelevant question:

"These nuns who were collecting in that district, did they return at all at a later date to try again?"

"As a matter of fact they did come again—about a week later. Actually on the day of the inquest, I believe."

"That fits," said Hercule Poirot. "That fits very well."

Inspector Morton looked at him.

"Why this interest in nuns?"

"They have been forced on my attention whether I will or no. It will not have escaped your attention, Inspector, that the visit of the nuns was the same day that poisoned wedding cake found its way into that cottage."

"You don't think—Surely that's a ridiculous idea?"

"My ideas are never ridiculous," said Hercule Poirot severely. "And now, *mon cher,* I must leave you to your questions and to the inquiries into the attack on Mrs Abernethie. I myself must go in search of the late Richard Abernethie's niece."

"Now be careful what you go saying to Mrs Banks."

"I do not mean Mrs Banks. I mean Richard Abernethie's other niece."

ii

Poirot found Rosamund sitting on a bench overlooking a little stream that cascaded down in a waterfall and then flowed through rhododendron thickets. She was staring into the water.

"I do not, I trust, disturb an Ophelia," said Poirot as he took his seat beside her. "You are, perhaps, studying the *rôle?*"

"I've never played in Shakespeare," said Rosamund. "Except once in Rep. I was Jessica in 'The Merchant.' A lousy part."

"Yet not without pathos. *'I am never merry when I hear sweet music.'* What a load she carried, poor Jessica, the daughter of the hated and despised Jew. What doubts of herself she must have had when she brought with her her father's ducats when she ran away to her lover. Jessica with gold was one thing—Jessica without gold might have been another."

Rosamund turned her head to look at him.

"I thought you'd gone," she said with a touch of reproach. She glanced down at her wrist-watch. "It's past twelve o'clock."

"I have missed my train," said Poirot.

"Why?"

"You think I missed it for a reason?"

"I suppose so. You're rather precise, aren't you? If you wanted to catch a train, I think you'd catch it."

"Your judgment is admirable. Do you know, Madame, I have been sitting in the little summerhouse hoping that you would, perhaps, pay me a visit there?"

Rosamund stared at him.

"Why should I? You more or less said goodbye to us all in the library."

"Quite so. And there was nothing—*you* wanted to say to *me?*"

"No." Rosamund shook her head. "I had a lot I wanted to think about. Important things."

"I see."

"I don't often do much thinking," said Rosamund. "It seems a waste of time. But this *is* important. I think one ought to plan one's life just as one wants it to be."

"And that is what you are doing?"

"Well, yes . . . I was trying to make a decision about something."

"About your husband?"

"In a way."

Poirot waited a moment, then he said:

"Inspector Morton has just arrived here." He anticipated Rosamund's question by going on: "He is the police officer in charge of the inquiries about Mrs Lansquenet's death. He has come here to get statements from you all about what you were doing on the day she was murdered."

"I see. *Alibis,*" said Rosamund cheerfully.

Her beautiful face relaxed into an impish glee.

"That will be hell for Michael," she said. "He thinks I don't really know he went off to be with that woman that day."

"How did you know?"

"It was obvious from the *way* he said he was going to lunch with Oscar. So frightfully casually, you know, and his nose twitching just a tiny bit like it always does when he tells lies."

"How devoutly thankful I am I am not married to you, Madame!"

"And then, of course, I made sure by ringing up Oscar," continued Rosamund. "Men always tell such silly lies."

"He is not, I fear, a very faithful husband?" Poirot hazarded.

Rosamund, however, did not reject the statement.

"No."

"But you do not mind?"

"Well, it's rather fun in a way," said Rosamund. "I mean, having a husband that all the other women want to snatch away from you. I should hate to be married to a man that nobody wanted—like poor Susan. Really Greg is so completely wet!"

Poirot was studying her.

"And suppose someone did succeed—in snatching your husband away from you?"

"They won't," said Rosamund. "Not now," she added.

"You mean—"

"Not now that there's Uncle Richard's money. Michael falls for these creatures in a way—that Sorrel Dainton woman nearly got her hooks into him—wanted him for keeps—but with Michael the show will always come first. He can launch out now in a big way—put his own shows on. Do some production as well as acting. He's ambitious, you know, and he really is good. Not like me. I adore acting—but I'm ham, though I look nice. No, I'm not worried about Michael any more. Because it's my money, you see."

Her eyes met Poirot's calmly. He thought how strange it was that both Richard Abernethie's nieces should have fallen deeply in love with men who were incapable of returning that love. And yet Rosamund was unusually beautiful and Susan was attractive and full of sex appeal. Susan needed and clung to the illusion that Gregory loved her. Rosamund, clear-sighted, had no illusions at all, but knew what she wanted.

"The point is," said Rosamund, "that I've got to make a big decision—about the future. Michael doesn't know yet." Her face curved into a smile. "He found out that I wasn't shopping that day and he's madly suspicious about Regent's Park."

"What is this about Regent's Park?" Poirot looked puzzled.

"I went there, you see, after Harley Street. Just to walk about and think. Naturally Michael thinks that if I went there at all, I went to meet some man!"

Rosamund smiled beatifically and added:

"He didn't like that *at all!*"

"But why should you not go to Regent's Park?" asked Poirot.

"Just to walk there, you mean?"

"Yes. Have you never done it before?"

"Never. Why should I? What is there to go to Regent's Park *for?*"

Poirot looked at her and said:

"For you—nothing."

He added:

"I think, Madame, that you must cede the green malachite table to your cousin Susan."

Rosamund's eyes opened very wide.

"Why should I? I *want* it."

"I know. I know. But you—you will keep your husband. And the poor Susan, she will lose hers."

"Lose him? Do you mean Greg's going off with someone? I wouldn't have believed it of him. He looks so *wet.*"

"Infidelity is not the only way of losing a husband, Madame."

"You don't mean—?" Rosamund stared at him. "You're not thinking that Greg poisoned Uncle Richard and killed Aunt Cora and conked Aunt Helen on the head? That's ridiculous. Even *I* know better than that."

"Who did, then?"

"George, of course. George is a wrong un, you know, he's mixed up in some sort of currency swindle—I heard about it from some friends of mine who were in Monte. I expect Uncle Richard got to know about it and was just going to cut him out of his will."

Rosamund added complacently:

"I've always known it was George."

## 24

THE TELEGRAM came about six o'clock that evening.

As specially requested it was delivered by hand, not telephoned, and Hercule Poirot who had been hovering for some time in the neighbourhood of the front door, was at hand to receive it from Lanscombe as the latter took it from the telegraph boy.

He tore it open with somewhat less than his usual precision. It consisted of three words and a signature.

Poirot gave vent to an enormous sigh of relief.

Then he took a pound note from his pocket and handed it to the dumbfounded boy.

"There are moments," he said to Lanscombe, "when economy should be abandoned."

"Very possibly, sir," said Lanscombe politely.

"Where is Inspector Morton?" asked Poirot.

"One of the police gentlemen," Lanscombe spoke with distaste—and indicated subtly that such things as names for police officers were impossible to remember—"has left. The other is, I believe, in the study."

"Splendid," said Poirot. "I join him immediately."

He once more clapped Lanscombe on the shoulder and said:

"Courage, we are on the point of arriving!"

Lanscombe looked slightly bewildered since departures, and not arrivals, had been in his mind.

He said:

"You do not, then, propose to leave by the nine thirty train after all, sir?"

"Do not lose hope," Poirot told him.

Poirot moved away, then wheeling round, he asked:

"I wonder, can you remember what were the first words Mrs Lansquenet said to you when she arrived here on the day of your master's funeral?"

"I remember very well, sir," said Lanscombe, his face lighting up. "Miss Cora—I beg pardon, Mrs Lansquenet —I always think of her as Miss Cora, somehow—"

"Very naturally."

"—She said to me: 'Hullo, Lanscombe. It's a long time since you used to bring us out meringues to the huts.' All the children used to have a hut of their own—down by the fence in the Park. In summer, when there was going to be a dinner party, I used to take the young ladies and gentlemen—the younger ones, you understand, sir—some meringues. Miss Cora, sir, was always very fond of her food."

Poirot nodded.

"Yes," he said, "that was as I thought. Yes, it was very typical, that."

He went into the study to find Inspector Morton and without a word handed him the telegram.

Morton read it blankly.

"I don't understand a word of this."

"The time has come to tell you all."

Inspector Morton grinned.

"You sound like a young lady in a Victorian melodrama. But it's about time you came across with something. I can't hold out on this set-up much longer. That Banks fellow is still insisting that he poisoned Richard Abernethie and boasting that we can't find out how. What beats me is why there's always somebody who comes forward when there's a murder and yells out that they did it! What do you think there is in it for them? I've never been able to fathom that."

"In this case, probably shelter from the difficulties of being responsible for oneself—in other words—Forsdyke Sanatorium."

"More likely to be Broadmoor."

"That might be equally satisfactory."

"*Did* he do it, Poirot? The Gilchrist woman came out with the story she'd already told you and it would fit with what Richard Abernethie said about his niece. If her husband did it, it would involve her. Somehow, you know, I can't visualize that girl committing a lot of crimes. But there's nothing she wouldn't do to try and cover *him*."

"I will tell you all—"

"Yes, yes, tell me all! And for the Lord's sake hurry up and do it!"

## ii

This time it was in the big drawing room that Hercule Poirot assembled his audience.

There was amusement rather than tension in the faces that were turned towards him. Menace had materialised in the shape of Inspector Morton and Superintendent Parwell. With the police in charge, questioning, asking for statements, Hercule Poirot, private detective, had receded into something closely resembling a joke.

Timothy was not far from voicing the general feeling when he remarked in an audible *sotto voce* to his wife:

"Damned little mountebank! Entwhistle must be *gaga!* —that's all I can say."

It looked as though Hercule Poirot would have to work hard to make his proper effect.

He began in a slightly pompous manner.

"For the second time, I announce my departure! This morning I announced it for the twelve o'clock train. This evening I announce it for the nine thirty—immediately, that is, after dinner. I go because there is nothing more here for me to do."

"Could have told him that all along." Timothy's commentary was still in evidence. "Never was anything for him to do. The cheek of these fellows!"

"I came here originally to solve a riddle. The riddle is solved. Let me, first, go over the various points which were brought to my attention by the excellent Mr Entwhistle.

"First, Mr Richard Abernethie dies suddenly. Secondly, after his funeral, his sister Cora Lansquenet says, 'He was murdered, wasn't he?' Thirdly Mrs Lansquenet is killed. The question is, are those three things part of a *sequence?* Let us observe what happens next. Miss Gilchrist, the dead woman's companion, is taken ill after eating a piece of wedding cake which contains arsenic. That, then, is the *next* step in the sequence.

"Now, as I told you this morning, in the course of my inquiries I have come across nothing—nothing at all, to substantiate the belief that Mr Abernethie was poisoned. Equally, I may say, I have found nothing to prove conclusively that he was *not* poisoned. But as we proceed, things become easier. Cora Lansquenet undoubtedly asked that sensational question at the funeral. Everyone agrees upon *that*. And undoubtedly, on the following day, Mrs Lansquenet was murdered—a hatchet being the instrument employed. Now let us examine the fourth happening. The local post van driver is strongly of the belief —though he will not definitely swear to it—that he did not deliver that parcel of wedding cake in the usual way. And if that is so, then the parcel was left by hand and though we cannot exclude a 'person unknown'—we must take particular notice of those people who were actually on the spot and in a position to put the parcel where it was subsequently found. Those were: Miss Gilchrist herself, of course; Susan Banks who came down that day for the inquest; Mr Entwhistle (but yes, we must consider Mr Entwhistle; he was present, remember, when Cora made her disquieting remark!). And there were two other people. An old gentleman who represented himself to be a Mr Guthrie, an art critic, and a nun or nuns who called early that morning to collect a subscription.

"Now I decided that I would start on the assumption that the postal van driver's recollection was correct. Therefore the little group of people under suspicion must be very carefully studied. Miss Gilchrist did not benefit in any way by Richard Abernethie's death and in only a very minute degree by Mrs Lansquenet's—in actual fact the death of the latter put her out of employment and left her with the possibility of finding it difficult to get new employment. Also Miss Gilchrist was taken to hospital definitely suffering from arsenical poisoning.

"Susan Banks *did* benefit from Richard Abernethie's death, and in a small degree from Mrs Lansquenet's— though here her motive must almost certainly have been security. She might have very good reason to believe that Miss Gilchrist had overheard a conversation between

Cora Lansquenet and her brother which referred to her, and she might therefore decide that Miss Gilchrist must be eliminated. She herself, remember, refused to partake of the wedding cake and also suggested not calling in a doctor until the morning, when Miss Gilchrist was taken ill in the night.

"Mr Entwhistle did *not* benefit by either of the deaths —but he had had considerable control over Mr Abernethie's affairs, and the trust funds, and there might well be some reason why Richard Abernethie should not live too long. But—you will say—if it is Mr Entwhistle who was concerned, why should he come to *me*?

"And to that I will answer—it is not the first time a murderer has been too sure of himself.

"We now come to what I may call the two outsiders. Mr Guthrie and a nun. If Mr Guthrie is really Mr Guthrie, the art critic, then that clears him. The same applies to the nun, if she is really a nun. The question is, are these people themselves, or are they somebody else?

"And I may say that there seems to be a curious—*motif*—one might call it—of a nun running through this business. A nun comes to the door at Mr Timothy Abernethie's house and Miss Gilchrist believes it is the same nun she has seen at Lytchett St. Mary. Also a nun, or nuns, called here the day before Mr Abernethie died . . ."

George Crossfield murmured, "Three to one, the nun."

Poirot went on:

"So here we have certain pieces of our pattern—the death of Mr Abernethie, the murder of Cora Lansquenet, the poisoned wedding cake, the '*motif*' of the 'Nun.'

"I will add some other features of the case that engaged my attention:

"The visit of an art critic, a smell of oil paint, a picture postcard of Polflexan harbour, and finally a bouquet of wax flowers standing on that malachite table where a Chinese vase stands now.

"It was reflecting on these things that led me to the truth—and I am now about to tell you the truth.

"The first part of it I told you this morning. Richard Abernethie died suddenly—but there would have been no reason at all to suspect foul play—had it not been for the words uttered by his sister Cora at his funeral. *The whole*

*case for the murder of Richard Abernethie rests upon those
words.* As a result of them, you all believed that murder
had taken place, and you believed it, not really because of
the words themselves but because of *the character of Cora
Lansquenet herself.* For Cora Lansquenet had always been
famous for speaking the truth at awkward moments. So the
case for Richard's murder rested not only upon what Cora
had *said* but upon Cora herself.

"And now I come to the question that I suddenly asked
myself:

*"How well did you all know Cora Lansquenet?"*

He was silent for a moment, and Susan asked sharply,
"What do you mean?"

Poirot went on:

*"Not well at all*—that is the answer! The younger generation had never seen her at all, or if so, only when they
were very young children. There were actually only three
people present that day who actually *knew* Cora. Lanscombe, the butler, who is old and very blind; Mrs Timothy Abernethie who had only seen her a few times round
about the date of her own wedding, and Mrs Leo Abernethie who had known her quite well, but who had not
seen her for over twenty years.

"So I said to myself: 'Supposing it was *not* Cora Lansquenet who came to the funeral that day?' "

"Do you mean that Aunt Cora—*wasn't* Aunt Cora?"
Susan demanded incredulously. "Do you mean that it
wasn't Aunt Cora who was murdered, but someone else?"

"No, no, it was Cora Lansquenet who was murdered.
*But it was not Cora Lansquenet* who came the day before
to her brother's funeral. The woman who came that day
came for one purpose only—to exploit, one may say, the
fact that Richard died suddenly. And to create in the
minds of his relations the belief that he had been murdered. Which she managed to do most successfully!"

"Nonsense! Why? What was the point of it?" Maude
spoke bluffly.

"Why? *To draw attention away from the other murder.*
From the murder of Cora Lansquenet herself. For if Cora
says that Richard has been murdered and the next day
*she herself is killed,* the two deaths are bound to be at
least considered as possible cause and effect. But if Cora

is murdered and her cottage is broken into, and if the apparent robbery does not convince the police, then they will look—where? Close at home, will they not? Suspicion will tend to fall on the woman who shares the house with her."

Miss Gilchrist protested in a tone that was almost bright:

"Oh come—really—Mr Pontarlier—you don't suggest I'd commit a murder for an amethyst brooch and a few worthless sketches?"

"No," said Poirot. "For a little more than that. There was one of those sketches, Miss Gilchrist, that represented Polflexan harbour and which, as Mrs Banks was clever enough to realise, had been copied from a picture postcard which showed the old pier still in position. But Mrs Lansquenet painted always from life. I remember then that Mr Entwhistle had mentioned there being *a smell of oil paint* in the cottage when he first got there. You can paint, can't you, Miss Gilchrist? Your father was an artist and you know a good deal about pictures. Supposing that one of the pictures that Cora picked up cheaply at a sale was a valuable picture. Supposing that she herself did not recognise it for what it was, but that you did. You knew she was expecting, very shortly, a visit from an old friend of hers who was a well known art critic. Then her brother dies suddenly—and a plan leaps into your head. Easy to administer a sedative to her in her early cup of tea that will keep her unconscious for the whole of the day of the funeral whilst you yourself are playing her part at Enderby. You know Enderby well from listening to her talk about it. She has talked, as people do when they get on in life, a great deal about her childhood days. Easy for you to start off by a remark to old Lanscombe about meringues and huts which will make him quite sure of your identity in case he was inclined to doubt. Yes, you used your knowledge of Enderby well that day, with allusions to this and that, and recalling memories. None of them suspected you were not Cora. You were wearing her clothes, slightly padded, and since she wore a false front of hair, it was easy for you to assume that. Nobody had seen Cora for twenty years—and in twenty years people change so much that one often hears the remark: 'I would never have known her!' But mannerisms are remembered, and Cora had certain very definite mannerisms, all of which you had practised carefully before the glass.

"And it was there, strangely enough, that you made your first mistake. *You forgot that a mirror image is reversed.* When you saw in the glass the perfect reproduction of Cora's birdlike sidewise tilt of the head, you didn't realise that it was actually the *wrong way round*. You saw, let us say, Cora inclining her head to the *right*—but you forgot that actually your own head was inclined to the *left* to produce that effect *in the glass*.

"That was what puzzled and worried Helen Abernethie at the moment when you made your famous insinuation. Something seemed to her 'wrong.' I realised myself the other night when Rosamund Shane made an unexpected remark about what happens on such an occasion. Everybody inevitably looks at the *speaker*. Therefore, when Mrs Leo felt something was 'wrong,' it must be that something was wrong with *Cora Lansquenet*. The other evening, after talk about mirror images and 'seeing oneself' I think Mrs Leo experimented before a looking glass. Her own face is not particularly asymmetrical. She probably thought of Cora, remembered how Cora used to incline her head to the right, did so, and looked in the glass—when, of course, the image seemed to her 'wrong' and she realised, in a flash, just what had been wrong on the day of the funeral. She puzzled it out—either Cora had taken to inclining her head in the opposite direction—most unlikely —or else *Cora had not been Cora*. Neither way seemed to her to make sense. But she determined to tell Mr Entwhistle of her discovery at once. Someone who was used to getting up early was already about, and followed her down, and fearful of what revelations she might be about to make struck her down with a heavy doorstop."

Poirot paused and added:

"I may as well tell you now, Miss Gilchrist, that Mrs Abernethie's concussion is not serious. She will soon be able to tell us her own story."

"I never did anything of the sort," said Miss Gilchrist. "The whole thing is a wicked lie."

"It *was* you that day," said Michael Shane suddenly. He had been studying Miss Gilchrist's face. "I ought to have seen it sooner—I felt in a vague kind of way I had seen you before somewhere—but of course one never looks much at—" he stopped.

"No, one doesn't bother to look at a mere companion help," said Miss Gilchrist. Her voice shook a little. "A drudge, a domestic drudge! Almost a servant! But go on, M. Poirot. Go on with this fantastic piece of nonsense!"

"The suggestion of murder thrown out at the funeral was only the first step, of course," said Poirot. "You had more in reserve. At any moment you were prepared to admit to having listened to a conversation between Richard and his sister. What he actually told her, no doubt, was the fact that he had not long to live, and that explains a cryptic phrase in the letter he wrote her after getting home. The 'Nun' was another of your suggestions. The nun—or rather nuns—who called at the cottage on the day of the inquest suggested to you a mention of a nun who was 'following you round,' and you used that when you were anxious to hear what Mrs Timothy was saying to her sister-in-law at Enderby. And also because you wished to accompany her there and find out for yourself just how suspicions were going. Actually to poison *yourself*, badly but not *fatally*, with arsenic, is a very old device—and I may say that it served to awaken Inspector Morton's suspicions of you."

"But the picture?" said Rosamund. "What kind of a picture was it?"

Poirot slowly unfolded a telegram.

"This morning I rang up Mr Entwhistle, a responsible person, to go to Stansfield Grange and, acting on authority from Mr Abernethie himself" (here Poirot gave a hard stare at Timothy) "to look amongst the pictures of Miss Gilchrist's room and select the one of Polflexan Harbour on pretext of having it reframed as a surprise for Miss Gilchrist. He was to take it back to London and call upon Mr Guthrie whom I had warned by telegram. The hastily painted sketch of Polflexan Harbour was removed and the original picture exposed."

He held up the telegram and read:

*"Definitely a Vermeer, Guthrie."*

Suddenly, with electrifying effect, Miss Gilchrist burst into speech.

"I knew it was a Vermeer. I *knew* it! *She* didn't know! Talking about Rembrandts and Italian Primitives and unable to recognise a Vermeer when it was under her nose! Always prating about Art—and really knowing nothing about it! She was a thoroughly stupid woman. Always maundering on about this place—about Enderby, and what they did there as children, and about Richard and Timothy and Laura and all the rest of them. Rolling in money always! Always the best of everything those children had. You don't know how boring it is listening to somebody going on about the same things, hour after hour and day after day. And saying 'Oh yes, Mrs Lansquenet' and 'Really, Mrs Lansquenet?' Pretending to be interested. And really bored—bored—*bored*. . . . And nothing to look forward to. . . . And then—a Vermeer! I saw in the papers that a Vermeer sold the other day for over two thousand pounds!"

"You killed her—in that brutal way—for two thousand pounds?" Susan's voice was incredulous.

"Two thousand pounds," said Poirot, "would have rented and equipped a tea shop. . . ."

Miss Gilchrist turned to him.

"At least," she said, "You *do* understand. It was the only chance I'd ever get. I *had* to have a capital sum." Her voice vibrated with the force and obsession of her dream. "I was going to call it the Palm Tree. And have little camels as menu holders. One can occasionally get quite nice china—export rejects—not that awful white utility stuff. I meant to start it in some nice neighbourhood where nice people would come in. I had thought of Rye. . . . Or perhaps Chichester . . . I'm sure I could have made a success of it." She paused a minute, then added musingly, "Oak tables—and little basket chairs with striped red and white cushions. . . ."

For a few moments the tea shop that would never be, seemed more real than the Victorian solidity of the drawing room at Enderby. . . .

It was Inspector Morton who broke the spell.

Miss Gilchrist turned to him quite politely.

"Oh, certainly," she said. "At once. I don't want to give any trouble, I'm sure. After all, if I can't have the Palm Tree, nothing really seems to matter very much. . . ."

She went out of the room with him and Susan said, her voice still shaken:

"I've never imagined a—*ladylike* murderer. It's horrible."

# 25

"BUT I don't understand about the wax flowers," said Rosamund.

She fixed Poirot with large reproachful blue eyes.

They were at Helen's flat in London. Helen herself was resting on the sofa and Rosamund and Poirot were having tea with her.

"I don't see that *wax flowers* had anything to *do* with it," said Rosamund. "Or the malachite table."

"The malachite table, no. But the wax flowers were Miss Gilchrist's second mistake. She said how nice they looked on the malachite table. And you see, Madame, *she* could not have seen them there. Because they had been broken and put away before she arrived with the Timothy Abernethies. *So she could only have seen them when she was there as Cora Lansquenet.*"

"That *was* stupid of her, wasn't it?" said Rosamund.

Poirot shook a forefinger at her.

"It shows you, Madame, the dangers of *conversation.* It is a profound belief of mine that if you can induce a person to talk to you for long enough, *on any subject whatever,* sooner or later they will give themselves away. Miss Gilchrist did."

"I shall have to be careful," said Rosamund thoughtfully. Then she brightened up.

"Did you know? I'm going to have a baby."

"Aha! So that is the meaning of Harley Street and Regent's Park?"

"Yes. I was so upset, you know, and so surprised—that I just had to go somewhere and *think.*"

"You said, I remember, that that does not very often happen."

"Well, it's much easier not to. But this time I had to decide about the future. And I've decided to leave the stage and just be a mother."

"A *rôle* that will suit you admirably. Already I foresee delightful pictures in the Sketch and the Tatler."

Rosamund smiled happily.

"Yes, it's wonderful. Do you know, Michael is *delighted*. I didn't really think he would be."

She paused and added:

"Susan's got the malachite table. I thought, as I was having a baby—"

She left the sentence unfinished.

"Susan's cosmetic business promises well," said Helen. "I think she is all set for a big success."

"Yes, she was born to succeed," said Poirot. "She is like her uncle."

"You mean Richard, I suppose," said Rosamund. "Not Timothy?"

"Assuredly not like Timothy," said Poirot.

They laughed.

"Greg's away somewhere," said Rosamund. "Having a rest cure Susan *says?*"

She looked inquiringly at Poirot who said nothing.

"I can't think why he kept on saying he'd killed Uncle Richard," said Rosamund. "Do you think it was a form of Exhibitionism?"

Poirot reverted to the previous topic.

"I received a very amiable letter from Mr Timothy Abernethie," he said. "He expressed himself as highly satisfied with the services I had rendered the family."

"I do think Uncle Timothy is quite awful," said Rosamund.

"I am going to stay with them next week," said Helen. "They seem to be getting the gardens into order, but domestic help is still difficult."

"They miss the awful Gilchrist, I suppose," said Rosamund. "But I daresay in the end, she'd have killed Uncle Timothy, too. What fun if she had!"

"Murder has always seemed fun to you, Madame."

"Oh! Not really," said Rosamund, vaguely. "But I *did* think it was George." She brightened up. "Perhaps he will do one some day."

"And that will be fun," said Poirot sarcastically.

"Yes, won't it?" Rosamund agreed.

She ate another éclair from the plate in front of her.

Poirot turned to Helen.

"And you, Madame, are off to Cyprus?"

"Yes, in a fortnight's time."

"Then let me wish you a happy journey."

He bowed over her hand. She came with him to the door, leaving Rosamund dreamily stuffing herself with cream pastries.

Helen said abruptly:

"I should like you to know, M. Poirot, that the legacy Richard left me meant more to me than theirs did to any of the others."

"As much as that, Madame?"

"Yes. You see—there is a child in Cyprus. . . . My husband and I were very devoted—it was a great sorrow to us to have no children. After he died my loneliness was unbelievable. When I was nursing in London at the end of the war, I met someone . . . He was younger than I was and married, though not very happily. We came together for a little while. That was all. He went back to Canada—to his wife and his children. He never knew about—our child. He would not have wanted it. I did. It seemed like a miracle to me—a middle-aged woman with everything behind her. With Richard's money I can educate my so-called nephew, and give him a start in life." She paused, then added, "I never told Richard. He was fond of me and I of him—but he would not have understood. You know so much about us that I thought I would like you to know this about me."

Once again Poirot bowed over her hand.

He got home to find the armchair on the left side of the fireplace occupied.

"Hullo, Poirot," said Mr Entwhistle. "I've just come back from the Assizes. They brought in a verdict of Guilty, of course. But I shouldn't be surprised if she ends up in Broadmoor. She's gone definitely over the edge since she's been in prison. Quite happy you know, and *most* gracious. She spends her time making the most elaborate plans to run a chain of tea shops. Her newest establishment is to be the Lilac Bush. She's opening it in Cromer."

"One wonders if she was always a little mad? But me, I think not."

"Good Lord, no! Sane as you and I when she planned that murder. Carried it out in cold blood. She's got a good head on her, you know, underneath the fluffy manner."

Poirot gave a little shiver.

"I am thinking," he said, "of some words that Susan Banks said—that she had never imagined a *ladylike* murderer."

"Why not?" said Mr Entwhistle. "It takes all sorts."

They were silent—and Poirot thought of murderers he had known. . . .